INTO THE BLUE

ZEA KAYLEIGH GALAN

To you,
In a world that taught you to dull your shine,
you still reflect light bright enough to blind them in the dark.

Listen to the official playlist for
Into the Blue

SPOTIFY

Hi friend! This is a **dark romance** story that is suitable for mature audiences only as it has dark themes such as murder, violence, illegal drug usage, and explicit on-page sexual content. It contains content that may be triggering to some.

A full list of the content warnings for this book can be found on my website at
www.zeakayleigh.com/cw

Join the Newsletter

Never miss an update about Zea Kayleigh, newsletter exclusives such as freebies and giveaways, first looks at new books, upcoming series, and events.

<u>SIGN UP HERE!</u>

INTO THE BLUE

BLUE DREAM

PART 1

If you've read the prequel novella, Blue Dream, move on to part 2: Into the Blue.

If you have not, this part is not a skippable portion of Blue and Diamond's story. You will be very confused without this information. I promise you won't want to miss the introduction to their dynamic!

Chapter 1

BLUE

I press my knife against his throat real slow to let him feel the weight of the moment. The steel glints in the dim office's lighting, but he doesn't move. It's either brave or stupid. My money's on the latter.

"I said," I murmur at his ear, "you answer to me now."

His pulse ticks against the blade. He's smart enough not to beg. Would do him no good anyway. Dumber men crack by now, start pleading or pissing themselves. Allen just breathes shallow, eyes locked on my men who stand at the door blocking his exit. He's not going anywhere until I can ensure I'm getting what I came for.

"From now—until I decide different," I finish without relieving any of the pressure from my blade. The glove I wear protects me from any blood that might spill, but also from any cuts since it improves my grip just in case whoever moves too much under me. I'm somewhat impressed that Allen isn't squirming more than this.

He swallows and I feel the motion against the edge of the knife. Still, he says, "I'm n-not your enemy."

I lean in a fraction. "Then why the fuck were there so many addendums to the contract I sent over?"

He lifts his hands like I don't have a knife to his neck and the sudden movement could cause a mistake that would cost him dearly. "It wasn't meant to be a threat."

"No?" I press the blade in just enough to make his skin tighten. "Then you're worse than I thought. Weak ass."

His mouth opens, then closes. I feel the shift when the realization settles in. He didn't just walk into a meeting to sign the dotted line. He walked into a test.

And he's failing.

I step back slowly, let the tension hang between us like smoke. My knife stays out. I don't sheathe it. I see the flicker of doubt hit his posture.

"P-please. It's how Manel would have wanted me to handle it. I was just following the procedure."

That's when I inform him, "If this deal falls apart because of you and your *procedures*, I'll make sure there's not enough left of you for your own family to recognize."

Now he's pale, his ruddy skin absent of all its usual ruddiness. This man, if left to his own devices, would lose this club to any given thug—like me, but they wouldn't have the kind of direction I do.

This place would be a mockery of what Manel would have wanted. I'm saving it from the ruin it was headed for.

"I'm not signin' any of 'em. What I sent over was already good. For you and for me. We straight?" I question, daring him to argue again as I clean under my nails with my knife's tip.

He clears his throat, hesitation still evident even as I take a seat across from him. "Y-yea."

Base thumps to a sensual beat just outside the door of the office. It contrasts the heavy feeling of my energy suffocating the space. I have no actual control over its presence, but I know when someone can feel my will and when they can't. Allen Sheedy certainly can, even from several feet away.

Redd and Marcell are behind me while Benito stands watch right outside. Two more of my men are in the rides we came in. I'm always five deep, if not more. Only an arrogant dick would be cavalier with their life when they move as much weight as I do. *If I have no ops, I'm already dead.* Everybody has a price on my head. I'll be damned if I give them the opportunity just by thinking I'm untouchable.

The man in front of me wipes his forehead. If I were Allen, I'd be sweating too. I take my time reading over the original contract a final time though Allen continues to fidget with just about anything on his desk.

This isn't a negotiation.

It's a leash and he should feel it tightening on him.

I slide the document across the desk to him and place the pen on top, silently telling him to sign. He looks at the papers and then back to me. "And I'll still be able to get my check at the end of the week? You know, Terrell made a part of my—"

I meet the shifty eyes of this man, smiling though I know it doesn't read anything like joy. "Don't like repeatin' myself much. So, I'll say this once and only once more. Everythin' will go as it has before. Only difference bein'—I'm takin' the bag home, not Terrell LaFayette Jr. Make sense?"

Typically, I'm not a gambling man. Too many factors I can't control.

But, when my real estate agent told me this property would be the best way to wash a good portion of the money I made, I took a chance. Needed to keep the money clean and there was only one way to do it. Came with the bonus of coming up on the jackass I'd enjoy bossing up on any day of the week.

Terrell Lafayette Jr. is a smug little piece of shit who rides the wave of his daddy's success like it's the fucking state fare Merri-go-round. He'd been snatching strip clubs and turning them into something I didn't want to happen to Off Topz. Didn't want the smack, snow or pixie dust in here and I didn't want to see more of his men when I was here to chill. Where there's snow, there's addicts and crack heads were just annoying. He'd have to get more of Fayes in here to control them. All in all, annoying and I'd rather take this place instead.

Junior fucked up somewhere along the way and couldn't afford to keep the place in whatever partnership he wanted with Manel. Like I give a fuck. Junior can keep losing and I'll keep scooping up more and more for my empire.

After my split from working with the Lafayette Family, the Fayes, I knew he was the first to feel the disdain I held toward the whole family. As *he should*. It's because of him I made the decision and I stand by it one hundred percent.

Off Topz is one of the best strip clubs in town, so I've been here more weekends than I can count. The food isn't half bad and the drinks are strong. Hell, the women they employ are some of the best in the state, I'm sure. It was neutral ground for everybody who does business in this area. You didn't have to worry about being shot at while you had a drink after a long day. And the days get to be very long doing what we do.

For the Duponts, to be in charge of this place, reaping the benefits of clean money and knowing the Fayes will still patron it is... frankly, good business.

Nothing makes me happier than good business.

Allen attempts to make space in the neckline of his polo shirt, pulling at the fabric as his throat works. I cross my arms over my chest and let the full weight of my impatience press on him before he splutters, "Ye-yes. Makes sense. I will let everyone know you have taken over operations. Will we have a ceremony or so-somethin' for Manel?" I don't respond quickly enough and he continues rambling. "He was a good boss. The girls loved him. He kept them safe. Made this club what it is. I—"

Manel Corolla was the late owner of Off Topz. He was a jovial man who laughed too much for my liking. However, I'd never fault him for the way he handled business. He kept the cops out of this place and made sure the underbelly of Clayton Terrace had a place to call home. Many deals were brokered and alliances were formed here. But most importantly, his untimely death led to solving a problem I had.

"Look. Don't care about any of that. If it don't interfere with the money, do whatever you want."

Allen swipes a hand over the back of his forehead again. "Okay." He looks over to the door where Redd and Marcell watch and wait for any signal from me to step in.

Benefits of being King.

But where there are benefits, there's plenty of drawbacks.

The biggest one right now is the inconsistency I've seen in my business. Money is moving weird through my ranks and runners are encountering more and more attempts to take what's mine or pinch a little for themselves without my say-so. The drawback of cutting ties with the

Fayes who previously handled all that business before. Now, it's solely my responsibility until I can figure it out.

The only ones who know about my growing concerns on the issue are in my court as king. Redd, my first regent or second in command, Vert and Geno, my second and third regents, respectively. Top tier and tight lipped. While there hasn't been a pattern to the way everything is going, I know I'm only as powerful as my power seems. If anyone gets wind they can come up on me, then there will be plenty others who think they can follow suit.

Hence, my acquisition of a proper... laundromat, if you will. My money is dirty and a typical accountant is out of the question. I had too many hands on my dough. It was too easy for mistakes to be made. Don't have time to chase down every little problem or dollar when moving green in the South has enough risks piled up against us.

Allen here might be sweating through his dry-fit polo, but he does good work. Manel talked about how he was never worried about the cash flow because Allen kept him on top.

Now, Allen is going to keep *me* on top.

I give him a smile, but from what I've been told, it does nothing to assure the person on the other side of it. It *shouldn't*. It's not meant to. "I'm not your point of contact from this point forward. My man will contact you with the details of the next drop." He'll deal with Vert and find out if things are the same or different between dealing with club owners and real criminals.

I grab the papers that have been signed and stand. "Cool, I'm out." I tuck my knife away and nod to my men.

Now, I'm gonna have a drink and see exactly how good it is to be King in another domain I now own.

Chapter 2

BLUE

It's a good night to make some money. Benito has a sack and I'm sure these boys wanna smoke a lil' somethin' while they kick back and throw some money on these asses shaking.

A server passes by me with some wings and a steak on her tray and I consider getting something for myself. I decide against it because I don't want to wait on the food. I might be ready to go once the green's all sold.

I'm about to say as much to Redd but something catches my attention instead.

Six inch heels lead up to the smallest skirt I've ever seen. The lights bounce off of the stretchy fabric as it hugs onto her curvy hips for dear life. The string that's holding her fishnets up disappears under the little scrap of black and sparkles.

I manage to rip my eyes away from the intoxicating sway of her hips to the blingy gems dangling from her belly button ring. It moves in time over her brown skin with her steps, just as tantalizing as her hips. A thin silver ring loops under her round nose, highlighting how cute the size and shape of it is. Another set of thin strings cross over her healthy waist to a set of titties that make me lick my lips. The same sparkling black fabric stretches impossibly tight over them creating an opening at the middle, begging for my face to be pressed between them. Mentally, I'm running my tongue between them, up to a juicy set of heart shaped lips and—

Fuck me, her sharp brown eyes are already on me.

The gloss on those lips shimmers as her mouth hikes up on one side and she winks at me. Winks.

I'm done.

Never been one to give two fucks about a stripper in this club. I've seen them all, and had my fun with more than I should have. None of them deserved my time, my attention, or my money. But fuck it, when you've got money to blow and a stack is the difference between you and *you-plus-one fun*—I'm gonna blow a stack or two.

It's been a while.

Since I started noticing too many *slips* and *coincidences* in the business, I've been hesitant to let anybody get close to me.

Nothing is more important than the money. When the money is not doing what I want, nothing and no one can keep my attention.

"You like that?" Redd asks when I'm still standing there outside of the office.

Now that all the contracts are signed and Allen is on game, I'm ready for this work day to come to an end.

This sparkling woman striding across the room would be the best way to do just that.

I scrub a hand over my face and shake my head. "Fuck. I more than like it."

She passes me by and I'm still standing here like a fucking lame with my hands in my fucking pants.

"I'll talk to A." Redd steps around me, but I put a hand on his arm. Redd is quick to act and second to think. If he sees it, he wants it and there is nothing, not a law or force, that could stand between him and getting what he wants. If I don't stop him, he'll do too much too soon. Though we're moving in the right direction, I'm still not in the clear to give my attention to anyone else.

"Nah." I shake my head, locs swinging around my face. I tie one around the rest to hold them back. "I'll watch for now."

Money machines rush like rain on a concrete pavement for the line of people trying to get one and five dollar bills cashed out to throw. The thunk of a bucket full of green stacks sounds off next to us as we walk deeper into the club.

The platform splits the main floor in half as three poles are all occupied by dancers moving around or on them to the tempting rhythm of the song playing. A DJ encourages the men salivating at the edge of the stage to throw their cash on them and bills start falling all around the women.

I pass the stage all together to the booth we normally occupy. While me, Redd, and Vert make our way over, Benito is already selling what he has on him. Moments later, our usual drink orders are placed on the table. Thanking the waitress, I pick up the glass and take a sip. The Jack warms as it goes down but my thoughts are somewhere else instead of the win I should be feeling after signing for ownership of this place.

"She's not out here," Redd comments over the music.

"Who?" I play dumb even though I've been looking around for the woman I already said I didn't have time for.

Setting his drink down, my friend gives me a look full of incredulity. "You think I'm blind or somethin'?" He makes a point of opening his eyes as big as they will go and blinking rapidly. He's a clown. Like I said, always doing too much.

"Never said that," I chuff and try to relax into the booth and stop looking for her.

"Yea, whatever." He scratches his short red beard and acts nonchalant as he delivers his next line. "She went to the black door. Means she's not workin' the stage tonight."

I look to my man, and he lifts his chin toward the hallway where the private rooms are.

No.

An acute pain starts behind my eyes as I think over what it means.

If she's working private rooms, then anybody could have her for the night. Unlike many of the clubs in the state, if someone buys a private room here, they have the girl for the night—not the hour.

Off Topz is a titty bar to stay above board. No bottoms come off on stage or on the floor. It's an easy way to get this place shut down if it did happen. The way Manel got around it was these private rooms—disguised as living quarters for the dancers. The laws had to know that's not what they were for but since these rooms were secure and no photographic evidence got out, they turned a blind eye.

From what I could understand, the club makes good money off those rooms. Whether I will continue that part of the club's dealings is undetermined. I never had any interest in all that, I'd just take a dancer to my place if I chose to. Rarely did. But I think back to the woman I saw for just a moment earlier and my brain short circuits.

The thought of someone else having her for the night is not a pleasant one. I slam the glass onto the table and step out of the booth, stalking over to the bar.

"Another?" The bartender, Chanel, asks. She used to be on the floor with the other dancers. Her pointy red nails clink on glasses she's setting out for a drink order that matches her bright red hair that's swooped to one side and then down her back. Before now, I probably would have tried it, but now she's an employee and it's not a good idea.

Ignoring her question, I ask my own. "Who's the new girl?"

Chanel taps on the ordering system with her knuckle since her nails are too long to make contact with her finger tips. My patience is thinning, but I know this is also how they look up reservations for the dancers, as well as, bar tabs.

"Oh," she smiles. "Talkin' about Diamond." *Diamond.* She looks up at me with her finger hovering over the screen. "You want her?"

Yes.

I don't say it aloud, but Chanel must pick up on my facial expression and taps away at the screen. "Room five, boss."

I am their boss now.

Don't really know if I want or need everyone spouting off about that though. "Look, be chill. Don't call me boss." She raises an eyebrow, but I add, "I *will* take another."

Walking back to the booth with a drink in my hand, I take my seat. It's gotten even busier in here since I've been at the bar. Benito is in the crowd and it looks like Lonny came in to help him divvy up the green. I nod my head, feeling even more affirmed in my decision to snatch this place up. This revenue only adds to the empire. Two birds with one stone—it's good business.

"I know you're not boppin' to this." Redd gives me shit, but I stop for a second to actually listen to what song is playing. It's a raunchy rap song by that artist from Memphis. I don't really care for it one way or another.

I wasn't dancing.

I *was scheming*.

"Shut up," I tell him, taking another sip of my drink.

Pretty soon the club is full and only standing room is available. I take out my cigar, gutting it and filling it from the stash in my back pocket. The musty smell of weed wafts into the air but my guys are so used to it none of them stop what they're doing to check on me. I'm quick to roll and lick the blunt to wrap it tight and tuck it behind my ear. The second one is faster and now I have one behind both.

"Imma take a step outside. You comin'?"

He nods and we leave out of the back door after shouldering through the busy crowd. Marcell and Benito are close behind, but they remain silent. They're working, not here in a social capacity. Vert hangs back in the club, probably being the broody shit he always is. Fucking vamp.

I light the end of my blunt when we get to the side of the building the lights don't illuminate. After a deep drag in, I say, "Got a room."

"No shit," Redd says, taking the blunt from me. He inhales and holds the smoke for a time before exhaling O's up toward the night sky. "I knew it."

"You didn't know shit," I say, snatching the blunt back from him.

He leans against the wall with a look I can't discern on his face. In a lower tone, so the other men can't hear, he says, "I ain't ever seen you look at a chick like that."

"So what?" I blow out smoke and watch it dance in the thick, humid night air.

"Nothin'."

"Nah. Say it."

He takes his time to finish the blunt without passing it back to me. I roll my eyes and light the next one without passing to him. He stomps the butt of the blunt in the concrete and kicks the roach over to the grass. "We were gonna just sign this shit and go. Now, we're stayin'?"

My voice is collected and calm as I answer him. "You don't have to do shit. Leave after this blunt. I don't give a fuck."

"Right." He looks agitated as he takes the last blunt from my fingers. His voice is distorted as he talks through the smoke in his lungs. "And leave the King by himself? Nah."

I tilt my head over to the two men keeping watch. "I have Marcell and Benito here. You should go."

Redd thinks over my words for a bit before handing me the blunt back. "Fine. I'll be sooo miserable meeting Steph in your stead." I narrow my eyes at him because I know for a fact I didn't tell him where we were meeting my real estate agent. He just bumps my fist before walking over to his car. Lonny rode with him, but I guess he's going back with me. From out the car window, Redd yells, "Enjoy that. You need a nut," with a big smile on his face. The clown.

I flip him the bird and he pulls out of the lot with a screech of his tires.

The hall to the private rooms is darkened and empty by the time I make my way back inside. It's hard to tell just how big any of the rooms are or where the door actually is if it weren't for the oversized chrome numbers on them.

I enter my code onto the keypad on the door and walk inside. Marcell and Benito wait outside the door and let it close behind me.

I huff a laugh at how the room is all black velvet and the lighting casts everything in a cool blue tone. Just for me.

The back wall is upholstered in tufted black velvet that several chains hang down over. I didn't request any type of bondage, but it's clear if I wanted to tie her up, I could.

Black linens stretch taught over the bed with small mahogany tables on either side. Opening one of the drawers, I see it's filled with lube and toys. There are some other *tools*, but I don't know what purpose they serve. I decide not to open the next drawer because I don't plan on using any of it tonight.

I grab a piece of gum from my back pocket and start chewing it to get the taste and the dryness from the smoke earlier out of my mouth.

Lying back on the loveseat just to the right of the bed, I relax in the silence of the sound-proof room and wait for the blingy woman to finally enter.

Diamond.

Everything about her glimmered and I like flashy things.

With everything I've had to do to earn the title of King, I deserve a treat.

This jawn is one treat I need to take a bite out of.

I hear the click of the door and look up to the sound of the club's music coming in and disturbing my brief moment of peace.

Her legs catch my notice first and I take a slow perusal of her. Again.

Still just as good as I remembered the view being.

"Shall I put something on for us, baby?" Her sultry voice slips around me like silk as she approaches a tablet on the wall which must control the sound system in here.

"Nah, not baby." I tell her. "Blue."

"Blue," she purrs. The sound of my name on her lips is a welcome one. Each deliberate step my way, creating a sway in her stride I can't look away from.

I don't know what this woman's doing to me, but I can't keep my eyes off of her.

"Well, Blue…" she runs a finger over the chains at my neck and falls into the loveseat. "I'm Diamond."

It's graceful and easy for her to drape her body over mine. Her ass in my lap and her legs crossed over the arm of the seat. Warmth radiates off of her, but it's the smell of magnolias that lingers around her, causing me to lean in.

I blow a small bubble with my gum as I assess her.

Not one ounce of intimidation comes off this girl. Like she already knows me or, more likely, she doesn't know enough to be afraid.

She takes two dainty fingers to my lips and before I know it, my gum is in her mouth.

My hand finds her thigh and the soft give of her supple skin underneath my palm distracts me for a moment. "What is it you came for, if not my playlist?" She blows a bubble herself and I'm still stuck on the fact I'm no longer in possession of my gum.

There's a gentle pull from her at the longest chain on my neck that catches my attention again.

"You're new," I say. My voice coming out thick with the fantasies of all the ways I want her blaring through my mind.

Big, brown eyes blink up at me. "To this club, yea. But every club is the same after a while."

She's not drunk or high or anything. All the dancers are usually one or more of those things.

I meet her eyes and they're unguarded as she looks back at me. "That right?"

She nods, slowly. "Unless you have something *new* to show me..." There's a tease in her statement.

Maybe it's a dare.

Something new? I can do that.

"Stand," I tell her and she gets to her feet. With a hand on her hip, and the blue reflecting off her brown skin, every one of her delicious curves is on display.

"Spin."

She's the picture of desire as the little skirt has risen just a bit for me to see the deep cleft of her ass is peeking through. *I want to bite it.* A little glimpse of the black g-string she must have on under this thing is all that separates her from my touch.

When she's returned to facing me again, she asks, "Will I do?"

Taking a deep breath in, I exhale the idea that I will not be giving this woman all my attention. "You will."

I pull the k-bar from my hip and cut the black fabric off her hips. I'm quick and even though she flinches, my knife is sharp enough to remove the skirt before she can register it.

In a mess of strings sliding down her body, Diamond stands before me in only a tiny g-string and an even smaller triangle bra top.

She does nothing to cover her body, but instead steps over the ruined clothes to bend at the waist over the bed.

Her peachy ass is on full display for me. So round and soft, I can't see the little slit just waiting for me tonight.

My eyes trail over the arch of her back to the lust glittering in her eyes when she says, "Does this mean we can start?"

Chapter 3
Diamond

Men are so easy.

It doesn't take much to catch their attention. No matter what kind of guy they *think* they are, if they're attracted to women—then they're an easy mark.

And Blue Dupont has just been caught in what will ultimately be his downfall.

Standing in a private room with just about two inches of fabric covering my body, I should feel exposed and vulnerable.

Except, I don't.

All the societal pressures and stigmas about modesty or even "purity" are an unknown concept for me.

That's what happens when you grow up the way I did.

Walking over to the neatly-made bed, I arch my back so my ass is on full display for Blue. "Does this mean we can start?" I ask with my forearms on the soft mattress underneath me.

I feel his hot eyes on me, raking over the position I'm in and it only takes seconds for him to get to me.

"Fuck, Diamond. You've got me bricked up," he says leaning over me but pointedly not touching.

Uh-huh. "So what are you going to do about it?" I kick a leg up for my diamanté heel to rest beside me on the bed. The position spreads me further so there is no mistaking what is waiting for him.

Take the bait. Take it and fall.

His fingers skim along my leg from my ankle, over my fishnets, to the exposed skin of my thigh and further to where the curve of my ass begins. His rough fingers graze the underside of my cheek there and I shiver.

"So what? You paid five grand just to have a conversation with me?" I drop my leg to the ground and flip, so my legs can wrap around him. He's pliant, allowing me to pull him into my body easily.

His teeth pull at his bottom lip as he takes his fill of what he can see of my body. "Nah. Saw you walk in and knew I needed to at least have some time."

This man is tall. At least 6'3", probably 6'5". And he's built, strong like... he's gotta work out. You expect that the higher up you go in an organization like his—the boss might be a little lazy. Probably let himself go. But this man looks like he's still working at the bottom.

Hungry and grinding.

I run my hands under his collar and feel the warm skin beneath my fingers. *Just because he's a mark doesn't mean I can't enjoy myself...*

"So, what exactly were you planning on doing with all this... time?" His hold on my waist is tight as he looks down at me on the bed with barely anything separating our bodies.

He smiles and it's not the kind of expression that's meant to convey happiness. It doesn't touch his eyes in a joyful way. There's an edge to this look and it's enough to make my core clench. His defined cheek bones and jaw are obvious under a neat beard. He is all edges, hardened and menacing without having to say a word. "Guess I was gonna figure out what you like and maybe show you what I like."

"That's an awful lot of maybes... " I hedge, begging him to make a move.

"Well, if you know what I want and what I should be doin' with my time here then maybe you should show me."

"There's that maybe again..." I tease. "I could show you, but I don't know if you're ready for all that."

His hold on my waist tightens a fraction as his eyes sharpen further on me. "Well, why don't you try me and see what's up?"

Surely, the King of Green is not *this* easy.

I know I said men are easy, but my expectations for what I was going to be up against are extremely flawed.

If my mother taught me anything, it's to tell them nothing. The most important rule is always to have the upper hand. *And knowledge is power.* Especially when it's knowledge of the competition.

When Terrell Lafayette Sr. fell for my mother, he left her high and dry when he found out she was pregnant. She was never the vengeful type. She was the "fuck you" and "do better without you" type of woman.

And she did do better. She went back home to Georgia and raised me with all the strength of a hammer. Pretty, smart and resourceful—like any good girl should be. Straight A's and an MBA to boot. From an online college but a degree is a degree. Like I said, knowledge is power.

She would likely still be the powerhouse she once was if she were still here.

But I want what Faye Sr. denied me.

An empire.

I could be running the business that should rightfully be mine right now. Instead, he gave everything to Terrell Jr, his sorry excuse for a son, who blew their biggest accomplishment all over hard drugs and greed.

Nothing is more important than the money.

But Faye Jr. doesn't know that. He's never had to earn and that's why he will be the downfall of the Fayes in Louisiana.

Unless I step in.

Blue Dupont is key to having the upper hand so I can take over my family's business. As the oldest, I should have first right to the succession of power. Dear old dad, never acknowledged me or my mother, so I'll get what's mine another way if I have to.

I'm going to come down on these families like the tool I was honed to be.

Untying the skinny straps from behind my head the two small triangles drop from my body. The man in front of me watches the glittering fabric fall and he catches his full lower lip between his teeth again.

His thumb slides up and over a nipple. They become hard and sensitive under his attention. His other hand is still holding me firmly, radiating heat through my middle and down to my core.

My head falls back and I moan when he fully grips my breast.

"Look right here. Don't look away," he says with gravel in his voice.

Shit, that's sexy.

My eyes meet his and the intensity of his attention hits me twofold. The presence of this man is a force within itself. It seems to expand from his body and take up all the space in the room. But it's also in his voice. I know he can control how much force there is behind his words. The ones he just said had so much weight behind them *even I obeyed.*

And obeying any man is about as low on my list of priorities as licking the concrete on Bourbon street.

It's then that I snap back to my task and make myself remember there are actually things we need to discuss before this goes any further.

"R-rules," I stutter out. Cursing myself internally—I have to get my shit together. *Another extremely unlikely thing for me to do.* I'm confident in my speech and have spent years perfecting my conviction to stand tall in a room of competitors. This man is absolutely my competition. *This is a job.* "You have to respect the rules in this room."

There, sounds more like me.

"Really?" He nods slowly, still keeping his gaze locked with mine. "Tell me then. Never been in one of these before."

He's never had a private room? That surprises me.

He probably doesn't need one. With the way he looks and the reputation he carries, I'm sure he has no issues finding a woman to warm his bed.

Warm his bed? Ugh, what am I? Geriatric?

I'm skeptical, but I lay out all the rules for him anyway. "No kissing on the lips. Consent is always verbal. Condoms, every time. No government names or identities. And finally, no recording."

All of these are the reasons why I knew this would be my way to get exactly what I wanted from the man in front of me. Sex work is not usually my bag. I've dabbled in it a few times at my old place, but it was too much for me to handle every night. I found my love on the pole and tend to stay away from the beds. Here though, I could at least be safe, all while I get the information I need. If he can't follow the rules then I'll be stuck trying to find another in.

He shrugs and relaxes. "Ain't gotta worry about any of that with me." He looks my body over from my clavicles to my hard nipples, down to my waist and bites his lip when he gets to the generous swell of my hips. His intense gaze lingers on my calf and toes and it's something I feel—like he's touched me there when he hasn't.

I am the product he has so generously paid thousands to possess for the night. And with the intensity of his inspection, I would say he is happy with his purchase.

"Good," I say, stepping out of his hold, allowing my hips to brush over him when I turn for him to see my ass again. "Have any ideas now?"

"Too many," he exhales.

Strong brows furrow over dark eyes that seem bottomless in depth. Deep brown skin like mahogany beckons my fingertips to explore. His locs are neatly styled and stop just below his shoulders. I wonder if he maintains them or if someone else does it for him. I can't see his arms though they stretch the limits of the long sleeve shirt he has on. Well defined and big enough to hold me up if we actually get to have some fun and try out any of *the ideas* he has *so many* of. He wears tactical pants like he's in the military or something, so they're baggy on his dense frame. Even still, I can see how hard he is for me. I won't lie and say I'm not thinking about what's hiding underneath that fly.

"Lay back on the bed how you were before." There is no leeway in his command. I purposefully take my time repositioning myself with my ass presented for him.

"Like this?" I ask primly, while blinking up at him. Looking as willing and desperate as I should for a client. But this time, I *am* very willing to see what this man will do next.

"Just like that, bae," he says. "Spread your legs. Wanna see that pussy drip for me."

A tingle shoots down my spine as I follow his directions and step apart. Cool air meets my lips. The string presses firmly against my clit, making me acutely aware of how turned on I am right now.

He wants to see me drip? He's well on his way with how he looks at me open and ready for him.

With two steps, he reaches me and the knife from earlier glints menacingly in his grip. A thick finger traces the waist of my g-string before he asks, "Can I take these off?" He didn't ask to cut up my skirt, but since I laid out the rules I'm happy he's taking them seriously.

"Yes," I respond quickly and with all the impatience I'm feeling. He lifts the fabric to slide the knife under. A needy little moan escapes me when my clit is pressed even harder against the thin strip of fabric.

He pauses and tugs on it again, but I try to stifle the second moan.

"Let me hear you. Paid good money for that needy moan you're tryin' to keep from me."

I huff out a breath and, blessedly, he frees me from the g-string with a swift flick of his wrist.

His knife is practically an extension of him. Men and women alike are terrified of what he can do with it. Talk of his venom treatment is what strikes fear in anyone who dares cross him. The shiny gleam of it tells me there is no venom on it now, but one wrong move and who's to say what might happen with just a nick.

He puts the blade back into its sheath and before I have long to think about the menace that was only millimeters from my skin, his index and middle fingers slide through my folds with embarrassing ease. "That gets you wet, huh? Maybe I should bring the K back out."

Did it? Turn me on?

Make me this wet?

I close my eyes, letting the feeling of his fingers running over the sensitive flesh between my legs light something inside me. "Did you like my knife between your legs, bae?" He asks again.

The words alone have me pressing my thighs together, trapping his hand between them. I've been doing this long enough to know *work is work*. It's better to enjoy it than to resist any positive feeling you can get from a client. Never have I ever been this wet so soon into a job though.

Is it this man? What power I know he holds, not just in the room but in the business I admire. Is it because of the way he handles that knife? Is it how he's touching me like I belong to him? Like he knows my body? Or am I just ovulating?

White hot desire sparks low, demanding more already and I haven't even seen his dick yet.

He pauses and I'm close to whining in frustration. "Need an answer or I'll take my fingers away."

"Yes. Yes, I liked it." The honesty flows from me on the wave of whatever magic he is working on my clit as he rolls the bud up and down between his fingers. Squeezing and teasing me with deliciously sure movements. His confidence is sexy as fuck mixed with the deep timbre of his voice. It's doing all the right things to me.

Suddenly something cold is at my entrance.

He doesn't stop playing with me.

I clench over nothing as I can't see exactly what is *almost* inside me. It's hard to think when he's getting me so close to coming. I turn my head to try and get a better look at what exactly he's doing, but it's no use.

He still wears all his clothes which do a good job of highlighting just how much I'm at his mercy right now.

"Fuck, Diamond. You're gonna soak my shit." Blue leans over my back with his lips so close to my ear when he whispers, "Are you gonna take this handle like a good girl and show me how bad you want this dick or am I gonna have to tie you up?"

Oh.

Fuck.

Chapter 4
Diamond

I'm fucked.

In the literal sense and in the figurative sense. And it's not something I was expecting.

The knife.

It's the knife that's poised right at my opening and I basically asked him for it.

I should be terrified that he has a weapon so close to the most sensitive part of me.

That fear tangles with adrenaline and creates a need that I can't comprehend.

I have never had a knife this close to me so many times and definitely not this close to my vagina.

But, I asked for this.

The handle of his knife slides into me with an ease I could only thank him for. He's the one who made me wet enough to coat the rough material that feels like it was ribbed for my pleasure as each one of the moulded ridges enters me slowly. His breath is warm on my neck as the thumb guard reaches my hole.

I'm breathy and spun up but I manage, "Blue, what are you doing to me?"

"Exactly what I want," he says into my ear, sending more hot lust down to my pussy. The handle is not exactly large, but it's bigger than I could have thought. "Show me how good you take it. Don't want any of that fake moanin' shit."

Fake moaning?

I feel my legs close to shaking with the quickening of how he's thrusting the knife into me. I have to remember this is work. He is a mark. I'm here for a reason and it was not to make a mess of his knife to the point of losing my mind.

But I am.

Losing my mind, that is.

Each ridge of the handle catching that spot inside me perfectly as my channel squeezes. He moves it in and out again. My head falls back. He has a hand in my hair so he can keep an eye on my expressions while I take his knife.

How is this so fucking sexy? If anyone had asked me if coming on someone's knife was a kink I was into, I would have disagreed.

Would have disagreed vehemently and likely cursed them out.

I would have been dead wrong.

But it's not just the knife.

It's the man and how expertly he does… everything. I was not prepared to be introduced to something new when I teased him earlier.

This is definitely new. For me, anyway.

As a glorified sex doll, I thought I'd seen it all but very few men have imagination.

I wonder how many other women has he done this with.

Fucking hell.

Slowly, so achingly slow, he removes the handle from my pussy before I have a chance to crest that wave.

This time, I do whine. "No—"

Did I just come close to begging this man?

Unfortunately, yes.

What is happening to me?

My eyes travel up to his and they shine in the darkness. He's smiling again. That same sinister look, but this time—I know there is something devilish behind it. No *sane person would think to put their knife inside of someone they just met.* It's likcly not an uncommon occurrence for him. I'm lucky that it wasn't the pointy side first.

His tongue peeks out from his lips to take a long lick of the mess I've made on the handle. It's sexual and absurdly intimate as his eyes never leave mine.

"Never waste a drop," he says before his tongue laves over the glove he was wearing to protect his hand, too.

I've never been jealous of anything more. I want to be that glove with his tongue laving over me.

Blue removes the glove and tosses it to the bed. His knife is back in the holster and I catch sight of the tattoos on his fingers. Snakes writhe over the lot of them, winding up his arm to under his sleeve.

I was so close to coming but never got there. With how easily he worked me, I know it was on purpose.

He knew and he left me hanging there.

"There's more where that came from," I say, lifting my leg so I'm spread for him again. His eyes drop to the wetness still dripping from me. Moments from reaching the blankets beneath me.

With an enthusiastic nod, he says, "You're gonna soak my face, bae. And you're gonna do it right now." Lying on his back, he beckons me over to him.

I'm stuck staring at the large man who, even on his back, fills the room with his big presence.

"I don't like repeatin' myself," he remarks when I'm still there looking at the man making me feel too many things I shouldn't be. "Crawl to me."

Oh.

Only a fool would deny Blue Dupont.

I crawl on the bed to him, stopping by his shoulder. "Leg over," he directs, patting the thigh closest to him just once. I raise it and he slides under me.

When I said no kissing. I'm glad it did not include these lips.

Again, I feel the exchange of control I'm giving him, even from a position over his face.

He demands and I've succumbed.

I don't feel a single loss when his tongue runs the length of my center from my still sensitive clit, to my opening, back even farther to my ass.

There is a rumble deep from his chest that resonates through me as I find a rhythm over his mouth. Fingers digging into my cheeks as he rocks me over his face, not shy about the slickness of me coating him and easing my ride. Other noises of appreciation pour from him like a direct line to my libido. The blue lights blur into a much brighter hue as his noises match the intensity of the climax I'm fast approaching.

My eyes squeeze shut when two of his fingers enter me and finally, finally I'm clenching on something that can get me where I want to go.

Blue is taking me somewhere I had not planned on going *at all*.

Lie on my back and say all the right things to lure him in?

Yes.

Sit on his face as he makes me reconsider if this is my new religion?

No. No *no no no no*.

Then, his teeth graze my clit and it's just the right amount of a shift in sensation to send me careening over the edge.

I reach for something, anything to sink my fingers into, to hold on to what little grasp of reality I could find. My body bows over and my bid for purchase in the sheets below us ends up including his long hair. I feel their resistance as I pull his locs in my grip, wave after wave of intense tremors wracking my body.

He hums in low tones contentedly through my core, keeping firm pressure on that spot inside of me until finally I'm spent and smothering him under my body.

After a few moments, when I try to catch my breath, I remember there is a person under me.

Blue sinks his teeth into the soft skin of my thigh that makes me yelp in surprise and scramble off of him. He takes a deep inhale once he's freed from between my legs.

I look at the spot where his teeth have left indents. *He marked me?* It wasn't hard enough to break skin, but it might bruise. *Will definitely bruise.* I know he couldn't necessarily breathe, but somehow I know he didn't do it simply because he wanted air.

By the time I stop thinking about it, he's up and over at the nightstand taking the package of wipes out to clean his face. "So, when do you work again?"

"Work again?"

He's not gonna fuck me?

What. The. FUCK?

He can't just—

Wait.

This is exactly where I need him to be. Even though I would like to finish what he started. I'll be spending way too much time thinking about whether or not I've developed a questionable knife kink because of this man.

"Yea." He puts another piece of gum into his mouth with the kind of cool, calm that is infuriating considering the turn of my thoughts. "What nights you here?"

Confusion still bangs around my skull and I can't keep the question in. "You're leaving?"

He doesn't answer, instead walking over to the door and knocking once.

Fighting the urge to let my mouth hang open, I'm still naked on the bed. I should grab one of those wipes for myself, since it doesn't look like he's gonna stick around—let alone clean me up. Before I can reach for the drawer and get what I'm looking for, the music from the club filters in as one of his guards hands him a bag.

Blue takes out five stacks of cash that are neatly bundled and puts them on the small table by the door.

"This the last time imma say I hate repeatin' myself." He turns to face me fully and allows the door to close behind him. "When do you work again?"

That weight of his presence presses against me, menace teasing along the edges.

I've caught his attention and that was the whole point of me being here. If I expect to get what I came here for then I need to keep it. Pissing him off is probably not the best way to do that.

"I work weekends through Wednesdays," I respond after giving myself the clean up he hasn't.

He nods, but doesn't respond right away. I take the pause in our conversation to decide what I'll do next.

My outfit lay in shreds on the floor, so I have nothing to wear out of this room. It smells of what we did and how I almost lost the whole damn plot because he made my legs shake.

I press into the left wall by the tablet and it opens to reveal the club robes that are kept in there. Allen told us we give nothing away for free—like I didn't already know that. As I shrug it on, Blue frowns in a way that feels too comical for the big man.

"What?" I ask, taking time to take my hair out of the collar and assess how I'm looking in the mirror on the closet door. I normally just blow-dry my hair and braid it to sleep so there is a soft wave in the length that remains voluminous around me. Right now, it's hot under my hair and under his scrutiny.

"Nothin," he responds, coming back into the room to stand behind me. In the reflection, I'm able to see how good we look together. It's a jarring thought because—what the hell? I'm not supposed to be thinking about *together.*

He. Is. A. Mark.

How I keep forgetting when he's touching me.

And he is. Touching me, that is.

His hands are on my waist and I know the touch is possessive. *Just like the bite he left me on my thigh.*

Is that what he does with all the girls he brings to the private rooms?

He doesn't get private rooms. Which I believe. Though if it's not in a room like this, I still know he's not lonely.

Especially not with the knowledge he clearly has about how to do... all he just did with my body.

Hell, I have not totally even recovered or processed what just happened.

I'm one of many and he's not my man. This is a job.

"Why didn't you fuck me?" I ask. There is no desperation in my tone, just curiosity. It was on the table and he… passed.

"Didn't?" His head tilts to the side as his hand trails up my side to below my breast. My nipple hardens and becomes much too obvious with nothing but the single layer of blush silk covering it. He watches in the mirror and I'm drawn to watch him, too.

"You never took your clothes—" My voice is breathy as his intention pulses heavy in the air without him having to utter a single word. His other hand matches the movements of the first and now my back is pressed to his front. "Off," I say, finally finishing my sentence on an exhale.

There is no mistaking this man is hard. The thick ridge of him sits between my cheeks. Its insistence is the beginning of what will likely be a Pavlovian response if anything from earlier is an indication of what I have to look forward to.

Who's to say there *is* anything to look forward to?

The man never even took his clothes off.

With my tits in his hands, he makes eye contact with me. It's intense and unyielding. "I don't pay for it," he replies, still playing with my breasts in his hands.

I blink several times and then I look over to the money that's so obviously sitting on the table. He follows my gaze and our eyes meet in the mirror again. "Told you I wanted some time with you. Time is money." His head nods once to the stacks again and he adds, "That wouldn't even start to cover how much my dick is worth." His sinister smile lifts on one side and I scoff.

"Well, I guess I'll never know." *That's it Rocky,* reel him in.

He crouches by the loveseat and picks up my outfit that he cut off of me, putting it into one of his cargo pockets. "Oh nah. You will. But when I'm ready for you."

But that's where he's wrong. He might have gotten me distracted for a minute earlier—okay, maybe longer.

There is still something I'm absolutely sure of.

He will never be ready for me.

I'm the one thing he never saw coming.

Chapter 5

BLUE

"And this woman you blew me off for is...?"

In front of my desk, my best friend looks just as pissed as I figured she would be in her pressed pantsuit. It's a deep navy color I know she picked because she's working at my place today.

When we were younger, everyone speculated she would be in the WNBA because of how tall she is and her love of the sport. Steph has always been about the money so she chose a different path. Now, she looms over me with her ball player height as smoke pours out of her ears.

Her temper is the least of my problems though. I give her a terse response. "She's new."

There was also speculation that her and I would end up together because we were on that court together more times than not growing up. It's because of her that I started going by Blue. She was nasty on the court, throwing elbows, fouling out. I had a black eye so often because of her sharp ass elbows. One day she said, *your eye is so black it's damn near blue.*

Then she just kept calling me that.

We were only in middle school and other kids caught on to it. They thought it was too funny that a *girl* gave *me* a black eye. Maybe it's a Southern thing or a Louisiana thing, but once you get a nickname, regardless of what it is, that bitch sticks. Can't ever get rid of it. I didn't care about losing to Steph or getting a black eye. What I couldn't abide was the disrespect to me and the base of it being the fact that Steph's a girl.

Turns out, Steph wasn't the only one who could throw an elbow or make someone blue with bruises. Bet I never heard anyone say "Blue," in mockery again. I own the name with pride, while they cower in fear.

It was many years later when I picked up a blade instead of using my fists. The tattoos only cover part of the damage my hands have seen. They definitely don't cover the damage I carry elsewhere. I flex my hands, feel the tightening of old scar tissue and begin massaging the digits. Years and four surgeries later, they still don't work as well as they should. I've adapted and most couldn't tell. For that I'm grateful.

"New?" She gives me an incredulous look back. "New... at the strip club?"

"She's a dancer, yea."

"And I waited at a brisket joint in bumfuck for an hour before Redd eventually showed up *without* the paperwork you were supposed to be having signed... because of a new dancer?" She was mostly upset because the barbecue spot I'd suggested we meet at was not a five star restaurant with table side service. She had gotten more uppity over time as her net worth increased. Something I knew only made Redd damn near feral.

Who am I playing?

That man is feral.

"He did sign it." I slide the papers across the desk to her and she finally sits in her plush leather chair across from me.

It takes her a moment, but she looks up at me and the incredulous look she had before is now twice as intense. "There is no addendum. This is the original offer I drew up."

Steph Perry has made a killing in real estate on the legal side, and recently—*not so legal* side, as she's been looking for ways we can expand the business as undetected as possible. We have several small businesses from restaurants to galleries, all keeping the money clean. The massive warehouse we're in now, is an actual storage facility for many of these businesses all operating under a larger corporation that I own. Off Topz was meant to be a joke on her part when she presented the option to me.

Honestly, what is more cliché than dirty business happening in a strip club?

And that's what made it perfect to me.

Little did I know I was going to see a woman who caught my attention moments after settling that deal. Caught isn't an accurate word for what happened to me. The moment I saw her, she was under my skin and I couldn't stop thinking about having her.

Still can't.

That has never been something I've experienced before.

From a young age, my dad had always told me women were only good for a few things. None of those things were worth repeating to you. I admired my pop for many things. His treatment of women, including my Ma, God rest her soul, was not on the list. In my mind, I had them very low on my list of priorities because a family was not something that could be possible for me.

Anything associated with me is a target. Just like my Ma, there is no way to save an innocent tied to us in this life.

Pa was a duffle-bag boy, and slung his shit everywhere. No finesse, process, or system. Went to prison twice and came out to keep selling again. He might not have been a picture perfect role model, but he always encouraged me to take the game he was running and do it better.

He had done well for himself. We lived comfortably and his reputation preceded him. Hence, all the lil' dudes who tried their luck with me. I knew it would fall to me to take over the Dupont name and be the successor this family needed. My little brother, Tony, wasn't built for this life and with everything I've done, keeping him as far from it is the luxury I've been afforded.

"Signed and notarized," I say, still looking at my computer and sifting through the files Redd sent me before Steph came barging in.

"Wow." She sits back in her seat, letting the folder close. She slicks a hand over her ponytail. "Makes my job a helluva lot easier. I'll finish this up then." Steph crosses a leg over the other. I can see the irritation she had earlier receding into nothing. "So, this new girl?"

She starts in on me, but I hit her with my own nosy ass question. "So, your barbecue dinner?"

She grimaces at me and I already know what she's going to say, but she says it anyway. "Nothing happened there. I ordered because I was hungry and the food was actually really good."

"That all?" I hedge. Redd might be a nosy fucker, but he won't give me more than crumbs when it comes to his fascination with my best friend.

One might think that my two best friends would be friends with each other. *Nah.* Redd has made it clear that he will not be sitting in a friend's territory with her in any capacity.

"That's all," she says through clenched teeth.

"And Redd—"

"Was annoying as shit, per usual. Why did you even send him if he didn't have the papers?"

"I didn't."

She looks genuinely confused. "So how did he..." She trails off and I let her.

There is no way I'm gonna confirm or deny anything about why Redd knew where she was.

She rolls her eyes. She knows I won't either. "Whatever. Don't change the subject. We're talking about your new girl."

"It's a temporary investment." She raises a brow. "I gotta be seen at the club I just bought. She's somethin' to look at while I'm there."

She scoffs and checks her manicure. "You'd be there anyway."

Steph was unclear of what I actually do outside of buying these properties. Everybody outside of the life could speculate. Rumors have some merit to them. Which is by design so as few of my people as possible would go down with me if I ever got caught up in some shit I couldn't buy my way out of.

And there is very little I couldn't buy my way out of right now. But the things I couldn't–it would be a tidal wave crashing indiscriminately over all of us.

She is probably the only person outside of Redd who knew who I really was. *And she still thinks I like being at strip clubs.*

"Wanna come next time?"

"No. I would not. Tits and ass don't do it for me." Then, she thinks on it for a bit. "You know… if they had ladies' night with like Magic Mike or something—I'd be down."

I narrow my eyes at her. "Not at my club."

"Well, the answer is no." She smooths the front of her suit after standing and pulls a stack of folders from her bag. "These are the next. Tell me if you want any of them. My picks are tabbed with red." She points to the ones she means with a neatly manicured finger. "And Blue?" She waits for me to stop looking over the files. When I do, she says, "If you like this girl, then don't let her get away."

I have zero intentions of doing so.

"Heard," I tell her and she gives me a satisfied nod before her heels click out the door.

As soon as she leaves though, I'm back to my computer. Reading over more of what Redd sent me about the newest dancer at Off Topz. I can feel the smile on my face. The selfie on her application captures the bold confidence I saw without question. Her big hair, like a mane, around a perfect face and juicy lips. I regret not getting a kiss, but I also know it goes against the rules of the club. I'll taste them soon enough. If they're anywhere near as sweet as the lips I *did* taste, those rules are protecting more than her.

The rules were just for a private room. *Right?*

No government names went out the window, as soon as I pulled her file. From the application I can see Rocky "Diamond" Owens was born Racquelle in Atlanta, Georgia. She has a degree… A masters? Fuck me. Beautiful and smart.

This is her third club and she has references…

If she's got these degrees, why is she still working at the club for me?

There's a link to her social media and I fall immediately into the rabbit hole of her strong legs and pole dancing.

Video after video of her suspended in the air from a single leg around the pole. She maintains crazy height, sometimes spinning at a pace I could never imagine. In some she's moving up and down the pole like gravity just doesn't exist. It's hypnotizing and some of the videos loop repeatedly before I realize I've been watching the same thirty-second clip for five minutes.

My dick is hard as fuck picturing her putting on a show just for me. At the same time, irrational fury assaults me thinking about how many people have gotten the private show I want to keep for myself.

I haven't seen her do any of this in real life and now I'm considering pulling her from the floor so she only works in the private room for me.

Need to see her soak my fucking knife like she did again. The same knife I've ended countless lives with, stained red so often it has its own rep.

I almost went back on my word and shoved my dick deep inside her. *Fuck, I wanted to.* I didn't even have any rubbers. That's how sure I was that I wouldn't be fucking anyone.

And if I hadn't stopped when I did, I probably would have tried to fuck her raw. Have my nut seeping out of those fat pussy lips so I could stuff it back inside her with my knife again.

What the fuck am I saying?

Vert comes into the office and the music from today's video is still playing on repeat. I know he knows how many times it's played at this point. She captioned it, "warming up for tonight" with a blue heart emoji after it.

A *blue fucking heart.*

Goddamn.

She's twirling slowly around the pole with both legs wrapped around and her hands trailing over her fuck-me body. She's got on another of those shiny, minuscule outfits—tight and tiny.

I'm already itching for my blade to take all of it off.

"We headin' over there, boss?" Vert finally asks from the doorway. I had forgotten he came in to be completely honest.

"Yea," I respond.

One night, became two nights, became three nights of watching Diamond twirl around the pole and stroll through the club like she was the one who owned this fucking place—not me.

For whatever reason, I let her do her thing. I didn't press her or demand the time I wanted. I watched and gave her space. Wanted to touch her but needed her to come to me on her own terms.

I couldn't show anyone I had an interest in this woman because she would have a target on her back in that very same breath.

And if I gave myself an inch with her for someone to see, they would know how much I want her. I'd absolutely take the full mile and that was dangerous for us both.

The first night, I walked in and sat at my usual booth, all my men with me. But I know she felt me in the club. From the pole, I saw her motions completely pause when I got into the area where all the raised platforms are. *She was playing with me.* Each time it was her slot on the stage, she glittered under the blue spotlights, making each reflective outfit look like her namesake. Bills steadily rained down on the stage.

Easily I'd blow bands just to keep the stage covered in mostly my money.

At the end of each performance, they would sweep the cash into the trench in the back for her to collect the money and have it counted backstage. By the time she was back on the floor, I fought every urge to grab her if someone else got her attention.

Twice, I had to enforce the "no touching" rules on the floor. I was close to catching a fucking charge for a woman I barely even knew. Less than a week I owned this club and I had to replace all the bouncers with my own men. None of which complained about the reassignment. Surveillance in a car at the same late hours was far worse than seeing some of Louisiana's finest women in as little clothing as possible for the same pay. I'm gonna win boss of the goddamn year at this point.

The rules are the rules though.

You don't touch what's mine.

My men threw out anyone whoever dared break the rules with my Diamond.

I was willing to pay for her time.

Anytime she wanted.

But I didn't want to block her hustle. In her element, she was like some mystical being as the lights glinted off her. Thick hair trailing her back. Little glimpses of her body teasing here and there. Strong legs always in fishnets.

One thing I'd never allow her to do again?

Take anyone to a private room if it wasn't me.

Dancers have the option to accept or decline a reservation of their room since there were so few limitations inside. If they were uncomfortable or just didn't want to, they could decline.

My name was the only one on the list and it was there every night. She has yet to show up for one.

Today, I'm getting my time.

As I wait in the room we had before, it takes everything in me not to be impatient.

When the sound of the club's music comes in through the open door, I sense before I see her realize she accepted the room with me and not Vert as I booked it.

She appears shocked for a moment, but then she collects herself quickly.

"Blue," she says, her sensual voice wrapping around me like it's meant to, "what are you doing here?"

Raising a brow, I ask, "Expectin' someone else?"

"Yes," she says simply.

Tonight, she wears black and silver stars over her full tits and another tiny skirt that has black stars over the silver fabric. Her belly button ring dangles with a spray of stars. Silver eye makeup makes her brown eyes look even bigger as she holds my stare when I meet them.

"Been busy?" I ask, though I know she has been. It's hard work to hide from someone as persistent as me.

"Thankfully," is all she says when she sits on the bed. *The bed.* Not on the loveseat with me. I suck my teeth, praying for calm because at this point, I'm ready to grab her and leave this fucking club.

Showing restraint with a woman is a completely foreign concept, but I knew letting her out of my grasp was out of the question.

What the hell is she doing to me?

Chapter 6
Diamond

Men are so easy.

As a second point to this list of reasons why I underestimated my abilities: it only took three days to settle myself deep in Blue's mind.

On the other hand, I did have him embedded in my thoughts too.

Far more than I'd like.

Yes, everything depended on this job, but I was finding it hard to separate the work hours from not work hours.

And dammit, he had ruined sex for me. Just one night with him and not a single toy in my drawer could get me close to the feeling I had in his possession.

On that vein alone, I wanted to taunt him.

Just like my orgasm that was evading me farther and farther the longer I was without his touch—he would wait for the time with me he wanted.

"Been busy?" He asks and I chuckle internally. *Hurts, don't it?*

Each night, I felt his energy barreling into me—up on the pole, across the floor, even the break room. My experience was all I had to fall back on to keep me unbothered and present in my tasks at work. It was like a warmth that held weight unlike any I've felt before. If I believed in magic, I would suspect he had something like it to press you without having to be close.

In this room now, I feel it—feel him.

My baser self wants me to present myself like a feast so I can feel what I felt before. But my more rational self knows, if I can just—for a moment—get my bearings, I can manipulate the situation how I need to.

Men are so easy.

Blue is a man.

"Thankfully," is how I respond as I trail a hand up my thigh to the garter clip that holds the stocking I'm wearing tonight and open it.

He sucks his teeth, a sign of displeasure though he still sits on the loveseat. He's not making a move and the restraint is evident in how his angular jaw ticks.

The stocking is quick to relax down toward my calf. "Could you help me with these? They're driving me crazy."

His eyes follow the line of my legs to my feet and then back up again.

Come on, Blue. Move when I say because I'm the one in control now.

He just leans back in his seat—half shadow, half man—with the kind of calm that screams predator, and I almost forget what I came here to do, again. His energy is begging me to fold under it, give him what *he* wants.

I double down in resisting just that.

A few seconds pass before I entice a little more in opening the other garter clip and the second stocking rolls down my leg.

He's up out of his seat then, taking long strides to get to me quickly. The man smells like sandalwood and sin. A slow burning scent, one that doesn't beg for attention but leaves its memory to haunt you long after he's gone.

Like him.

He watches me, strong arms stretching against his sleeves, tattooed fingers clenching in the moody blue lighting. Calculated. Dangerous. Beautiful in the way a knife is beautiful right before it ruins everything.

Or simply changes the way you think about pleasure.

"You're quiet tonight," he remarks and it feels like he's making a point before kneeling in front of the bed. He rolls one stocking down with slow movements, lingering against the smooth skin of my calf. I fight the shiver from the heat his touch leaves behind.

His voice is the kind that curls around your spine and tells your survival instinct to sit the hell down. I hate how easily I want to let it.

"I'm thinking..." I hedge.

He looks up at me from where he kneels. "'Bout what?"

You.

What it means that I never questioned your authority over me and let it feel something like concern for my well being that curls something low in my belly.

What it means that I wanted to tell you everything about my plans instead of allowing them to weaken your outfit further.

I definitely cannot tell him that.

"About the girls who had you before," I lie, knowing it'll make him pause the sensual touch he has on my leg.

He does. Slight tilt of his head, that faint tick in his jaw again. "There's no girl who's *had* me before." There's an inflection there that does the heavy lifting of his meaning.

I nod, as if that settles it. But inside I'm screaming because that was a petty question. *Why does it matter if there was someone before me?* The fact he reconfirms for me without complaining about repeating himself again is significant somehow.

And Blue... Blue smiles at me like he knows.

That unhappy smile is doing dangerous things to me.

He knows there was no reason besides a slight insecurity driving the question.

Like he's waiting for me to confess to the irrational possessiveness I feel.

I won't. This is all a game.

I sit across from him, the hem of my sparkly skirt is riding scandalously high on my thighs. His eyes don't flinch. They never do. He doesn't ogle. *He studies.* As if he's already dismantled me and is simply waiting for the pieces to stop moving.

"You trust me, Blue?" I ask and hate how breathless it sounds as he's still touching me proprietarily.

He chuckles deep and low. "Trust you to do exactly what you need to make money."

Right. I'm a dancer at his club.

I swallow hard. That line? That line should've put me back on mission.

Instead, it makes me wonder what it will be like to make money *with him* instead of for him.

Damn it.

I cross one leg over the other to buy time. I hope he mistakes it for nerves instead of guilt.

"I know who you are…" I hedge.

His eyebrow raises, "And who am I?"

"The King." I roll my shoulders back. "They call you the King of Green and the Dupont name is dangerous in the South."

His eyes hold mine, still unflinching. "That's me," is all he responds with, watching my face for anything that will give him information.

I can't blow this.

"I should stay far, far away from you. You're no good for me."

His head tilts toward the door. "Haven't left yet."

I shake my head. "I heard something tonight."

His brows slam down. "Go 'head."

"I heard someone's leaking info to the Fayes." There. Simple. Just laying it out. I did actually hear someone. Though the reasons why I was listening were purely selfish.

If I can establish that I can be useful in more than just sex, he will see me as more valuable to him.

At least, I hope so.

I need him to.

The corner of his lips drop and he stands, looming over me.

That's the moment I realize I've pushed too far. Not because he lunges, or raises his voice.

No.

Blue just leans forward, slow as molasses but infinitely more lethal.

"If I thought you would be sniffin' around my business," he says, "you wouldn't be sittin' in here, teasing me. You'd be in the bayou with venom in your veins and your pretty mouth shut for good."

Chills race across my skin.

But I'm not afraid.

God help me, I should be afraid.

Instead, I look into his eyes and wonder what it would feel like if that intensity was for me instead of aimed at me.

I'm losing control and daydreaming about things he could do with me too often.

And when he reaches for his knife, stopping in front of me with his presence swallowing me whole, I do something stupid.

I look up at him with hunger instead of fear.

He reaches down, fingers catching the hair at the nape of my neck, the blade's edge a breath away from my throat.

"Tell me why I shouldn't do just that," he demands.

You have to play this right, Rocky. You have to. "Because I can help you."

"Careful, Diamond," he sneers.

I should back away.

I don't.

I breathe him in—sandalwood, weed smoke, and something rich and ruinous. Then I whisper the words that will damn us both.

"Maybe I don't want to be careful."

Because even though I came here to dismantle him and take what I deserve... Part of me is starting to wonder what it might feel like to belong to the King himself.

"I don't mix business and pleasure so if you aren't one, then you're the other. And I'm in no mood to fuck around with my business."

Fire blazes in his eyes, hot enough to burn me where I stand. The control he has over me is intoxicating and addictive.

I want to surrender to him.

But I can't. This is where I need him.

Too emotional to think straight—to get sloppy and let me in.

"Neither am I," I breathe.

He has to take me.

I'm held with his grip in my hair, too off balance to do anything but let him hold me here. Any sudden movement and his knife will end whatever ambitions I could have had.

So I stay there as Blue's gaze burns over my vulnerable form as he thinks about what he will do next.

My heart is thundering in my ears.

I'm at his mercy and he has a reputation for showing none.

Finally, he lowers his knife and returns it to his hip. Before I can feel relief, his lips crash into mine. My back meets the bed, but the weight of his big body pins me in place. The hard feel of him, making a place for himself against my soft curves.

His tongue is battling with mine as we fall into whatever has been stretched thin between us like taffy. Everything we haven't said or done since that first night here becomes inconsequential.

Goddamn, this man can kiss.

He's just a mar—

My skirt rips with ease from my body. His hands are burning a path to my top to rip it off of me next. His mouth hasn't left mine, all while I'm one tiny g-string away from being naked for this man. Again.

It feels so good to have my body in his hands. I'm burning from his touch and how he brands himself into my skin.

His fingers find my center and I was wrong. That g-string doesn't mean shit when it comes to this man. His fingers enter me without any hesitation.

No.

Not enter. *Fill.* Two of his fingers are filling me because of how big they are and how tight I'm already squeezing them.

He hisses and grabs my breast roughly. "This pussy is beggin' to be full of me. Fuck, you're so tight."

His lids are heavy as he watches me take his fingers.

There's something crude about being naked while he's still in his clothes again.

The self control he has in not pulling his dick out and just fucking me like he so clearly wants to is another turn on I wasn't expecting.

I moan as he manages another finger inside. It's a stretch. It's too much I think.

He sees my expression, "You'll need at least one more to fit me," he clarifies.

A shiver runs down my spine. My lower belly clenches and clenches.

Four fingers.

Oh. My. God.

So big.

"I know, bae. Even if I wanted to, I'd hurt you tryin' to fuck."

He tries for a fourth finger anyway and I never make it.

I'm too far gone.

I'm over the edge and cum rolls down his hand over those snake tattoos freely.

"Look at how juicy this pussy is for me." He slides me up the bed to make room for himself between my legs.

I have to be able to see him.

I've been spoiled from my first O on his face. My hands carefully gather his locs so they don't get covered in my cum and he looks up at me for a moment with an emotion in his eyes I don't know how to name.

I don't get long to wonder about it because his mouth covers my clit to my opening, tongue dancing from top to bottom, driving me into another plane. My hips buck off of the bed and he does nothing to keep me in place.

Instead he slides those three fingers from earlier back inside me. I'm a little more relaxed now. He's able to get his index finger into the second knuckle while his middle is putting pressure at the top of my channel. It is a kind of dexterity I didn't know to be aware of. I'm stretched and stuffed—bordering on coming again when I know it hasn't been enough time.

"I ca-can't! Blue! It's too much."

He backs off, only to take his pinky out of my pussy and slide it into my ass.

"Ohh," I exhale as he easily fills both my holes. All while my clit is still being tormented in his mouth.

He hums, that deep rolling sound that comes somewhere from his chest, and I break.

A scream tears from my throat from the magnitude of this orgasm and the shock of how responsive he makes me.

I don't get a chance to come down from the high before he's pressing me.

"Tell me who's snitchin'," he says, the command rolling easily from his lips. He thinks he's got me in his hands when he couldn't be more wrong.

He's playing exactly into mine.

Body boneless and still on the high, my words come out in a sigh. "Dejuan. I saw him talk to Jay last night in a booth in the back. Isn't Jay a LaFayette?" *I knew he was.* And I also know Dejuan was only working under someone else's orders.

I need to know Blue trusts my word and what he would do when I give it.

"He is." He scratches his beard and the movement is agitated and quick. "What you hear?"

"He was confirming a drop? Jay slid him an envelope and left quickly after."

Blue gets off of the bed, going for the wipes to clean his face and hands again. This time, he doesn't just leave to get my money and go.

He leans over me, our noses brushing as he cleans me with one hand and the other on my face. It's gentle and affectionate. So out of place here even though it feels right.

"Don't care if you don't want to be careful. You will be careful in whatever it is that you're doin' sniffin' around the Fayes. Don't trust any of them around what's mine."

His.

I don't answer, too stunned that my plan is working so well. I nod instead and he leaves again, only returning briefly to leave my stacks on the table.

Chapter 7
Diamond

"Who you?" The elderly man who looks so much like me asks from his doorway.

I fidget with the hem of my tee over the waistband of my pants as he squints at me, trying to figure out if he really is seeing me. I know from pictures and the times I've seen him from afar, we are almost identical. Whatever are in his genes—they're potent. Both me and Terrell Jr. could be twins with how similar our features are.

He couldn't deny the resemblance if he tried.

After everything went down with Blue, I knew I had to at least try another way. I sat in that room considering any possible way that I could ally with Blue instead of making him my enemy. But it's too late with the truth already burning under my identity and what I came here to do.

Now, I stand in front of my biological father hoping for no more hiccups in my plans. Terrell Sr. and my mother weren't on speaking terms when she left the state. I'm certain that never changed even after.

She's gone now and he's an old man in retirement.

Maybe he will react differently to meeting me for the first time over a quarter of a century later. He's too close to seventy for me to just spring this on him but I must.

Years ago I was bitter and sad that he was never in my life. But now, I need to keep in mind that this is business.

I'm not here to get the dad I never had growing up.

I'm here to take everything he built and do better than he ever did.

"My name's Racquelle." I hike my purse onto my shoulder a little higher. "Do you mind if we sit for a bit and talk? Is that okay?" I say with as much decorum as I know how.

He nods, and unhurriedly opens the door wide enough to allow me inside. Why he would let a complete stranger into his house, is unclear to me. He must have some sort of security measures. *Maybe he doesn't.* That makes me more uncomfortable than it should.

His home is large enough to accommodate at least six rooms and as I walk through the foyer to the sitting room, it's clear that he made this home cozy and peaceful. So different from what the outside world must be like for him.

We end up in a little nook that's by a large bay window overlooking a lush garden outside with sculptures and a pond. The plush brown chair that's available across from him is framed in ornately carved wood that matches the carvings of the coffee table. He must have been reading the memoir that is closed with a bookmark sticking out of the top. The book sits next to a glass of what I hope is tea and not liquor this early in the morning.

I sit my purse on the table and cross my legs at the ankle. There is no point in beating around the bush with small talk so I plainly tell him, "I'm your daughter."

His face scrunches up, deepening the creases in his brow and around his mouth. "My what now?"

"Do you remember Genesis? Genesis Owens?" He shakes his head. I was really hoping to not discuss her dancing career, but I will give it a try anyway. "Krystal? She used to dance at the Golden Splash Cabaret before it burned down." My mom had left Louisiana long before the club was destroyed but that doesn't matter here.

I see the recognition in the lines of his weathered face before it turns to a sour expression. Quickly, I keep talking so he won't say something bad against my mom before I'm able to say what I need to. "I know you two were not on the best terms when you ended things, but I'm not here to talk about that or make it any better. She passed last year."

He doesn't speak for a moment as he processes what I've said. "So, what are you here for?" No condolences or anything. I shouldn't have expected there to be any from him.

I sit up a little taller. There is a reason why all of this is happening. Each move on my part has to benefit the goal. *Show no weakness, Rocky.* "I want to talk about business."

My father sips from his glass and returns it to the table. I note that he never offered a drink to me, but ignore that thought when he speaks again. "What kind of business?"

Gotta be frank, this man is no more concerned with me now than he was when I was standing at the door. Maybe I should have spent some time buttering him up but I don't know if I could with how little he gives a shit about me being here.

"You left everything to Junior. We both know he is not the best person to lead this family. He's making a mess of everything."

There's silence in the space between us, so I continue sharing what I know about Junior's bad business decisions.

"He's losing properties, tainting partnerships—he's costing this family so much more than it's profiting. To hide the losses from you, did you know he's moving smack into your clubs? A friend of mine is currently in rehab because of him." There is so, so much more to the story of his destruction but I don't elaborate further.

He leans away from me. Either surprised at my boldness or the fact I was privy to what should be family-only information.

But I am family and Junior is a hot fucking mess who is going to run this family into the ground.

Senior shakes his head, repeatedly. He must know or suspect that what I'm saying is true. He can't be that far removed from the business. "I don't even know you. You're a stranger to this life and these people. Why are you here tellin' me this?"

"I want to help you. I can be the head this family needs." I know how I sound coming here as a stranger, asking for what he's worked his whole life on. But I am his daughter and more deserving and qualified than his son.

He smacks the idea away with a scoff. "What makes you think you'd be a better leader than him?"

"I've been studying for this. I know what is going on in your business better than you or Junior do right now. I know the imports and the exports—running better than anyone. Let me show you what I can do. Don't let him ruin the LaFayette name for good."

I'm trying to give him a lifeline. If he gives me what I'm owed then it will be far better for him and his son than if I take it.

This is his first and only opportunity to make a smart decision.

There's compassion in his eyes for a moment and then he pats my hand. The gesture is condescending and I despise it instantly. "That was a lovely speech sweetheart, but there is nothin' I can do to help you. What's done is done. Either way, ain't how it works in this family. No one would respect or listen to you if I just told them to. I'm old and tired and I just wanna live out the rest of my days in peace. Terrell is the head of this family. It's been said and done."

My mind whirs a hundred miles a minute as I try to find a way or the words to say to get him on my side.

I don't get a chance because a ruckus comes into the room led by the man in question. He sips from a styrofoam cup, rattling with ice.

He sees our dad first and starts to say something before his eyes cut to me. "Who this?" Each of his steps is sluggish and it's like he's moving through mud or something to get to me. His bloodshot eyes are alarming, but it's the purple stain to his lips that gives me pause.

"You still sippin' that shit, boy!" Senior shouts, standing from his chair to snatch the cup out of his son's hand. He's able to with ease since Junior reflexes are absolutely shot. Senior sniffs the cup and gives his son a look of disdain. "Told you stop drinkin' that shit when you workin'. Hell, you won't listen to shit."

Senior takes the cup with him to the kitchen, leaving me in the room along with Junior and three of his goons. I square my shoulders as Junior looks me over. It's not hard to look like the better person when he's fucked up on cough syrup at mid-day when he should be working.

Before I came, I thought I looked too frumpy in a light tee and jeans to ask my father's approval in taking what should be mine. With my hair brushed back into a ponytail and light make-up, I'm presentable and polished. Something just seemed wrong with showing up in a suit—he likely wouldn't have opened the door. This was my next best option.

Here Junior stands looking like he rolled off his bedroom floor five minutes ago. Not only are his pants too big and his shirt wrinkled to-be-damned, he reeks like a stale bar and it's likely because he wore this exact outfit out last night.

The three men behind him, we'll call them scary thing 1 through 3, look marginally more put together, but the menace on their faces as they look at me is enough for me to realize how unprotected I am right now. It might take too long to get to the gun in my purse if any of them try something.

Senior returns from the kitchen with something in his hand that he gives to Junior. The younger man flops onto the couch in the sitting room across from the nook we were just in. I wince at the thought of his smell setting into the tan fabric of the couch. He begins tearing into what I can see is a breakfast sandwich.

Senior didn't even offer me water, but he made a whole breakfast sandwich for the man who is single handedly destroying everything he worked for. *Fine.* The other men grumble about how they didn't get a sandwich, but I decide it's time for me to leave.

"Thank you for your time," I say to my father. It sounds cold and formal because it is. This man is no more family to me than a stranger on the street. Even with the knowledge that we're blood, he wouldn't consider trying to save himself and I won't either. I grab my purse from the table and Senior follows me to the door after a brief nod.

I don't bother looking back at the men in that house. Like the rest of them, they'll learn that I'm not to be underestimated.

"And he didn't listen to a word you had to say?" Liezel's voice is tinny even on speakerphone as I scroll through my tablet looking at the numbers in front of me. I lie on my bed in the minimally decorated apartment and huff. All the strategies I planned to lay out for Senior, now for my benefit only.

I'd be lying if I said it didn't hurt a little bit that he wasn't at least interested in talking to me more. If I found out that I had a daughter, I would at least want to know her last name.

Could I imagine what it was like for him and the women he had dealt with before and after my mom? No. But at the very least, there should be some flicker of intrigue there. I'm a badass, have my life together. Fuck, I came to him with solutions but he didn't ask as single question.

Maybe I was wrong. It's not just Junior who has no respect for his legacy. Senior is just as stubborn and unconcerned with the future.

As a woman who has been on the periphery of this entire business for the last five years, I know that it is not a friendly one for my gender. America is not the land of the free. It's the land of men thinking they know everything while the women have to clean up their messes.

Here I am, doing just that, but I'm not giving it back after.

On the whole, the Lafayette's were responsible for supply chain management, inventory control, and organizing shipments. This is at its core simple business logistics of any product. It gets complicated because everything they're running is illegal.

Weapons and weed.

I'm impressed by how successful my biological father had been with no degree and only experience to guide his decisions. What I've learned about our legacy is inspiring and I know that I could build upon that in a way that would be positive. We could have more. His accomplishments are something of note not meant for trash like Junior.

At one point he and Blue's father, Nate, were allied and it was an unstoppable partnership. From what I could tell, the Duponts only had the weed on their mind but the Lafayettes made their name originally in smuggling weapons into the country. They were mutually beneficial as the sale of one was conducive to the sale of the other. That was until Senior decided to step down and give Junior control.

It was all a rapid decline from there, including pissing Blue off and losing that partnership. I'm not sure what sparked that feud. I don't think anyone knows besides those two.

"He listened to what I had to say. Then he patted my hand in the most condescending way possible."

"Ouch." There's a pause and then she says, "And what did Blue say?"

"Nothing. I'm not telling him. It's pointless and without the true support from the Lafayette's, I'm expendable and unimportant. He can't know any different until I get where I need to. Pussy is not that good," I huff again. "Besides, he hasn't even fucked me to use the all powerful P in its truest form."

Liesel laughs. "Girl, stop. You have that man in a tizzy. Booking out your private room, cock-blocking you. He replaced the staff just because he wanted to protect you." I had been keeping my bestie up to date on all my progress with Blue. She never forgets any details. That's why she's my bestie.

I shake my head though she can't see. "That's not enough. He's clearly just possessive and doesn't play well with others. That isn't going to get me where I need to go."

"You just need time. I know you're the most qualified for the job and you know it, too."

"I'm no miracle worker, Lee. If Junior breaks this family beyond repair, even all my practical knowledge couldn't put the pieces back together. He's ruining it and it's so bad it almost feels intentional."

"Could it be intentional?"

"No. Who knows how much Senior did or could have taught him. He's just a trainwreck of a person. He smelled like they actually scraped him off of a club floor when I met him in person."

Liesel gasps loudly into the phone. "He was there? Holy shit. Go back to that part!"

"Not really. He walked into the house after I came over. He was sipping dirty sprite and Senior cussed him out. I left soon after that. I don't trust him not to try anything if he knew who I was."

"You don't think Senior would tell him that you're his sister."

It feels like a punch to the gut, but I admit, "He doesn't care, Lee. The man has probably had many *long-lost kids* pop up asking for something. He was jaded. Not even the least bit surprised. More... annoyed? I don't know. Neither of them are viable options, I have to go about it the hard way."

"That's your specialty," she reminds me. "I'm sorry, babe. It's his loss. You're a badass daughter. Gennie knew it and keeping him out of your life was probably for the best." She always knows what to say.

I sigh, ignoring the twinge in my chest when I think about the loss of my mom. She lived the life she wanted and I know she's in a better place now. "Right. So, the hard way it is. Tell me what's been going on back home."

Chapter 8

Diamond

Two weeks have passed since I was formally rejected by my father. In the grand scheme of things, it changed nothing. I would get what I needed from Blue and take over brutally when I had to.

The problem was I saw Blue less and less since the night I told him about Dejuan. Maybe he suspected something of me and was creating distance because of it.

He did say that he didn't mix business and pleasure. This could be my boot.

I tried not to worry about it, but it was hard not to because… I missed him.

No, no, no. Not in a romantic way. Romance was completely lost on the man at this point. The first night we met was contractual. And I supposed, every meeting after will be as well.

However, I'm still empty inside where there should be… him. I feel like I've been teased to a breaking point and it's getting serious without anyone to scratch this itch.

What was he doing telling me how big he was? If that wasn't a taunt, I don't know what is.

About as much as me twirling on the pole and ignoring him is.

Not the point.

It's Saturday and I thought I'd see him, for sure. But instead, I felt someone else watching me too closely since my second set tonight.

Not Blue—he always watched like a king surveying what he already owned. This was different.

Menacing and slimy is how this man's attention felt.

I caught him leaning against the bar, sleeves rolled up to show a cuban link bracelet and not enough respect to the bartenders.

Jimmy LaFayette. As far as family goes, he would be my second cousin and that only makes the ick much stronger. He likely has no idea that we're family, but if we weren't—I still wouldn't appreciate the way he watches me. Only malicious thoughts are behind those eyes.

He had the kind of face girls in the club pretended to like—angular jaw, eyes like empty pits, icy gold fangs. His taper fade and scraggly beard did not do anything for me. I suppose I developed a taste for shoulder length locs and a trim beard since I've been here.

Jimmy doesn't come here often, but when he does, I make sure to avoid him from the sleazy energy coming off him alone.

Tonight, I'm his target it seems and I can't escape his gaze.

I didn't show that I figured that out. Didn't flinch, didn't waver. I know better than to give a creep the satisfaction of fear. But the minute I step off stage, I feel him trailing behind me like a stain I can't wash off.

The break room is small, and too damn quiet for a Saturday. Not a single girl is in here and that was suspicious in itself.

Where is everyone?

I make it halfway to my locker when the door shuts behind me with a loud, deliberate click.

"Diamond," Jimmy coos, voice as fake as the gold chain strangling his neck. He has no sweet intentions coming into this room.

I don't turn around from my locker. I don't keep any weapons in here because we usually don't have to. In a pinch, I might be able to use my heel if he doesn't suspect what I'm doing. "Don't call me that."

He laughs and the sound grates on my nerves. "But that's what you go by, ain't it? 'Sides, I think it fits. Precious. Pretty. Real easy to hold against the light and see straight through."

I turn then, asking, "You need something?"

He takes a step forward, licking his teeth. "Just came to introduce myself. Officially. We're family, after all."

My stomach drops.

My blood turns to ice.

He knows.

Did Senior tell him?

How did he find out?

Who else knows?

"How long you been spyin' on us, cousin?" he spits, closing the space between us.

I force a breath in through my nose. "I didn't spy. I've just been working. More than any of you ever do."

My response knocks the smirk off his face. His empty eyes grow even darker when he says, "You got a lotta nerve sayin' shit, when you been strippin' under his roof."

Blue. Of course.

To the Fayes, I was betrayal wrapped in glitter.

Seems rather dumb to me since I tried with Senior and he flat out wanted nothing to do with me. *How could I be betraying anyone?* I'm loyal to me and mine alone in this feud between them.

"You don't think he cares what blood runs through your veins?" Jimmy hisses, stepping in close enough I can smell his cologne that's too sweet and too sharp, like rotting flowers. "You think the King's gonna protect you when he finds out your daddy's name?"

I don't move. I couldn't. My whole body goes still.

He was baiting me.

"Say it," he taunts. "Say who you are."

His fingers brush my jaw, and the heat of fury rises up before fear ever could.

"Say it, or I swear I'll—"

I move first.

My hand snaps to his wrist, twisting hard enough he hisses.

"Touch me again, and I'll break it," I say, voice like steel.

He yanks away, holding his hand to his chest. "Bitch! You'll regret this! Lucky boss said not to hurt a hair on your head."

I slap him before I even realize my hand moved.

The crack of skin on skin echoes like a gunshot in the narrow room.

He stumbles back, one hand to his cheek, murder in his eyes. "You're. Dead."

"No," I tell him with conviction, chest heaving, heart pounding. "I'm just getting started." I could say more, but I stop myself because he's not worth it.

"You think Blue's gonna keep you after he finds out who you are? After I tell him?"

"You tell him, I'll survive. You lay a finger on me again, you won't."

Something in my voice makes him hesitate. Then, like the coward he truly is, he sneers, adjusts his collar, and walks out without another word.

I stand there, breath shallow, adrenaline singing in my limbs. *I'd blown my cover.*

I get my bag out of my locker and rush off to find a bouncer to escort me to my car. I was supposed to be on stage at least one more time, but I'm far too rattled to hide that fact. I'll deal with the consequences of it later.

Right now, I desperately need to get out of here.

Back at my apartment, I stand under the spray of water. I search for any semblance of calm, but I can't find it with so many unknown variables floating around me.

How much does my half-brother know? Did my father tell him? What does he plan on doing with that information? How long am I safe here before one of them does tell Blue who I am? Should I just tell Blue myself?

When I get out of the shower, I quickly go through my routine of detangling and moisturizing my hair, skipping the blow-dry all together. I opt for just two braids, knowing that I'm not going into work tomorrow anyway.

I *can't.*

Even with the bouncers there, I have no idea how many targets are currently on my back.

I do the only thing I can think of at the moment. I call my best friend. "Lee?"

"Babe, wassup?" The music dies down as she goes to my old break room. "Why aren't you on the floor?"

Tears are already rolling down my face. "I think I fucked up." My voice catches in my throat and I wipe my eyes. "Lee, they know who I am."

A beat, then, "Who is *they*?"

"The Fayes."

"Fuuuck. Fuck, fuck, shit, fuck. Do I need to come get you? I can be on a plane tomorrow—"

I hear the clacking of her locker being opened as I'm sure she's already grabbing things to come get me. "And risk you, too? No! They sent someone to confirm who I am tonight. Some sleazy cousin of mine. But they know."

"Well, shit girl. What can you do? What can I do?" I have no idea what I can do. This is a lot. Maybe too much. I thought I could come here and get this done but maybe I shouldn't have come by myself. I have no one to look out for me like Lee does back home.

I think I'm in over my head.

I know that Blue is not how I thought he'd be. But my blood would threaten to turn me in like I betrayed them and for what? They couldn't possibly have proof that I had been listening to their conversations or searching through their business. It's far too late for that. They never suspected even with countless months of gathering data before I got to Louisiana.

There's three short knocks at my front door and I pause.

"Someone just knocked on my door," I tell my friend.

"Don't go see who it is. Have you ever seen a scary movie before?"

I'm already up and walking over, tying my robe at the waist securely. "This isn't a scary movie. Just stay on the line."

"Racquelle Owens, listen to me! Do not open—"

There is no peephole on my door, a red flag in itself. So I have to open the door a sliver to see who's there.

When I do, I instantly know that I shouldn't have.

"Nice place, Diamond," he coos in that same fake sweet voice.

Chapter 9

BLUE

"Think you want to see this boss…" Vert says, interrupting me mid-swing.

My hands are already covered in red as I turn from where Dejuan is tied to the chair in the middle of the main interrogation room.

I'm unhinged and at my limit after getting nowhere with this rat. He confessed to telling Jay exactly where our next drop was happening so my men could be bum rushed before they reached Louisiana state lines.

But he won't tell me why or who has convinced him to turn on this family.

We got him off the streets. Kept him out of jail more times than I can count. Kept his pockets fat so he could feed his three kids.

And yet, here he is running his mouth to Faye trash behind my back.

I grab the tablet Vert hands to me and wait for what was so important he came in here while I'm working.

On screen I see Diamond walking past the bar. Several heads turn to follow her and that doesn't surprise me. I hate that I'm missing the opportunity to see her on stage tonight, but I couldn't wait any longer once I got my proof.

On camera I've got Dejuan meeting with Jay another time outside of the here-say Diamond told me. There is no mistaking he's doing this family dirty. I could never excuse betrayal. That is the hard line no one is allowed to cross.

Nothing is more important than this family. If he has betrayed my trust, then he's betrayed all of our trust.

Normally, I'd let one of the soldiers handle some little shit who wronged us. Depending on how high up they are, I'd sic Redd, that feral motherfucker, on them. But for a snitch like this, I'd rather handle it myself. Even if it exposes the ways I have to accommodate to inflict pain on others without my knife.

If I start with the knife, I don't have enough time to drag out the process. Using a hammer fist punch or my elbows does the job pretty well when it's not often that I am the one on this side of things. Grateful that it's rare for me to enforce my rule.

I'm watching my dancer sway through the crowded club on this tablet. Complicated feelings crop up when I look at her there without me. Too many and most of which I need to keep under wraps for now. After Diamond turns the corner to the break room where the dancers get ready and touch up, a man enters the room after her.

My eyes flick up to Vert who is already grimacing at the screen. "Keep watchin'," he says, tapping the screen to the next clip. There are no cameras in the break room, for obvious reasons, so I don't know what happened inside, but in this next clip I see the man leaving, holding his hand to his chest. Then Diamond is rushing out after him, but going the opposite direction to the parking lot. Chris, my bouncer, is taking her to her car and she leaves.

My jaw ticks when Dejuan groans behind me when his head lolls to the side. I check to make sure he isn't about to fall over. The bindings are still secure on him so he can wait for what's coming to him.

When I look back to the tablet, the man who followed Diamond is now in his car. The timing is too suspicious and I hate to ask, but I have to know. "Where's he now?"

"Marcell just saw his car pull up to her complex. He's probably at her door."

"Fuck!" I shout into the cold room, the sound echoing back. The regret I have for telling Marcell to not engage, only surveil, taste like acid at the back of my throat. "Get him on the line," I bark.

After one ring, Marcell picks up wasting no time in updating me on the exact information I'm looking for, "She opened the door. He forced himself inside. Should I go in after him?"

I don't know who this man is to her. I don't get the feeling it's any good for him to be there when she left from work early after he followed her.

I don't fucking like that shit at all.

"No. I'm on my way. Get close, but don't engage."

"Heard," he confirms and I curse again. Ending the call, I dial another number and when the line connects, I demand, "Where you at?"

There's crunching in my ear like Redd's eating something. "South Point. Why? What happened?"

"Go get the truck," I tell Vert and he leaves without a word. To my second, I question, "Why are you in Steph's neighborhood?"

He doesn't answer my question, the pause pointed and unhelpful. "What do you need?" He finally asks and I let him change the subject.

"I need you to send me Diamond's address."

"You're askin' me why I'm in Steph's hood in the same breath that you're askin' for Diamond's addy? Hmm."

He's not wrong, but I don't give a fuck. I need to get over there right now. "Don't *hmm* me, asshole. Just send the address."

"I'm going," Redd says. "While I got you on the line, what perfume does Steph wear?"

"The fuck? Dude, stopping playin' with me. Are you almost done?"

"Yea. Sent. You need me?"

I should probably have him come here and finish what I started with Dejuan. I decide against it. "Nah, enjoy bein' a creep."

"With pleasure," he says, hanging up on me.

Turning back to Dejuan, my patience is already frayed and I'm sick of working him over anyway.

I barely feel the spray of blood against my face as I give him peace in his death. "Get him out of here," I tell the two guards at the door and wipe my knife on his shirt.

"Boss, I think we should go with you," Vert says when we park next to the Camero Jimmy came here in.

"Keep watch from here. If anythin' you know you what to do." Having my men watching her is one thing. But letting her know just how much she's gotten under my skin is another. I don't want to make anything worse with all five of my men trailing behind me when I go check on her.

With a nod, I step out of the truck into the muggy night air. It's an unwelcome feeling since I'm on edge and pissed that I'm going to find another man tonight who won't live to see another day.

There's a long hallway that leads to the last door on the second floor where her apartment is. It's well lit, but I wait in the alcove of another apartment door to keep from plain sight. From the lot on the opposite side of me, Marcell, Vert and my other men can see clearly onto this floor.

It's not long before Jimmy leaves her apartment with a smug look on his face. I've seen him around and never liked the dude.

I like him even less now.

Bad news for Jimmy.

As soon as he passes the recessed area I've been waiting for him in, I wrap my arm around his neck, locking my hand behind my wrist so that I can put as much pressure as possible to his throat without him being able to breathe.

I don't need my hand strength at all for this maneuver and I'm happy to show my strength when it comes to this bastard.

Knocking the back of his legs, he loses his balance and is at my mercy in the attack with no way to right himself, even as he claws at the sleeves of my jacket from the concrete.

"What are you doin' here, Jimmy," I ask in an even tone. This man is no match for me in size as I have about four inches and a hundred pounds on him.

He's not getting free until I decide he can... *If I decide he can.*

"I-I was just followin' orders," he whimpers, like a scared little boy.

He should be very fucking scared. My worst suspicions were that Diamond was in trouble because of me. He wasn't just acting alone, someone sent him. That is infinitely worse. It's not just this piece of shit that has taken notice of my attachment to the curvy dancer.

"What goddamn orders?" I bark.

He wheezes so I give him just a bit of extra room to take a deep breath. When I feel like he's had enough time to recover, I press my knee into his back and he begins to sputter out, "Boss didn't like she was dancin' at your club and you spendin' all this time on her."

How the fuck does Junior know that?

Demanding to know the answer to that question, I question, "Who told him?"

"I-I-I don't kn-now. Was just supposed to rough her up, scare her. Let her know he knew about her."

This stupid piece of shit doesn't know how close I am to ending his life for daring to get close to what's mine. Through my teeth, I continue to press him for more information. "So, you followed her home instead?"

"Look, man. She hit me, alright? I couldn't handle that disrespect. Boss said don't hurt her but there's a lotta ways to give a lesson. You know what I mean?" *Give a lesson.* The fuck does that even mean. This sack of shit will be the only one learning any lessons.

There is a special sleeve just behind the sheath that holds the venom I'm most known for administering with this blade. Right now, it gleams with the special blend of venom that remains stable in a mixture of my own making. I don't have to cut deep for the toxins to start affecting him.

But I want to.

"No, I don't," I growl in response to his asinine question. I cover his mouth with my hand. He doesn't get another word out before I press my knife to his neck and let it sink in slowly.

For minutes, he writhes on the ground before I leave him there. It will take less than thirty minutes for his body to completely shut down and no ambulance or EMT could help him even if they pulled up right now. Only I have the anti-venom on this side of the Earth. He will be long gone before they even know what happened to him.

He won't be worth any of those tax dollars going to waste. He is destined to be gator chow. With the week I've had, it seems that my gators will be eating good.

Now, all I have to do is call my guys and get this cleaned up so I can check on my dancer.

Chapter 10

BLUE

"Blue?" Her voice is strained as she holds her robe tighter together at the neck. I did an okay job of cleaning up my face and changing my clothes, but there's no hiding the way my anger vibrates in the air. "What are you doing here?" She looks at me skeptically, and that anger returns.

She likely thinks I'm here for some fucked up reason like the man I just deleted from existence moments before. She looks around behind me to see if anyone else is here with me.

They're all in the truck we came in. Jimmy's body in the back, prepared to sink to the bottom of the bayou after my gators have a turn.

When she really looks at me, she reels back. "What happened to you?"

I take that opportunity to walk in and close the door behind me.

She knows who I am and what I'm known for. For once, I wish she didn't—that no one did.

I wish that I wasn't coming into her spot for the first time wearing not one, but two, different men's blood.

I wish that the reason I was coming over was a different one.

But wishes don't have shit to do with why I'm here.

Jimmy was after her.

I need to know why.

"Had a talk with Dejuan," is what I grunt out. It's not an answer to either question she's asked me since I got here. Why am I talking to her like she's the one who did something wrong? I need to calm the fuck down.

While I take a minute to attempt that, I look around her place. There's not a lot to it. She hasn't been in Clayton Terrace long, but this apartment looks impersonal and bare. No boxes anywhere, so I wonder where the rest of the decor is. It's the bare bones of a living space. She makes more than enough for this place to look at least a little more lived in. Where are the photos, stupid little knickknacks or hell, a candle? This is just furniture and a TV.

She takes inventory of my person and I don't help her fill in any gaps. At this stage, I make my way to her kitchen. Washing my hands in her sink is useless, but I do it anyway. I didn't wear my glove and now blood has started to sink into my skin. The tattoos on my fingers look more menacing decorated in red this way. Blood is one substance that even dark skin can't hide.

She's followed me into the kitchen, maintaining a distance from me that I don't like but understand. Leaning against the door frame, she asks, "Was he the rat?" *Huh?*

Oh right. Dejuan.

I turn in the kitchen. Leaning against the sink opposite of her, I observe what state she's in. She looks familiar in a way that I can't place. Not just because I've been picturing her in my mind non-stop.

She has no makeup on, her hair is damp and in two braids I'd be happy to wrap around my tainted fists. Her legs are bare under that robe and so are her feet.

I like how she looks made up in her shiny outfits and all, but I like this natural version, too.

I could get used to seeing her like this.

Clearing my throat, I gruff, "The rat? Nah. A rat? Yea. And so I guess a *thank you* is what I owe you."

Shock breaks out across her face and I wonder why that is. "Thank me? I just told you what I heard."

"You helped me with somethin'. Maybe more than I know right now."

"Well…" She bites her lip, making moves to exit the kitchen. I'm not letting her get away from me. Not when she's so close. It's not very large and with the mood I'm in, my being here is likely suffocating for her. "If that's it, I accept your gratitude. I'll see you at work."

My hand shoots out to the opposite side of the door jamb, preventing her from walking away. "Holdup. Where you goin'?"

She blinks and then crosses her arms over her chest. "I want to lay down. I've had an... unpleasant night. We can talk another time."

I lean over her, my stature large enough to block the overhead lighting to cast her in shadow. "We'll be done talkin' when I say we're done. Heard?"

Her eyes narrow the smallest bit but she doesn't try to leave again. *Good girl.*

"Saw you leavin' the club early tonight. Why?"

She looks in the direction of her front door. It's visible over the breakfast bar on the other side of the counter we're against.

It's too much speculating. I fucking hate speculating almost as much as I hate gambling. I wanted the facts and figures. If I can't see it for myself, plain and simple, then I'd come to my own resolution about it. Those resolutions were hardly preferable for the other person involved. *Elimination was as simple as it came.*

I barely know Diamond—aside from what Redd was able to uncover, which was a fuck ton. You could tell a lot about someone from what the government knows and paperwork. Hell, her social media is revealing, but not in the ways I want to know.

Ever since I paid for her in that private room, she's been on my mind. I haven't been able to get her off of it. Fighting it is dumb at this point. Once I can figure out why this woman has my attention, then I can let my fascination go and get back to the money.

"A guy started harassing me. I didn't feel safe, so I came home but—" She abruptly stops, glancing toward the door again and then back at me.

She starts gathering her braids into a ponytail behind her head, swirling it around putting it into a bun or something. The long column of her neck is exposed. With her hair up now, the line of cleavage that was hidden before is visible. The swell of her tits are obvious in a way that makes my hand twitch to grab them and feel them again. She notices me watching her slide a hand under the fabric to just above them. It's not to cover her nipples but rather points out that she isn't wearing anything under the robe, when the fabric slides down her shoulder. A shoulder I'd like to kiss and nip when she slides on my dick, saying my name—

She never finished her sentence and the rational part of my brain recognizes that.

It was clearly a diversion tactic.

Goddamn, this woman. I take my good girl back.

I grab her chin and force her eyes to mine. "But what?"

There's an emotion I can't read in her eyes when she spits out, "But he followed me home. He left just before you came over."

I already knew this. I had my suspicions, but to know that he was here and she didn't want him to be—makes my blood boil. A new fury takes over me as his painful death doesn't feel painful enough. He had to go for touching what's mine. But he upset her, made her feel unsafe in her own home.

Not my Diamond.

"What'd he do?" I grit out through my teeth.

Her gaze meets mine and I force myself to wait for her answer. There is an uncertainty there that I don't like.

I'm not like that slimy fuck who just left this plane of existence. I'm not a good man. My morals are skewed heavily toward the money and keeping my people good. But I don't want her to be afraid of me.

I can't have that.

I release her face and take a step back. She breathes more easily as my rage tempers to something far less cloying in the small space. I take several steps back until I'm sitting on the back of her couch. Taking my jacket off, I lay it on the couch next to me.

Finally, her posture returns to something that resembles the same confidence she shows at Off Topz.

"The man, Jimmy, he's a Faye. I think word might have gotten out about me—"

"Why didn't you call me?"

Her delicate brows tip downward as she looks me up and down. "Is that something I was supposed to do?"

"Yea! She has me on the phone already," a voice says into the room, but I don't know where.

She blinks and then looks down at her phone. "Shit. Sorry, Lee, I'm gonna call you back."

"But it's getting good! I still—" Diamond ends the call and looks back up at me.

"My friend back home was on the phone while he was here. She was ready to call the police if necessary."

"You think pigs could've saved you?"

"Who else would?" She asks with a raised brow and her hands on her hips.

I don't know what possesses me to say these next words. I can't take them back even though what they imply is a pale comparison to how I feel. "I'm here, ain't I?"

Maybe I expected relief or some gratitude from her, instead she crosses her arms, pushing her tits up and exposing more of her neck. "So what? I don't even have your number or ever see you outside of the club. Why would I rely on you?"

Standing from the couch, each step takes me closer and closer to the woman who has infiltrated my thoughts and caused me to take two lives today. I keep walking her backward until her back is pressed firmly against the wall. Her hands are on my chest, trying feebly to keep any space at all between us.

"Cause you belong to me. And if *anyone* other than me threatens you, makes you feel fear, and causes you to leave your place of work, then I have every right to ensure that it's the last thing they'll ever do."

Diamond's neck is craned back in order to keep eye contact with me. Her dark eyes do nothing to hide how wide her pupils are. She doesn't speak for a moment. I hate that she isn't confirming.

"Tell me you know it." I hold her by the neck, her pulse racing under my palm, her breaths shallow only faintly brushing along my cheeks. "You are mine, baby. It's too late for you to escape that now."

Her hands slide from my chest to my waist, no longer maintaining distance between us. "Not baby. Racquelle," she murmurs low into the sliver of air that separates us.

My Diamond.

My Racquelle.

Something snaps.

Restraint blown.

I take her lips with mine, claiming her in this moment and for every moment after.

This is *my woman.*

Her smell.

Her touch.

The way the heat between her legs beckons me closer, deeper.

I'm helpless to resist.

She has her legs wrapped around me as I hold her up against this wall. Her tongue swirls in my mouth and I'm losing all sanity.

Why did I come here?

I don't remember.

She's alive—alive in my grasp, panting as I massage through her fat lips and over her clit. She's coating them completely, the sound of her wetness loud in my ears as blood fills my dick. It's painful to not be inside her right now.

Flicking my pants open, not bothering to remove my belt or take them off completely, I pull my dick out over the waistband of my boxers.

Impatient and desperate to fill her with all of me.

I pause for a second, her slit hugging me as she rocks over the length slow and methodical.

This is a woman who knows what she's doing.

My woman who knows what she's doing.

I curse and my head falls back. Only for a second though. I need to see her face, feel her losing her sanity right along with me.

With a handful of her titty, I grit out, "Gonna stuff you full. Right now. Can't wait."

I couldn't.

I had seen her break over my fingers, my knife, had her flood my face—I don't know what I'll do if she doesn't agree.

A life, several, had been paid for me to get to this point. To see that I wanted her more than I could fathom possible. Now, I have to face facts. Refraining from fucking her wasn't about what my dick was worth. It was about what I was willing to sacrifice to indulge in her. *I'd pay what it costs.* I'd end any life that threatened hers. I'd be the protection she needed to ensure I could keep her and keep her safe.

Diamond nods her head frantically, reaching between us to better position me at her entrance. "Yes. Right now," she huffs and the crown is kissed by her warmth.

"Take a deep breath, Racquelle," I command. She shivers and then my hand is on her throat again. I hold her in place, eyes flicking between either of hers as we join for the first time.

The crown of me will be the biggest struggle for her tight little cunt to take. Even with prepping her and fitting as many fingers as I could, I know it doesn't compare. Worry starts to color her features, but I shush her, "Keep breathin'. You can take me. Show me what a good girl you can be." I encourage her and hold back as much as I'm able as I ease into her.

She moans into a groan and I feel her dripping over me, down my shaft and onto my nuts.

"That's it. Open up for the King." Once the crown slips into her, I pause only for a moment. Our eyes are locked on each other and she wraps her arms around my neck. Racquelle is slippery and warm and only a direct order from the big man upstairs could make me stop what is coming for her.

I don't know how she knew, but she's coming along for this ride. I punch my hips upward in one swift movement. It's quick as she cries out. Her hands wind through my locs, holding on in any way she can when I start bouncing her on my dick, fast enough for her robe to fall to the side, her sexy as fuck body jiggling in time with each one of my thrusts.

Skin slapping skin, she soaks my boxers.

My name starts as a low chant from her throaty voice, "Blue, Blue, Blue," but it turns into a plea as she tightens and clenches on my shit.

My balls are drawing up and I want to fill her up with more than just my dick. I want my cum leaking out of her. I tell her as much, "Want my nut to be leakin' from you for days. You gonna take it all, Racquelle?"

Her eyes roll back with her head as my name continues pouring from her lips.

She's so close.

She's so close, but I'm nowhere near close to letting her be done with me.

She will never be done with me.

I carry her to the couch, clumsy from too much blood flowing south. I step wrong, knocking my shin into her coffee table. Pissed and too focused on not missing a moment of the magic grip Racquelle has on my dick, I kick out and the table goes flying into the wall. Something else smashes to the ground with it. Neither of us stops to see what it is because the deeper angle she's riding my dick at is too fucking much euphoria to pull away from.

Her hands grab onto the back of the couch, she's smothering me between her tits.

Fuck, I'm in heaven.

I don't dream often any more. But this, this is my dream. From the moment I saw her, this is exactly where I wanted to be.

I lick and suck, trying to leave a mark. Claiming her in every way I know how.

I can just barely make out her breathy pants while she rides my dick like a cowgirl. With my hands on her ass, I move her body closer to mine so her clit is rubbing over me while she gets to that edge.

"Blue, please. Blue..."

We're both falling, crashing. My nuts tighten and she goes silent as her orgasm wracks her body. Each clench of her core on me is torture and pleasure as each pulse of cum spurts into her.

It starts to drip from her, but I use my fingers to run it up to lubricate the hole I am definitely claiming next.

My finger rolls around the puckered hole and she moans into my shoulder, still trying to recover from the first orgasm.

I'm already stiff again.

One O isn't enough for me. It will never be enough for her after this.

I test once, twice and on the third time she lets me in. So tight and so responsive. *Fuuuck, I need in.*

She sits back, pushing my finger in, to the second knuckle.

"Oh god, Blue, you feel so fucking good filling me up," she gasps at the second finger I add.

"Ride me like that. Go 'head. Put that ass to work." I smack her ass hard with my other hand.

She cries out, but does what I said, rolling her hips before bouncing to a sexy rhythm I match to reach deeper inside her. I'm filling two holes already, but it's not enough.

I pull her face to mine, kissing her deep. Easily, I'm able to undo whatever she had done to her hair and get that braid wrapped around my fist.

With her head pulled back, my fingers in her ass and my dick stuffing my nut back inside her, she looks like the sexiest vision I've ever seen.

"Tight and warm, smellin' like magnolias and keenin' like a goddamn vixen. Give me that O, bae."

That does it.

She gives me everything, squeezing me so tight I'm dragging over her spot again and again as she comes.

"That's it, bae. I want all of it."

I will never be done with her.

Chapter 11
Diamond

Despite the fact that summer is over, it's blistering hot outside. I worry for my frozen meals in the short walk from the grocery store to my car. I'm not parked that far, but I feel a thin layer of sweat down my back and under my hair. My shirt sticks to me and I walk a little faster toward my trunk.

Taking my keys out of my purse, my sweaty hands drop them and I curse.

This is not helping me get into my car any faster.

When I stand, there's a shadow over me and I turn, my back pressed to the car door. "Can I help you?" I spit in frustration of being taken off guard.

The man in front of me is not smiling but sneering at me. Unease trickles down my already sweaty back and I start thinking of ways to get away from this creeper. It's not uncommon for me to have an unsavory interaction with men, given my job. But in Clayton Terrace, it seems to be happening far too much for my liking.

I think back to Blue and last night, how he was the one to ensure that Jimmy would never make me feel the way I did ever again. Right before he fucked me into oblivion. I'm still a little sore from his size and the rough way he pounded my pussy like it infuriated him.

If I was missing out on a WAP this good, I'd be mad, too.

My thoughts turn salacious only for a moment when a whole different set of thoughts take hold.

Guilt freezes me since I'm keeping what would be the most important information to share with him at this point in my back pocket.

But a woman is nothing without her secrets.

Especially in the life I want to lead.

The people I want to lead.

There's too much time where I'm there frozen and two more men box me into the space where I stand. Their size makes it near impossible for me to see around them with any success.

The one on my left with a fade that has two large scars at his temple speaks first, breaking the sound of my heartbeat in my ears. "Terrell wants to see you." *Oh no.* These are the men from the LaFayette place that were hanging around Junior.

"For what?" I screech. The sound is full of nerves and probably the appropriate amount of anxiety.

"Didn't say. Come along and don't put up a fight."

Like hell.

I'd fight tooth and nail to not go anywhere with scary thing 1 and scary thing 2. If I leave with them, nothing will end well for me.

My eyes dart to the left quickly, but not quick enough. Scary thing 1 puts a hand on my door handle, keeping me from setting the alarm off and drawing attention to us. The one who spoke first grabs me and I struggle for only a moment before I feel a prick in my neck and a hand over my mouth.

I thrash and try to yell.

My head goes all lightheaded with the lack of oxygen I'm getting right now.

I'm gonna pass out.

Darkness is coming for me and fast.

I'm—

The first thing I check is my clothes. It's an effort because one of my hands is tied to a pipe that's above my head. It's already fallen asleep, completely useless, but the other works just fine. My clothes are all still there. Nothing feels sore in my body like I've been sexually assaulted, but my head is killing me.

Unfortunately, I have had these protocols drilled into me from a young age just given my background. It's second nature to tick these off the list.

"Bout damn time. I was sick of waiting for your ass."

I blink and try to move my head around. Try to find the body that belongs to the voice.

Fuck.

No.

NO.

no.

Terrell stands there in the light, only marginally more put together than the last time I saw him. It's dim and I don't know where I'm at. I look for clues, but it's useless since I can barely see anything.

"What do you want?" I croak out. My head is throbbing as I sit up.

His voice grates on my nerves as he rebuts, "Nah. Don't work like that. You've been runnin' your mouth too much already. I'll do the talkin' now."

"Don't know what you're talking about." I cough. My throat is dry and it feels like I've been sucking on cotton balls. "Can I get some water?"

"Sure," he says, nodding to scary thing 2.

It happens too quickly for me to realize what's happening. Water splashes me in the face and it's ice cold. I squeal and try to protect myself from the liquid, but I can't do anything with my hand still attached to the wall. One hand manages to rise, but the other jerks. Immediately, a twinge of pain fires in my shoulder. It hurts like hell with pins and needles running up and down the limb.

"What the fuck?" I yell. "What the fuck was that?"

Another dousing of water and I'm shivering. Junior is a giant sack of shit! It's already cold in here but with the water soaking my clothes, it's quickly lowering my body temperature.

"You done?" He asks with no expression other than irritation. *What does he have to be irritated about?* I'm the one who got taken against my will by the very man I'm trying to destroy. Now, I'm freezing cold and wet.

Let's also go back to how my arm is completely dead hanging from the wall!

I remain silent since I don't want to be doused with water again. I don't know what plan he has for me and it's best that I allow him to at least tell me what is in store for me so that I can come up with some kind of plan to get away from him as soon as possible.

"Good. You shut your ass up." He paces to the side, making me track him through the dark space. "Imagine my surprise to find out the woman who went to visit my Pa the other day is none other than *the Diamond* everybody has been talkin' 'bout at Off Topz." His arms fly up beside him, spread wide with incredulity. "And she's my sister! What do you know?"

"Half," I retort. The pressure increases behind my eye as the headache from whatever they gave me is leaving my system as quietly as a marching band. "So what?"

His head bobs and it's an impatient gesture. "I send Jimmy to go check things out and now...?" He looks around the room dramatically. "No Jimmy."

He takes several steps toward me to close the distance between us. At *least he bothered to take a shower today.* The last time I saw him, he reeked of alcohol and cough syrup. He's much more lucid today and I wonder if that bodes well for me.

With the look in his eye, I'm going to guess that it is worse for me. Much worse.

"Jimmy was a pig," I respond trying hard not to shiver. It's more than a little difficult. I'm achy from the shock and generally uncomfortable as I count more and more men in the room. Every single one of them leers at me and they come closer to where Junior is pacing. Not looking at me in a way that I would want at the club, but like I'm their next meal and they don't plan on leaving any meat on the bone.

"My sister, whorin' herself out for a Dupont? You're no sister of mine." He tilts my chin up with a finger, demanding, "What have you been tellin' Blue, huh?"

"I didn't say nothin'." I try to turn my head and rid myself of his touch, but it only pisses him off.

The blow catches me off guard.

I reel backward, my shoulder on fire as I twist around from the force of his slap across my face. I taste blood in my mouth and spit it back at Junior.

It hits his shirt and he grabs my hair. "You don't know what you got yourself into. I have no use for any bitch who sluts herself out for the Duponts anyway." He pulls the shirt over his head, exposing his bird chest. I cringe when it hits me in the face. "Let's see how much he likes you when you get this makeover."

Makeover?

A blow to my ribs comes first. I had been too busy watching Junior to notice that the men in the room had surrounded me. I don't catch who delivers the first hit before another comes to my back.

I cry out, unable to protect myself when I take a fist to the face that stings instantly. I feel the skin separating over my cheek, blood running down my face at the impact.

Dangling helplessly, I take more hits and time seems to slow as I fight with my consciousness.

How did I end up like this? An actual punching bag and for what?

Eventually I blackout though I know I'm still being attacked. Turbulent and tumultuous darkness blessedly consumes me again.

I wake again, this time in the trunk of a car. It moves and jostles me. I try to scream, but there's tape over my mouth and around my hands.

Frantically, I look for any way to free myself. One of my eyes is completely swollen shut and the other is bloodshot and sore. It hurts just looking in the dark space that's only illuminated by a safety light.

Music plays loudly around me, I can barely breathe in the tight space. Weed smoke seeps from between the backseat and into the trunk. It's getting thicker and thicker as we drive along.

I don't know what to do. I can't reach for an escape latch. It's dark as hell back here.

My body is one giant bruise. Pain assaults every part of me like sizzling fire. It's a miracle I'm not dying from internal bleeding. I don't even know for sure that I'm not.

I hurt.

Am I going to die?

The car stops moving and the music playing from inside does too.

Should I be relieved or more nervous that we've reached our destination—whatever that is?

Not an ounce of daylight remains. It's so dark that I don't know where I am when the trunk opens.

It's scary thing 1 here to take me somewhere. I'm like a rag doll losing her stuffing as he drags me from under my armpits. My right shoulder is blazing the hottest with pain but only muffled sounds come from where my mouth is taped.

There is only one security light above a metal door that I can make out through my good eye. This building is massive and I can't see where it ends or begins in the relative darkness.

Another unknown location. I must still be in Louisiana at least. Other than that I don't know where I am.

"In case it wasn't clear—you're not welcome with the Fayes. We see you around," he sneers, "and no one else ever will again."

With a boot surging quickly toward my face, I lose consciousness again.

Chapter 12

BLUE

"Boss," the staticky voice of one of the men at the back comes through on my desk.

Redd looks over to the radio and grabs it before I can. "This Redd. Wassup?"

Neither of us were supposed to be working this late, but for the third time this week, there was a delay in the package over state lines. Blue Dream, our biggest seller and the newest cannabis strain we offer, gone like smoke. Unlike the one from Colorado, this one from California was missing a quarter of the shipment from one truck.

How does a quarter of the weed just disappear?

Tracking down illegal shipments of weed should be easier since we are paying more than the government does for dispensaries in that state. There are plenty of extra funds to be able to secure the packages in some kind of way. Aside from hiring private security or developing some kind of trackers to put in every package, there isn't a way. It's not USPS insured or some shit.

Granted, we're able to move more weight without the stipulations and guidelines of red tape registered dispensaries regulations face, but it's the fact that from point A to point B, shit is missing.

When I took over for my father before he passed, all I had to worry about was the boot, Louisiana. Terrell Senior was still handling moving this shit. He'd run it from Mexico, and we'd distribute it.

Easy.

Fucking cake walk.

Now cutting them out is proving more difficult because I can't have eyes everywhere. I can't rely on the people I've put in place. I can't rely on the dealings I've made.

That is becoming more and more clear.

I just don't know why.

Colorado was easy when it was Colton and his men. My brother may not have been a part of this in any way, but his best friend, Drea, had been my first key into how I could expand the Dupont name past state borders and take advantage of American produced weed. Getting the good shit and charging even more for green where they couldn't get it legally in the US.

Medical grade marijuana was nothing to sniff at. Profit margins were higher because everybody wanted this shit in comparison to the reggie I was dealing with before. I don't know if it was because Senior was making bad choices on suppliers or if the quality degraded from the region he got it from.

Either way, I had to level up if I was going to expand. After making that connection with Drea's ex, I began to really hit my stride. My next connect in Cali was easy. Same process, just a new location.

It was—until it wasn't.

This is more calculated than just randomly picking off something by accident. *Someone is hitting us slowly.* Making me distrust my men, forcing me to chase down these itty bitty ass problems while something larger is surely brewing.

With Redd behind the computer screen doing whatever he does, I'm stuck thinking over every interaction I've had with all parties involved. Time passes before anyone says anything over the radio.

"Umm, someone left a body here. She's at the back door, boss." I snatch the radio from Redd's hand. He rolls his eyes, focusing back on the screen.

It's been two days and I haven't heard from Diamond and she's not been to work. What we had was only the start. I'd hoped to finally put some of the fun extras in the private room to work, starting with those chains on the back wall above the bed.

She wasn't there though.

Figured she was just uncomfortable after Jimmy accosted her. But I told her that I'd taken care of that problem. I put my number in her phone and aside from the first call she placed so that I'd have her number, my phone was dry.

She never hit me up and she wasn't working.

My gut churns thinking about what could have happened to her. A suspicion enters my mind and I don't want it to be true. I grip the radio so tightly that the metal stings against my damaged hands. "Who is it?"

There's a pause before a crackling response comes through the radio again. "Don't know. She's not conscious."

She.

Fuck, no.

I look over to Redd and he shrugs. Pressing the mic on, I ask, "Dead?"

"Should I check?"

"The fuck? Yes." I'm already headed down the four flights of stairs to the security at the back.

The secured and barred doors buzz to let me through. I can still hear Redd following behind me, but I don't wait for him.

Normally, we receive any illegal product through these doors. It's a precaution to have the men here to keep an eye on any deliveries and to make sure someone can't just walk out with my shit. The other door on the west side is for standard deliveries for any of the legal fronts.

The only people who know of this entry are the ones involved with the green. This reeks of Junior and I need to get to the bottom of it.

"Open the door," I bark when the outside door is still locked.

With another buzz, I'm able to push through and I see her there at the foot of the short steps leading to the door.

My Diamond.

Racquelle.

The concrete runway is empty for once, My steps pick up. Rushing and practically leaping off the steps to get to her, my black heart cracks wide open at the state she's in.

"Fuck." I brush the hair from her face with shaking fingers. "Fuck, baby."

The tape over her mouth is my first priority. It's stuck to her bedraggled hair and over her bruised and bloody face.

Whoever did this, taped her up after they pulverized her.

My fury mounts as I take my time trying to get the tape off as gently as possible. I know I'm not gonna be able to keep from hurting her further.

Each millimeter it releases, I wince.

Who the fuck did this?

I'll kill them.

It takes me a few minutes, but I'm able to get the tape off her face so she can at least breathe better. She still hasn't moved, but Redd is there by my side now.

"Shiiit," he says, before turning back to the security door to call for someone to bring a car around.

I don't know where to grab her.

She's beaten so badly, that I'm scared I'll hurt her more by even touching her.

With my arms under her torso, there is the faintest movement of her lips as I try to get to her hands behind her back. A low, suffering moan escapes into the humid night.

"Racquelle. Racquelle, can you hear me?"

She mumbles something finally. She's alive. *Thank fuck.*

Cutting the last tape from her wrists and ankles with my knife, I tell her, "Gonna pick you up, okay baby?"

I don't wait for her reply when Vert comes over to help me pick her up with as much care as we can.

Normally, I'd be pissed to even see another man with their hands on my Diamond, but anything to make her more comfortable right now is better than putting her through anymore pain.

Her head rests on my lap as we take that drive back to my spot.

Redd makes all sorts of calls as I stroke the hair from her face, counting each nick and bruise that's visible in her dirty, bloodied clothes.

There's a car already waiting for us there. It must be the doctor we use for our soldiers to come check her over. I'm grateful that Redd is at least on top of things as my thoughts turn more and more murderous.

We park and I try to lift her head. Racquelle jostles, startled and disoriented. "Just let us carry you inside. I'm not tryin' to fight with you on this. I got you."

She settles and I watch diligently as the doctor examines her on my bed.

Three broken ribs, a dislocated shoulder, two black eyes, countless butterfly bandages and unknown substances keeping her mostly unconscious.

I hope that she wasn't awake for any of it.

I told her that I would ensure that if anyone hurt her, I'd make them regret it in the worst way.

Rage and hate mix at toxic levels in my bloodstream as she lies in the bed looking like she does.

I'll find who did this, and I'll make them pay for what they did to my Diamond.

INTO THE BLUE

PART 2

Chapter 13

Diamond

When I wake, the room is awash in Blue.

From the way it smells, to the energy that surrounds me—it's all him.

It takes a few moments for me to blink and realize that I'm not at home or in my apartment. I'm also not in that dim room where my half-brother ordered his men to attack me either.

"How are you feeling?" The deep voice from my left says.

Blue.

I turn my head and sure enough, it is him. He shifts, one hand covering the fist that he holds to his lips at my bedside.

That's my fist. He's holding my hand in his and kissing the knuckles with reverence that I can feel down to my core.

Looking down at myself, I see that the other arm is in a sling. I'm bandaged and in a bed. My clothes are changed and I seem cleaned up for the most part.

Did he do this?

"I'm... ow," I wince when I try to move. There's something tight around my middle, binding me.

"Don't move around yet. Your ribs and your shoulder are fucked. Matter fact, you're not in good shape at all." He looks concerned, but there is something more intense in his eyes, when he says more firmly, "Don't move."

"How did I get here? I—" My words halt as I remember being dragged from a trunk. "How long have I been here?"

"'Bout three days." I expect more information, but he doesn't elaborate. I'm sore and my mind is foggy. I don't know what to think about being in Blue's space.

Truly alone with him.

The last time that I saw Blue, he was showing me a side of him that I had only glimpsed before. In the club, in the private room, there was always this intensity about him.

A desire that I could succumb to.

He was a mark and I knew that. But I couldn't make my body listen to me.

I had gotten caught up in what was purely his will.

Even after I had just seen him, I knew that I needed to see him again.

It was dangerous.

I was in danger far before I allowed him to take over all my thoughts and tell him my name like he deserved to know the real me. Like maybe he deserved to see the real Rocky.

I should not have been associated with him in the first place, but it was necessary.

What I didn't account for was how unhinged Terrell Lafayette Junior is. I have no idea what he knows of me now and that is the most dangerous part of all this.

I felt unsafe around Junior and my instincts were absolutely right. I should have screamed when I first felt those men corner me.

It's unfortunate that it's always the worst idea to give men the benefit of the doubt. *That doubt is there for a reason.*

Now, I'm reaping the consequences of my poor judgment.

He could have killed me, but he didn't.

Somehow, I know that's worse.

There is no time to flounder in the should-haves when I'm still in an unknown location. And though Blue is the lesser of two evils, I am vulnerable and exposed in his presence. Physically and... *sigh*, emotionally, too.

Damnit. He is my mark.

I fucked around and damsel'd too damn hard.

I need to get to my phone.

Taking my hand from his, I do my best to sit up even against his direct order. It hurts like a bitch, but I can at least get a better look around the room I'm in.

Dark furniture, abstract paintings on the walls, and a—"Is that a tank? Wh-what is in there?"

He stands to his full height, coming over to the bed and adjusting some pillows behind me before sitting on the bed next to me. It's then that I realize how truly massive the bed is.

He's a big man, so I could guess he would have a bed that matched. But... this thing is like two kings side by side. Built for orgies or something—it could easily hold six people.

"Snakes. Got two of them," he simply informs me like it is the most normal thing in the world.

"Snakes?" He shrugs, and I squint to try and see anything more clearly through the glass. The enclosure spans the length of the room. With how large it is, it must be custom made. I hedge, "Like... a garter or..."

"Mexican Black Kings. Sativa and Indica. They're sunnin' right now."

"What does that mean?"

"They're cold blooded. Need sun or light to keep their temps up." He points to a corner where a large lamp is illuminating a clump of blackness.

Then I see it move.

Slithering along the rocks and onto some leaves and sand, it pauses at the other end of the tank. It's *absolutely massive*. It's got to be longer than I am tall or pretty damn close. Its tongue flicks out and I see that Blue has made silent steps over to the tank. For a man his size, he sure does move quietly. He slides the top open and he reaches an arm in.

Slick as oil, the massive snake starts winding up his arm and behind his hair to the other arm. "Sativa, meet Racquelle."

My pulse quickens and I try to scoot away from him. I've never seen a snake this big in person or one in real life. It's far too comfortable outside of the glass that should be keeping it away from me.

He looks genuinely perplexed. "You scared of him?"

"Uhh, yea! What the hell? That thing could eat me!"

"Nah," is all he says, letting the reptile slither down his wrist and to his waist. He's wearing a sash of this black snake that glimmers cobalt in the blue lighting. The scales are so smooth and shiny that it looks like an oil slick on his black shirt. If it weren't for the way it's moving, I may not have even known it was there. The single chain Blue's wearing around his neck moves every now and again, setting shimmering reflections around. "Sativa ate not that long ago, prefers rodents or other snakes over people anyway. My gators though—not as... discernin'. If you're unlucky, you'd find out that they think meat is meat."

That freaks me out way more. Like the venom, it's common knowledge that he makes people disappear by feeding them to his gators that are loyal only to the hand that feeds them.

"Well, I'd rather not test my luck today. I have enough things trying to kill me."

Sativa has made his way back to his neck, settling his head among the loose locs that hang from Blue's head.

I wince again when I try to move away from the big man and his big snake.

"Who did this?" He asks, gesturing to my general state. Should have known that he would not miss me wincing. I'm glad he hasn't come any closer with the snake though.

"I don't know," I lie. Another to add to my list at this point.

"Don't lie. Remember what I told you? Can't keep my word if you don't give me somethin'."

I chew my lip, thinking over my options.

Telling him the truth of why Junior attacked me is out of the question. "I'm pretty sure it was the Fayes. They didn't like what I told you."

Vague, so vague, but I'm toeing a line here. I have no idea if they knew I was the one to tell Blue about Dejuan. Couldn't be sure that Dejuan is still alive, but using context clues, I don't think he is. But I did tell Blue about Jimmy and I know for a fact that Jimmy is missing because of me.

Missing.

Gone.

Very dead—if the blood on his hands and face were any indication. I saw it clear as day in my apartment, but dare not comment on it. *Am I less guilty than him?* Each choice I've made was a step in many steps to get to my goal.

Blue nods his head. "Gonna take care of it." Walking back to the tank, he allows the snake to slither back down his arm into the enclosure where it disappears under some rocks. *I'd never see it coming,* I think as the snake moves out of sight. "First, gonna take care of you."

Running a hand over my head, I realize that he must have washed... and detangled my hair from the attack. It's even got some product in it that makes the long braid it's in smooth and neat down my back.

He's been taking care of me.

In jogger sweats and bare feet, he comes to my side and holds an arm out. The same one that he casually handled a snake with care. I don't miss that symbolism for a second.

From handling one snake to another.

I move as slowly as I can with his help. He keeps me steady as vertigo makes my vision wavy when blood rushes. After a moment, he's supporting me out of the room down another hallway with dark decor and luxe wood furnishings. The carpet is plush under my feet and I am thankful that walking isn't painful. He stops at a doorway with a heavy looking door. "Mind if I smoke first?"

It strikes me as kind of weird that he's asking. "Only if you're not gonna share with me," I say.

He grins and it's unlike any of the ones I've seen before. This one actually looks... pleased? That is so weird to qualify, but not once have I seen him look this way.

He pushes the door open and I see why the door is so heavy. It doesn't reek of old weed smoke, but it's faint in the air, probably from the fabric in the room. He sets me on a plush charcoal chair that instantly swallows me up. I'm sinking into the stuffing, but it's comfortable and not putting too much pressure on my sore body. He flicks a switch on a machine in one of the large windows. There is some kind of film over them so the room is dark enough that I can't see outside well. I'm sure you couldn't see inside either. A low whir comes from the machine and it must be what pulls the smoke out of the room.

He walks through the space gathering things.

A jar from a shelf full of them. Each one filled with slightly different shades of green from a pale citron to a deep, purplish hue. Some of the dried cannabis is tinged with red or yellow. A true connoisseur's collection.

A packet of cigarillos from a box with all different flavors to choose from. He picks a navy colored one with blueberries on it.

A tray from a table beside the shelf of jars.

Then a little baggie with small white foam cylinders. Cigarette filters.

Blue sits in a chair similar to mine and begins working on his project. He's efficient as he uses a nail to slice the brown tobacco leaf in half to empty it of the shredded tobacco. A few minutes later, he's broken down the sticky green clumps of weed from the jar. It has a blue-ish hue to it and there's white fluff sticking to his fingertips as he sprinkles it inside the leaf by small pinches of his index and thumb. Finally, he sets the white filter in one end and licks the edge of the leaf as he rolls it closed.

The blunt is tight and plump.

He sets it on the edge of the tray and repeats the same actions for the second. It couldn't have been more than ten minutes and he's ready to go. I didn't think that there could be anything sexy about rolling a blunt but here I am—practically drooling.

I smoke, sure. I know about selling weed, procuring it, distributing it, the local laws of many states if caught doing any of the aforementioned things... But this? Oh, I shouldn't have seen him do this.

He makes rolling blunts look like a craft. A skill or art form that should be awarded. Maybe it is. I've only seen it as a means and not a medium.

Setting the tray down, he puts one blunt behind his ear and lights the other. He takes an inhale in, holding it for a moment and then blows it out. I press my thighs together. This shouldn't be as hot as it is.

"When did you start smoking?" I take the offered blunt and puff shallowly, aware of my sore ribs. Instantly, tingles of ease settle through my bloodstream.

"It's crazy people think that because my Pa sold the shit, I was like nine years old with a blunt hangin' out of my mouth." He takes the blunt back and his eyes watch me, gauging my reaction.

I didn't think that, but it's hard to tell what kind of exposure he would have had. It's not like there were history books about these crime families. All I know is from word of mouth.

"I didn't take my first inhale until I was eighteen. He figured if I could get a Marlboro then I could at least puff somethin' better." There's a tightness around his eyes as he tells this anecdote about his dad.

"You looked up to him," I state though it could easily be a question.

He doesn't confirm but instead conveys, "He was human. He was raised in a different generation. He had ambitions that were bigger than anybody around him could grasp. He achieved them. He gave that drive to me. So, I took it."

He took the drive and that much is clear with all he's done since his dad stepped down. He didn't just become King with that step. It took time and effort to build this empire further. "What didn't you take?"

"Wish I hadn't taken how he treated my Ma. He didn't fight for her or keep her safe. His eye was glued to the money and everythin' else fell to the side. Even me and my lil' bro. But he saw us as his legacy, so neglectin' that was bad business. Nothin' a Dupont hates more than bad business."

He doesn't light the other blunt like I expect.

Long limbs unfold to his massive frame and I feel small under the man but also under that honesty. *He is as much a product as I am.* His father shaped Blue and set him on the path he wanted for him.

I wonder if Blue wanted this life or if he just took it. I don't ask.

He tosses the filter into a bucket and turns off the fan in the window. By the time he's back over to me, I hold my hand out for him to pull me out of the chair. He pops a stick of gum into his mouth and instead of having to take it from his lips, he hands me a piece, as well.

Blue helps me to the hallway again and we reach a spacious kitchen with the same dark wood as the rest of the house with matte black appliances. It's so much like a cave in this place.

A very luxurious cave with cherry wood and hidden corners.

He helps me sit at a bar stool in the kitchen that overlooks the stove and sink on the opposite side. My observations of him are slow because of whatever we smoked, but I'm no less aware that he's getting things to cook.

He's... feeding me.

I expect some kind of munchie meal or stereotypical stoner food like instant ramen and grilled cheese but by the look of the ingredients—it won't be that.

He pulls a large knife from a wooden block on the counter and expertly filets a chicken breast into thin cutlets before seasoning them and setting it aside. He methodically portions then rinses some rice and presses a button on a rice cooker before coming back to the first counter and cleaning it. Whatever this meal is, it beats the frozen junk I've been settling for by a mile. He chops some vegetables and I watch in fascination. If watching him roll a blunt was sexy, then this is basically pornographic.

As mundane as it is, I've never been on the receiving end of something like this. Yes, my mom cooked for me. But, my dating life is virtually nonexistent because of my job. Kinda hard to balance both when either expects to be *the only one.*

I know what he can do with a knife and all of it turns me on like a horny little cat, apparently. He definitely has activated some kind of knife kink for me because, "me next," is poised on my lips. I don't get the chance to embarrass myself because he is the one to break the silence between us.

"How did you become a..." he pauses, bent over with a tray in his hand. I get a glimpse of the writhing tattoos over his strong back as the t-shirt rises up a bit and I try not to bite my cracked lip. "A dancer? Always a story there." He's back to cleaning the counter, now that he's put the vegetables in the oven, but I want to go back to the mystery tattoos I've yet to see.

How is it that I still haven't seen this man naked?

A few moments pass where I try to think of how to answer this question. It's not complicated, but I find myself wanting to be honest even though I know I can't be fully. "I guess, I'm following the family business, too. My mom danced and I grew up around it to an extent. I knew all the other women who worked in her club. My best friend is the daughter of a dancer. It was just normal to me though I know how people see us—judge us. My mom never glamorized the life or let me see it as anything other than it was. She taught me to dream big and I am. My story doesn't end with me dancing at Off Topz." There. All of that is true.

Liezel has been my friend and support as we both navigated life as young girls who had seen too many things, too young. Our moms weren't saints, but they kept us fed, clothed, and off the pole until we were old enough to make our own decisions. We could have done anything else, but community is hard to find and even harder to leave. And every single one of those ladies were family to me. That's why it hurts so badly to lose members.

I miss my girls, but I'm here for a much bigger reason.

The chicken sizzles in a pan and he tends to them before asking, "Where does it end?"

"I don't know yet." I rub my chin, realizing that I must look like death with no makeup covering my swollen and sore eyes. Why had I not thought to do any kind of primping in all this time? *Shit.*

"Maybe I could help you with that," he hedges. I fight back a smirk because even looking like the thing that got caught in a lawn mower, I still played my role perfectly.

You already are, more than you could ever know.

Chapter 14

BLUE

There's a woman in my house.

This is not just *any* woman.

Fuck I look like having any regular ol' woman staying in my crib?

This is a woman that could make me change my ways.

The fact that she's still here is proof of that.

In the fifteen years I've lived in this house alone since my dad passed, I've never let a chick stay over. Yea, I might bring them back here, but the score is settled before they walk in.

You can come, but ultimately, you gotta go.

I've been taking care of Racquelle though. Best I know how. Had Vert and Geno go get her things from that apartment and now she wants for nothing. That place never looked like one she cared about anyway. No personality or indication that she was planning on staying there.

Now she doesn't have to.

Redd managed to find her purse and phone on the side of the highway so she's got a way to tell her friends and her family that she's okay. She has relaxed a lot more since she's been able to contact them. As much as anyone can who's been jumped by a bunch of cowards.

I could have had someone come and cook for her and help her around the house, but I don't trust anyone to be around her when she's just a fragile thing.

I might be a monster, but I take care of mine.

I'm also a man of my word. When I claimed her, it wasn't a fucking throw around phrase or some shit. I will keep her safe from this point forward. By any means necessary.

There was no need to have more people in my house. I wasn't going to leave her side. If she needs it, I'll be the one to get it for her.

I could do anything that I would have been working on in the warehouse, from my home office. Anyone who I needed to meet with there—they could come see me at my home office.

Not that I've been getting any work done that I need to. I've gotten no closer to answering my missing product or rat problem. Having Allen on my books has shown me that I'm still profitable. But for how long if I can't count on product to come to my guys on time?

I've got Vert on it for now. He managed to raise the prices by ten percent to make up for the product loss with all the men under him selling in Louisiana.

It's a bandaid. A flimsy one, but since Racquelle is starting to feel better I'll be able to get after it with a more hands-on approach. I just need to see if the rat will expose themselves.

That is exactly what this is like.

Rats don't take the whole loaf. They chew through the middle.

Racquelle's ribs aren't giving her problems any more and she's not really had to use her sling. She even started working out when I go to my gym in the back of the house.

I have all the equipment I'd need to stay in shape, so I don't have to be in public just to workout. I prefer to do it alone and that's not really possible when it's unsafe, and dumb as fuck, to go to a place consistently every week with none of my men with me. I've got plenty of privacy to train in peace here.

Occasionally Redd or Vert will join me, but they prefer the gym Redd trains everyone else in. A luxury I can't afford.

Opening the door to my home gym, I walk past the treadmill and squat rack to where Racquelle has set up.

She's working with dumbbells today to test the strength of her shoulder. They aren't heavy, but in the mirror she watches her reps from the bench. With a call to the doctor, he was able to refer me to someone who could give me insight on workouts that would be helpful for her recovery. I still think it's too early for her to be going this hard, but I can't stop her. I'd rather be here to help her.

"Need some help?" I cough to hide my instant regret of the cheap line. Racquelle is capable and would be just fine on her own if it weren't for me in the first place. Too bad for her that I'm not an experience that she will be able to shake.

She watches me walk over in my long tee and exercise shorts with intrigue.

Her eyes never leave me when she releases the weight from over her head and back to the bench.

I sit behind her, our thighs touching. She picks the weight back up and I spot her, though we both know it's unnecessary. I want to touch her anyway. At least she'll still be able to work out while I do it.

I haven't touched her in a sexual way while she recovered here. I don't deserve an award or something for not taking advantage, but it's been too many long as fuck weeks since I had the ability to touch her in a way that wasn't sterile.

The way this started between us was contractual, but I now know that I would have pursued her regardless. It took one look and I knew I needed to get close to her. I want what we have to be less of what it once was—to become something real and genuine.

Our first rep together is easy. I count them out, making sure to watch her form. By the time she gets to eight, I can see her struggling even though she could have stopped at any point.

"Don't have to hold yourself together for me," I attempt to assure her.

She doesn't flinch when I take the dumbbell from her. That's what makes me the most furious. Not the bruises. Not the swelling that's finally started to go down. Not the cuts that have seamed up.

It's the fact that she's trying to pretend like none of it hurts.

My voice is low, "You're not gonna impress me here with how much pain you can take."

The gym is not where I want her to show me how much pain she can take. With how undeterred she was with my knife at her throat showed me that she could handle plenty. The memory sparks something low in my stomach. Even then, she wasn't afraid. Or maybe she was and didn't show it.

This isn't the same thing though.

I watch her jaw tighten, then she reaches for the weight with her good arm. "I'm fine. Working out is good for me." She transfers the weight and presses it up again.

"Nine," I say, correcting her form as she lifts the dumbbell laterally. Her shoulder tenses and she winces.

I see it though she tries to swallow it down.

"Keep your core tight," I murmur, resting my hand over her middle. "Don't lean. You cheat yourself like that."

She nods once, face blank. Trying to prove she can do this alone.

I hate that about her.

Not the strength—never that. Her strength only makes her more fucking sexy. I don't know anyone that could have gone through what she did and be this determined to move past it like it didn't happen.

Not in my world.

It's the lie she's telling herself that she has to hurt quietly. Like she hasn't earned softness. Like she can't be soft *with me* when I've given her every opportunity to be.

I'm not the most romantic guy. Fuck, it's not like I've even been on a date in a decade. But I've been taking care of her. I know I've been doing a decent job of it, too.

"Ten," I say, and she lowers her arm slowly.

I'm still watching her closely in the mirror. "You good?"

She nods again, but I move before she can speak. I close the space between us, wide legs bracketing her hips, pulling her back until her spine rests against my chest. We sit like that for a time so she can rest.

I can't make her stop pushing herself, but I can be here to support her if and when she needs me.

"Go for another set." I pick up the other dumbbell and place it in her hand.

Her shoulder twitches and she bites her lip until color drains from it.

"That's it," I murmur against her ear. "Slow. Controlled. Got you." My palm supports her bicep through the extension.

I stand behind my words. I mean it when I said I have her. I have to keep her safe from the fucked up parts of my world. *This happened to her because of me.* The guilt is foreign but well deserved.

I'm keeping her.

Even when I shouldn't.

The smell of her, even a little sweaty from what she was doing before I got here, is intoxicating. I'm always drawn to her. Wanting to lean in and have more. Her body's soft where mine is hard and it kills me to know someone touched her without permission. That they intended to hurt her and did so.

She didn't deserve that.

"You shouldn't be doing this so soon," I mutter, fingers ghosting over the curve of her elbow, checking for tension.

"I need to feel strong again," she breathes, meeting my eyes for the challenge. Her statement hits me square in the chest.

Strong.

I don't doubt her strength, but that strength was never supposed to be built out of bruises.

"You already are," I say. It slips out before I can stop it.

She lowers the dumbbell, lets it drop to the mat between her feet, and leans back against me fully this time. As we sit here together, her heart beats against mine.

"It's not enough," she whispers. "Maybe, I'm not enough."

My eyebrows draw in with confusion. "For what?"

She shakes her head slowly, chaotic thoughts flitting through those eyes that search mine in our reflection. "I shouldn't be here and you know it."

"I don't know shit. You're mine," I clarify. "Even if you don't want to be. Even if you're fighting what I've already told you. Gonna take care of it."

I had Redd tracking the Fayes movements for a good while, but never with the effort I had been recently. Redd was completely on board to end any Faye life since they were directly responsible for his brother's death. I had him held back because at the time it was not good business to burn that bridge. But now, it was a matter of going to war if I retaliated in any way.

Their attack on Racquelle was very clearly the first act of war.

Nothing is more important than the family and Racquelle was a part of that now. Nothing in my conscience could let her go when the last time I let her be, without me and my protection, things ended the way it did.

But that fucker Junior was hiding. He wasn't in the state and no one could get a location on him. As soon as Junior showed his face, it'd be the last time he would take a breath.

Wrapping my arms around her, I'm content with the fact that I can hold her without her wincing in pain. She turns her head just slightly, enough that I can see the corner of her mouth curve—not a smile, not really. Just a silent challenge.

"I never said that I didn't want to be," she says. I kiss the edge of her jaw, slowly making my way to her neck on the side of her tender shoulder. "Just that I shouldn't be." She doesn't pull away.

"I would take out every single one of them," I whisper into her skin, "just to see you safe with me." Her breath catches with my words or my touch, I can't tell.

My hand moves to her waist. We're not talking anymore, not really. We're hovering at the edge of something raw and deep.

If I can feel it, I know she feels it, too.

She doesn't stop me when my fingers slip under the edge of her leggings. Our eyes on the path my hand is taking.

My middle finger grazes the little bud that's already sensitive. "You've been missin' me." My finger slides lower to find her wet, not wet enough to take me, but slick enough to get there.

"You've been treating me like glass," she exhales. My index and ring finger encase her lips and give me a little leverage in these tight pants to sink inside her. Her head tips back when I'm able to get to that second knuckle.

My nose drags along the curve of her neck, taking in the scent that is so Diamond that I'm taken back to that first night I had her in my hands. "You right." I nod along her skin. "You like it when I make you shatter, don't you?"

It's impossible to go slow when I know what the answer will be, but I wait for her to tell me anyway.

"Yea, Blue," she says and I waste no time sliding another finger in, too.

That tension in her back melts away as she gives into me. It's soothing in a way that I could not have expected. Knowing that I'll be giving her this moment of peace, that she expects the release I'm about to give her—priceless.

She may not be completely there, but I will show her that she can be soft with me.

I start working my fingers in and out while my other hand slides under her sports bra to find her stiff little nipple. She bites her lip, but the moan is still clear as day.

"That's right, bae. Lemme hear you," I whisper into her ear. "I want it all." Something too dangerous to say out loud, but I say it anyway because it's true.

"Mmh, what's this?"

My teeth grind at the entirely unwelcome voice interrupting us.

Racquelle stiffens in my arms. *Fuck.* All that work to relax her and it's gone. Evaporated into the air.

Now, I'm really pissed.

I let my hands slide away from her slowly as I summon patience. "What you want?"

He takes one step into the room, and I'm up out of my seat to keep Redd from coming in any further. I quickly adjust myself and hustle to the door.

I don't care who it is, I don't want anyone seeing my Diamond like this.

"Later," I tell her and mean it. She nods before standing, tight ass on display in her leggings when she makes her way to the treadmill. Her shoulders roll back and a new mask of unaffected casualty resides where her undoing once was.

I fucking hate that even more.

"Called you a few times before I came, but you didn't pick up." I walk out of the room toward my office and my second follows me.

"I was busy."

"If my honey was sitting up at the crib, walkin' around in that, I probably wouldn't be pickin' up the phone either."

"What?" *Fuck.* "Wassup?"

"You need to go talk to Colton. He is supposed to be keepin' shit in line. If he's not, then he needs to know that we aren't cool wit' it. We got those shrooms and wax coming."

"What happened now?"

Redd walks over to the computer to pull up the information he's talking about. I take a seat on the corner of the desk, looking over his shoulder to see just what the fuck is going on. "Multiple inconsistencies with the timelines. He was supposed to deliver on the last two late packages, today. He's talkin' some ra-ra bullshit and I'm thinkin' he's not cut out to lead like he said he could. That was too big an upfront investment to allow some whenever-the-fuck delivery times. What the hell did we pay for?"

"You check his lines?"

"The best I could, which is really well. He hasn't made any calls that would make it seem like he has any sort of foul play happenin'. It's the same guys and the same movements. His truck is takin' the same routes." He shows me the map that tracks those routes and they all match the ones that have been laid out for them.

"If I go, it needs to be silent. I can't move with the whole team. The last thing I need is for word gettin' out that we have any weakness. Even perceived. Two men, max"

He nods. "You could be there tomorrow if you leave tonight."

I look back toward the gym and grimace.

"She's gonna be fine here." My jaw ticks again. "Well the only people who know she's here are top tier and security is tight on the premises."

"Double it."

"For?"

"Her." I'm not ready to leave her. I don't want to leave her in my territory without me here. She will be protected by my best men. I'll have eyes on her for the most part. But it wasn't that long ago that I was scooping her broken body from the ground outside my warehouse.

It's too soon, my heart and mind tell me.

Nothing's more important than the money.

Fuck.

"It's only a few days," Redd reasons.

"I know." I scrub a hand over my face. "Book the flight."

Chapter 15

BLUE

"Even with the favor of the law, I'm not superman, dude." He tries to explain, but I really don't give a fuck about his excuses.

September in Colorado isn't half bad. It's cooler here than it is in Louisiana, but I don't mind it. It makes long sleeves more bearable for a trip I didn't want to take. Sitting in the shade of his Douglas fir on benches outside of Colton's home isn't the worst way to spend my time. It's the company that makes it irritating. The whole point of delegating was so I didn't have to make trips like these.

I can't stand to have this uncertainty and have my information be filtered through so many mouths. That trust I had is dwindling by the day. I can't afford to wait for shit to fuck up before I take action.

This hazel-eyed, military-cut wannabe is a pet project that I have very big plans for. When I met him, he was doing small business. Selling to his friends and just outside their circles. After all, cannabis is legal in Colorado. All you have to do is present a valid ID and be older than twenty-one to get your hands on it.

His in with me? Selling medical grade at a wholesale price.

I bought out his operation within a week of meeting him randomly on a visit to see my brother.

Is Colton Flagg a good man? No, definitely not. He knocked up my brother's best friend and the weekend I met him, he sent one of his guys to pick her up after her car broke down on the side of the road. One. Of. His. GOONS. *Not him.* When he wasn't doing shit besides sitting up at the house. Sorry absentee dad type of shit. It's why I feel no ways about using him as a pawn in this setup.

Like I said, I bought him out fairly easily. But I knew he had enough money to at least put the mother of his only child in a decent sedan. The hoopty she was rollin' in was junkyard fodder long before I saw it.

Could never be me.

But I digress, he is not a good man—which made him the best man to carry out the operation I had him on at present.

It was simple.

No record, easy in to the Colorado Police Department. Kiss enough ass to rise up in the ranks and bam—He's a sheriff overseeing the safe transport of my green over the state border.

A difficult task because the law is more strict here since there are plenty of people trying to smuggle *Colorado's finest* beyond the border. But using him to crack down on my potential competitors created a wide open market to exploit the arbitrary laws around cannabis, and now mushroom, production to suit my needs in the South, where it suits lawmakers to crack down on these substances.

This had been years in the making all while he tested the limits of his power in moving small shipments to me on different pathways. It was smooth as the quantity increased and the number of runners we employed increased. It was large enough that I figured my separation from the Fayes wouldn't hurt us.

The quality made up for the quantity in the meantime.

Now, I'm looking at the man who assured me that it was no problem to increase this shipment. Yet! A third of the product is gone.

"You told me that it wouldn't be a problem. Now it is. Think I came here to *chat*?"

"I've kept my eyes open. It's not any of my guys. I've been watching them all. It's just gone."

"You some kind of magician?" I ask.

"N-no," his hand is on his belt, too damn close to his gun. It makes my men antsy.

"Go 'head and put your hands where we can see them. I'd hate for a misunderstandin' to become a different problem entirely."

His hands raise immediately. "I wasn't—Look, I'm doing everything that I can."

"If that were the case, then you'd have a lead on how my shit went missing."

"I can't keep an eye on everything when I still have other responsibilities to the county. This only works because I'm respected at my job."

"A job I provided for you."

"I know that." He sighs, scratching the back of his head. "There's an opportunity that I see coming soon. I could replenish what we lost without raising suspicion. I just need a bit of time."

I consider his words, my hand resting on my knife. Haven't had to press him for anything since I'm the reason he's no longer a low level dealer. He's only steps away from becoming a quartermaster in this family. *That means something.* "What makes you think I have time to spare for you?"

"I'll be able to move three times as much. There will be no eyes on me or anything."

My eyebrows lift, completely unbelieving but intrigued by the possibility. "Three times as much?"

"Yes, I'll move as much more. My guys will do what we need to."

"How much time are we talkin' 'bout?"

"December. Christmas time. They hold a retreat and I can play my part to get that in the works. If I'm controlling the planning of it, then I can make sure they're out of the way."

I scratch my beard, considering again. "Don't like the risk you're takin'. I'm gonna have some of my own men on it."

"Of course. I could show them—"

Holding up a hand, so he'll stop talking, I inform him, "No, you'll leave transportin' to them. If you're clearin' the way then they'll just need to drive the routes."

"But—"

Shaking my head, locs flop into my face and I pull them back. "Nah. I'm still missin' part of what I'm owed already. Haven't ruled you out as a suspect yet."

Under his breath, Colton murmurs, "You're not the only one taking advantage of this opportunity."

"What was that?" I sneer, not liking how he won't speak up when saying something that will piss me off.

"Competition is high," he says more firmly.

My knife is out and my men are close behind me. The blade is exposed, even as my hand remains at my side. "Is that a threat?"

"Not me. Never me. But you know, I worked with the Fayes on many occasions. Knew those guys. They can't be happy about the ties being cut."

I nod once and my men are at Colton's sides. "You think for one second, that I give two fucks about what you or any of them think about the decisions I made for this family?"

"No, but—"

"No, period." My knife is poised right under his ribs. He wears no protection under his uniform, and that was a mistake on his part. One to add to a long list of them, I'm sure. "End of the sentence and the discussion. You sympathize with a Faye more than the Duponts losing product, such as yourself?"

Quickly, his head moves side to side before he rushes out, "Christmas, I'll get everything exactly where it should be."

"You will, I'll make sure of it." A final nod to my men and they escort Colton out of my sight.

"Hello?"

I look down at my phone to make sure I called the right number. Three diamond emojis tell me that I did call the right person. Putting the phone back to my ear I say, "Damn. Didn't save my number?"

"Don't take it personal. I don't save anyone's number." Her sharp tone is a welcome one. I was hoping that she wouldn't be upset when I was gone. Leaving her in the house by herself with strict directives to my men to not let her go anywhere without me, would be irritating to anyone. But she hasn't complained about it. Just her usual little attitude.

"Oh." I lie back on the pillows. "I'm just anybody?"

The smile in her voice is evident. That makes me feel less irritated about not being there with her right now. I didn't feel suffocated or crowded like I thought I might with a woman staying with me. Can't even lie and say that it was a temporary thing when I moved all her shit in. *What little it was.*

I have no plans at all to move any of it out.

Or to let her leave.

At some point she'll be healed enough to get back to Off Topz.

Am I going to be able to be okay with her at risk in my club again?

The number of bodies I'm accumulating on her behalf is bound to grow when she does. I need to find a better way to deal with all this. Because if anyone even thinks of hurting her again, I'm past the point of talking it out.

"If I had a list, you'd be somewhere near the top of it."

"Yea?" I question and she makes a noise of agreement on the line. "What number?" I light the blunt I rolled earlier and start blowing it out the window while I wait for whatever she'll say next.

There's silence for a bit then, "Four."

Despite the shitty rating, I laugh. No one would be so brazen with me. I've never met a woman who was—outside of Steph and to me, she barely counts. "What would change that?"

Even on the phone, her voice is sultry, wrapping around me like an embrace. "I don't know. You have a habit of leaving me high and dry when I wanna get off..."

I run a hand through my locs. "Fuck, that's my bad." I never apologize for business decisions. *I never had to.* It was not something that ever came up. Racquelle is making me see things completely different. I had fucked up in leaving without telling her. *Even more because I said I'd finish her later.* "Let me make it up to you."

"Mmmh," there's rustling on the other side of this conversation and I wonder if she's in my bed. I had been sleeping in the guest room before I left. I didn't want to hurt her somehow while I was sleeping. That would be changing as soon as I got back in town though. "How are you gonna make it up to me?"

I guess it's the obsession playing up, making my dick hard as fuck just listening to her talk on the phone. "What you got on?"

"The sheets."

"My sheets?" I bite my lip at the image. Diamond's body is a work of fucking art. Like I made this woman in my dreams and she just appeared. Curvy in all the ways I like, a coke-bottle brown skin lil' thing. She's soft everywhere I like and she knows how to drive me crazy off those curves. I really fucking hate that I'm here right now. "And what else?" I ask, taking my last hit from the blunt before putting it out on the window sill.

"Nothing."

"Fuuuck," Running a hand over my face, I know I'm in for it. "Didn't know I was callin' for a good time."

"It's me," she purrs. "You called for a great time."

Placing the phone on speaker, I sit up. "I'm not fuckin' around. Are you gonna play with that little pussy for me?"

Her mischievous smirk is obvious from the tone of her response. "Grabbing something right now."

Mine stretches to match hers. So willing to play. "What you grabbin'?"

My phone vibrates and a picture message pops up. *I just got a dick pic from my girl.* "This one is as close as I'll get to what you feel like."

The toy is clear and girthy but definitely not as big as I am.

Lust crawls up my throat and I grab myself over my cargos for now. "It'll do."

"Good," she says and I hear the snap of a bottle opening.

My mouth drops open. "You got the lube already?"

"You said you weren't fucking around, right?"

A groan rumbles in my chest. *I wish I was there to see this.*

"Let me see," I command.

The tone for a video call plays in my ear. Suddenly, I'm looking at her lush titties and bare pussy spread on my black sheets with the lighting glowing around her. I don't know if seeing her is better or worse. I'm bricked up and pressing against my fly.

"Are you gonna keep your clothes on for this?" She asks while squeezing one of her full tits.

I take my pants and boxers off, not bothering with the shirt. Don't have lube or some shit like that. I settle for spitting into my hand and stroking my shit for her to see how hard she's made me.

She chuffs and shakes her head, rubbing the tip of the toy over her clit. My eyes are glued to the way her lips blossom open. The deep pink calling to me. "One day you'll take that shirt off."

"One day," I say to her pussy. "Pinch those nipples. I like 'em hard for me."

She listens, using her forearm to lift them and rolling one between her fingers. I bite my lip, wishing it were me giving them that kind of attention. Cupping and squeezing them. Wishing I could have my mouth over them.

"Harder."

Her moan is loud in my quiet hotel room and I relax on the bed again. Her breathing is getting faster, as her other hand is still rubbing the toy over her clit.

"Put the toy down for a minute," I say. "Show me how wet you are."

Racquelle uses her index and ring fingers to spread her lips for me. The middle circles her opening, gathering the slick moisture there.

"Damn, bae. Want to put those fingers in my mouth."

"Just the fingers?" She asks and slides the middle finger in all the way. Her lips form a perfect "O" as her brows pucker in concentration. She starts moving the finger in and out, probably reaching for her g-spot.

"Nah," I manage though my focus is solely on how she's teasing herself. I stroke myself a few times and squeeze the head to hold off on coming. It'd be easy as she's putting on this show. I need to last so I can see just how far she'll let me push her. "Put the rest in."

"Okay… Like *this*?" Her voice catches on the last word as her tight hole stretches to accommodate three more of her fingers. I remember just how warm and snug my fingers were inside her.

"Just like that. Be good for me and hold the camera right up to that pussy. Wanna hear how wet you are."

She giggles, actually giggles, with three fingers pumping in and out of her. "You're a freak, Blue."

"You knew this." My cheek hikes on one side. "Now let me hear that needy pussy. Wish I could taste it."

She moves the camera how I asked and I'm about to bust.

Every sound is driving me crazy.

I need to start stroking myself harder.

"I want to see you. It's been too long," she breaths.

I find a pillow to prop the phone up on and place it so she can see my hand twisting up and down. There's enough pre-cum now that sliding over my tip and back down is smooth. I'll just have to imagine that it's her juices for now. "Almost forgot you were missing me," I tease.

"I didn't," she says, moving the phone back so I can see all of her again. "Can I use my toy now?"

"Yea, just hold it against you for now." Her toy is clear and I'm gonna need a minute to prepare for the sight of her stretching around it so I could see *everything*.

Goddamn.

This woman is mine.

I've never done anything like this and she is making it so I'll never be able to go back to the basic shit I had before.

"Want to see you take all of it." The intensity of her eyes reaches me through the phone. They burn with the same need I'm feeling. "Slide it in."

Racquelle spreads the lube over her toy quickly and completely, before shoving it inside.

Just like the first time I fucked her.

"Are you imaginin' it's my dick fillin' you like this?"

"Yes," she moans, pushing the toy back inside herself.

"Don't be selfish then," I say. She blinks, twisting the toy. "Rub that clit, too. I'd never leave it out."

A happy laugh escapes her, "You're right," she confirms using her other hand to rub circles over the bud.

She's writhing on the bed, trying to find the right pace to fuck herself.

My fist is rough and fast on my dick as I watch her try to get there without me.

A sick part of me hopes that she can't.

I need to be the only one who can make her cum like I do.

Am I jealous of a silicone cock replica?

...

No.

"You're gonna have to fuck yourself harder than that if you expect to come, beautiful."

"I'm trying," she pants and I can see that she is.

"You're gonna have to try harder than that. That toy will never replace how it feels to have my dick between your thighs. How it feels to be split apart by me so that I can take you higher and farther than anythin' ever could. You need my hands on you, ownin' your body and showin' you how good I can make you feel."

"Oh, god," she cries, the fine tremor in her thighs my clue to keep going.

"Not, god. Blue," I correct her. "It's me who you need to shatter and break you, so I can put you back together with my tongue, my lips, my fingers and my dick. If you want to come it will be because I allowed you to and I'm the one who took you there."

"I n-need you... Oh, Blue. I'm so close," she whines.

"I know, bae. I'm gonna take care of it as soon as I get home. Now show me you remember how well I work your body and give me the cum I've been waitin' for."

"Ah—Fuck!" She shouts, body clenching as she continues pumping the toy inside her as best she can while coming for me so beautifully.

From her sounds alone, I'm spilling over my hands and dripping down my arms.

The thought of wasting it comes to mind as I'm cleaning up my hands in the bathroom and wiping my dick off to get dressed again. Should be stuffed inside her not swirling down the drain. I realize that I'm far gone already and I don't want our call to be over.

Lying back onto the bed, I demand, "Tell me what you been doing all day," caked up like a simp fool. I don't care as she tells me all that she's gotten up to in my absence.

Chapter 16

Diamond

"Rocky, I need an update."

It had been weeks since I felt safe to contact Liezel. She's been holding everything down admirably, but I was the brains of this whole operation. I couldn't wait any longer to check in with my team.

"I'm still following the plan as outlined. He's noticing just how big the problem in Colorado is for him now. We can't let up." It was something I was counting on him to take issue with. The direction he took was outside instead of repairing from within.

I, more than anyone, would agree with him not repairing the partnership with the Lafayette family—only because Junior was still in charge. My shoulder ached recalling what it was like to dangle from that pipe the last night I saw him.

What he did to me was confirmation that this man had absolutely no understanding how to be a leader. He did not deserve anything that had been afforded him including, but not limited to, Blue Dupont.

I didn't need further convincing when he turned my perfectly profitable club, The Chrome Flame, back home into what it is now. The gratitude I had for my foresight was never something I took for granted. I was able to get so many girls out of there before they got hooked on that shit and either lost their lives or became indebted to the monster, himself.

The work I'm doing was in large parts a *fuck you* to Junior, and Senior for that matter, but also showing how undervalued we, as women, were. Dancers are more than just products, but we're people too. People who hold far more power than they would like us to believe.

"So, just keep going as normal?"

Though she can't see me, I nod my head. "Yes. I'm gonna see him tonight when he gets back, so I won't be able to call you for a while. He's reluctant to leave me alone after... Junior."

Lee sighs on the other end of the phone before she adds, "It's kind of sweet. Are you sure you can keep this up?"

"What?" I scoff, though it feels forced and a little fake. "You think him being somewhat decent is gonna ruin the mission?"

"Ruin it? No. But falling for him will make this much more complicated. He eliminated Jimmy Lafayette and Dejuan Jones. Jay Shorn is also MIA right now. It seems that he's killed or made them all go missing." She pauses and I consider her words. She delivers the next line with a punch. "You are the common thread for all of them."

"Falling for him?" I echo back to her and my thoughts begin running. "He's protecting his business the only way he knows how."

"Or... Or he's protecting the woman he has feelings for."

Grimacing down at my phone, I don't like what she's alluding to. "Be serious, Lee."

"I am. None of his actions fit the profile we made for him. He would never do this for a woman." I sit back on the bed that he's given up for me to sleep in. *He gave up his room, so I would feel comfortable recovering here.* I'm not going to point that out to Liezel while she's already on a roll. "We couldn't identify any consistent partners over the last four years. The only woman he is seen with repeatedly is his real estate agent and the relationship is not at all romantic."

"I'm not falling for him," I say, but the words taste more false. "I want to partner with him."

Maybe *partner* is a more fitting word in more ways than one.

Falling for Blue is like being weighed down by the finest luxury all while gasping for air below water. The truth of what he is steals every good thing I've held onto about myself. Every little thing that I promised myself, I'd never compromise on.

How can I be a good person when I know how red my hands are by loving this man?

Falling into Blue? I shouldn't.

Should not.

Does him saving me, giving me the life I want, excuse all the lives he hasn't spared?

There's good in him.

I *know it.*

But there's bad beyond measure.

I know he'll never truly share how deep the blue goes. None of that matters because he's claimed me as his.

Once you're in the blue, you'll never get out again.

I know that his empire wasn't built on strictly legal means and neither will mine.

Blood is already running and I'm directly responsible.

We aren't in this business to win awards.

We're in it to make money.

As long as I have the upper hand with him, I can at least make sure that I keep my life now.

I decide to change the subject altogether. My feelings for Blue and his feelings for me are completely inconsequential to the job. "Are you staying safe? I miss home so much. I miss you."

My starring role as Rapunzel in this tower was vital for the story. I could complain and be honest about how much I hated being stifled in this house under his protection, but I needed to remain the helpless little woman in his eyes in order to keep his trust.

He can't know my true intentions for being here.

I couldn't go back to Atlanta now anyway. I knew that was where Junior was holed up to avoid Blue. Coward.

The birds chirp idly from her porch. She must be smoking before her shift. Normally, we'd be sitting there together. "You know Lidia never lets me out of her sight. I might as well say she's my personal bodyguard."

A little chuckle escapes my lips. "And you want me to face facts? You're not doing it yourself."

Her exhale is a brief moment of static on my end. She's definitely smoking without me. "You're right. She is my personal bodyguard."

I laugh at her obliviousness. "Pot meet kettle."

"Couldn't tell what you're referring to. My regular has been feeling very generous, since I've been with the flog. You think I should start demanding to be called Mistress or Domme? Mistress Lee does have a good ring to it."

"Gets my vote." I cross my legs under myself as I settle back onto the couch. "You could finally use some of that fetish wear. Surprised you have money for food with how much there is."

"A girl's gotta have hobbies," she laughs. "Don't worry about what I'm doing in my free time."

"You could be making so much more if you truly offered yourself as a Mistress. OH, I know who would enjoy being your test dummy. I guess, test subby is more accurate."

"Ruben isn't *that* willing. I feel like I've been training him to be more submissive. The flog was just on a whim—"

"No, Lee. I meant Lidia."

"Lidia?"

"Yea."

"No. That's not a thing."

Lidia had worked at the club long before Liezel or I started on the pole. She is a staple in The Chrome Flame and for good reason. Strong, takes no shit, and keeps the girls safe. Especially, those of us who were in high demand. But there is only so much that she could do against new ownership without losing her job.

I knew for a fact that she had a soft spot for Lee. When Junior started spewing his shit into the club, Lidia was the first outside of Lee's door to make sure none of them touched her.

None of the coked out patrons and none of Junior's men who were passing it around like candy.

"Come on. Studs like to be dominated, too. You'd be so good at it," I assert.

"I don't think so. I'm not ready. Plus I have all this on my plate with you." She's not wrong. With my Rapunzel status, she's having to take on more than she usually would.

"Not for long, I—"

"Racquelle," Blue's voice calls me from the front room. *I didn't think he'd be home already.*

Hurrying into the bedroom, "I've gotta go. I'll text you okay?"

"Okay. I love you! Be safe! Safer than last time," she scolds.

"I will. Bye," I say, ending the call and lying on the bed waiting for Blue to come find me.

As usual, his energy reaches me before he does. A shiver rolls down my spine as I recall how I came in this same spot last night with his instruction.

"You didn't hear me?"

"I was just taking a nap." *A nap? Really?* I sigh at the bad lie and ask, "How was your trip back?"

"Too fuckin' long," he whines. He drops the designer bag from his shoulder onto the ground and flops onto the bed. His head rests in my lap. It's not sexual but certainly proprietary.

His long hair fans out onto the covers separating us and I run my fingers through it. He groans and while the sound of his voice at that level is inherently sexy, I don't get the feeling it was meant to be.

"You're gonna make me fall asleep," he comments as I continue playing in his hair.

"Maybe you should sleep."

"Nah. It's not sleep on my mind."

"Tell me what is." Maybe I'm prying but if I can get any additional information from him while he's relaxed and unguarded, then I'm going to.

"This trip didn't go how I expected."

"You were just visiting your brother..." I hedge. "He wasn't happy to see you?"

He doesn't flinch, but there is a moment's pause where he must have forgotten that's what he told me he was doing in Colorado. I, of course, know different.

"Nah. He wasn't. I'm thinking that I shouldn't have even gone. I'm more pissed than I should be about it."

"Family is hard."

His eyes blink open, "Your family is?"

I suck in a breath before blowing it out. "I think that maybe it will get easier over time to acknowledge that my mom is no longer here, but it gets harder I think. I have my club family, but being here it's not the same."

"What happened to your Ma?"

"Overdose," I say simply and then wipe the corner of my eye. "You never really get over the could-haves. She was still so young. I know we joke that even at eighty-two, they're still a baby. But she really is gone too soon. She wasn't even graying yet."

He wipes another tear from my eye. "Mine neither. She was the only good thing about this house. Sometimes I hear her callin' my name to come inside or to put the dishes away."

"Is she who gave you the nickname?"

"Blue?" he questions, adjusting himself to be more comfortable in my lap. "Nah. She was the last person to call me by my given name." He considers that, looking off into the distance. "She hated Blue."

He chuckles softly, "I remember her sayin', 'Spent all this damn time pickin' out a nice name for my boy and he picks somethin' dumb. A damn color.' She didn't ask if I picked it, but I guess in a way I did."

I had assumed that it was a family given thing or some story behind it. The turmoil in his eyes suggests that there is much more to it. "If you didn't pick it, who did?"

He bites his lip before breathing out slowly. "Man, Black people will give you the most crazy nicknames for dumb shit. My friend used to call me that because she gave me a black eye that looked blue. Playin' ball, being kids, y'know? The teasing, jokes were relentless from the other kids for months. It fucking stuck. Then, I earned it."

"Earned it?" I ask.

He's silent for a long time. I try to be patient, twisting his locs into something of a style while he breathes deeply with his eyes closed over whatever memories he's fighting.

Then he gets up and pulls the shirt over his head.

At first, I'm taken back by his sudden nudity. Then I start looking over the art inked on his pronounced chest and strong, sculpted shoulders. I knew that he worked out, we often did together. His body is perfection, lickable and taut. All that toned mahogany brown skin, begging for me to explore the art he's decorated it with. He spends so much time training to make sure it looks that way. I suppose he can't rely on gators to save him if anything were to go awry in his day to day.

Until this point, I never saw him without a shirt on. What catches me off guard completely are his arms.

The scar tissue.

So many scars.

My eyes widen against my better judgment telling me that I should keep my mouth shut and look away.

But he's showing them to me.

I won't look away.

I take a hand in mine, turning it so that I can see his forearms. This right one is worse than the other. At first glance, you likely couldn't tell. There's so much ink, shading, shadows, and snakes writhing along the strong length of his arm.

Underneath the ink though, angry lines where his arm was opened, had to be surgically, with how precise all the incisions are. Those would maybe not have been noticeable if it weren't for the keloids.

Raised and jagged along those incisions.

Some look like they have been reduced but formed again.

I look up at him and he's watching my face, hard as stone. No emotions in the line of his mouth or the cut of his gaze.

"What happened?" I ask tentatively.

He takes one of my fingers and runs it over the scar closest to his wrist, it's the least raised scar. I can tell from the way the skin jumps that it is not a comfortable feeling. "My thumb collapsed. A bone splintered. Took months before my dad believed I should see someone. By that time, two different tendons had been damaged and partially severed. Hand almost shattered from overuse and inexperience."

He takes my hand to feel the next scar up from this one, more raised than the last. "They had to search for the tendon that split and replace the one in my thumb with a piece of it higher in the arm." His skin is warm as he guides me to the next scar.

"Why—" my words come out choked, but he doesn't allow me to trip over the clumsy way I was going to ask just why his dad wouldn't take him to a hospital.

"Told me that a man knows how to fight. I fucked my shit up bein' a pussy." He sucks in a breath and continues, "Said to use my left and figure out how to manage without it. That it would heal in time."

"But it didn't," I whisper.

Looking over his hands, I try to see what's underneath the tattoos there. So many nicks and if I look closer, I could see the smaller incision marks on his thumb. A couple on his other fingers.

"Nah. It didn't." He shows me the other arm. "So, I used my left like he said. And I didn't learn anythin' from the first time." The sound he emits is one of old pain and resignation. "As much as I hurt the kids who called me out of my name, I hurt myself two times more."

The scars on this arm aren't as pronounced. But imagining him having to use it while his other hand was damaged is too painful to imagine. I wince even as I softly run my fingertips over these surgical scars.

"I met Redd by then. He had learned much more than I had havin' been a light skin with curly red hair and freckles. They been messin' with him long before people got on my ass. He taught me how to fight without using my hands the same way. First one to recommend a knife instead."

My eyes are still stinging, thinking about that young boy who endured that with no one there to protect him. Hands ruined trying to defend himself. "Will you tell me your given name?"

I knew it. Of course I did, with how many files I had on this man. But I wanted him to give me permission to call him by the name his mother called him.

A silly and selfish thing to ask of him.

He tilts my chin with the hand that suffered the most damage. Emotion so fierce rests behind deep brown irises that have experienced so much. "No one calls me by it. No one is allowed to." My eyes drop preparing for the rejection, even when I know I don't deserve to have that kind of access to him.

He lifts my chin again, "Look at me."

"It's okay. You don't have—"

"To do anythin' but stay Black and die, I know." A small smile plays on his lips when he says, "But I want to tell you."

"Okay," I murmur, eyes flitting left and right between his.

A *snake, I am.*

A *manipulator, I am.*

None of that would stop me from taking this little piece of him.

"It's…" I lean in, even as he pulls me toward his face with his touch at my chin.

Our lips are moments from touching.

His breath on my lips sends tingles along my nerves and my eyes close. "Milo Leonel Dupont," he confesses between the seam of my lips.

The kiss is unlike any of the ones that preceded it.

He's gentle, soft with me. Softer than I deserve but as soft as I yearn to be with him. His vulnerability tastes like serenity on my deceitful tongue.

Blue takes his time to show me what it means to belong to him and hold those painful parts that need to be shielded from the world. I don't know if I can bear to hold them when I know I'm unworthy.

And yet, he continues to kiss me slowly.

Unbearably slow as his true name rings around in my head though his voice was so low I almost missed it.

His hands are roaming my body. The covers that once separated us, forgotten and gone.

"You always smell so damn good," he pants, rolling me over to straddle him. His nose pressed into my neck, buried in my hair.

I kiss his forehead to his temple, down his chest over other scars he didn't tell me about, to his taut stomach, tongue running over the grooves there until I reach his joggers. His length is pressing against the front of them.

He watches me from where I kneel between his legs, hands poised to remove this final barrier between his dick and my lips.

He helps me by lifting his hips, so that I can take the pants and boxers off at once.

Before me, he's completely naked.

This is an achievement.

Something to brag about.

I don't know anyone who could have the same badge on their vest.

I could understand why he never took his shirt off with me before. There's too much raw vulnerability there. Too much to explain and give power to.

But I saw it.

I see him.

His dick bobs in front of me and I've never been more eager to slide my lips around someone as I am right now.

He gave me the power, not knowing that I should be the last person he exposes himself to.

Lust and greed mingle in a dangerous dance through my blood, kneeling between his legs like this.

It's too late to take it back now.

Milo.

The first drag of my tongue up the thick vein along the underside of his dick is the surge of power I didn't expect. He grits his teeth and a hand combs the hair from my face so he can see what I'm doing better.

"Fuck, yes. Put that hot mouth on me," he barks.

Oh yes.

This is gonna be good.

The dark wide crown of him is tight with need and smooth as I hold back his foreskin with my fist. It's barely a grip that I can maintain. Either my hands are small or he's really just that big. I have to get my other hand involved just to fully enclose the shaft.

Licking all around the flared head, I take my time going from side to side with the tip of my tongue. Then in tighter circles around the sensitive opening, my tongue flattens down that vein again.

"Yes, bae. Take me into that mouth," his commanding tone requires me to. It's somehow sweeter because of what he's called me. What he always calls me when he's hard and horny for me.

It was a stretch for me to get my lips around him. The wide head of him pulling my lips taught and drool begins to run from my lips. I use it to help me stroke his length all while my cheeks are stuffed with him.

A shallow bob is still a bob nonetheless when it's all I can manage. I rely heavily on my hands to give him head and I'm proud of that. This is expert level management of a big fucking dick.

I couldn't fit it down my throat if I tried.

Gagging over him trying to get close is messy work when more drool coats him and I'm still giving it my best.

I don't think he can take it anymore. With a hand in my hair, he pulls me off of him with a pop and straight to his lips.

Here is the rough and commanding man who ruined sex with any other person in my eyes. The brief sting at my scalp pales in comparison to the pleasure that I know he'll give me.

Wasting no time, he's pulling my sleep shorts off and burying his face between my legs.

He's voracious and unyielding as he pays my sensitivity no mind.

He wants my cum and he wants it now. Tongue fucking my center, lapping at the juices coming from me like he's dying of thirst.

I throb and buck, trying to control this orgasm, but it's coming too fast.

Nonsense noises fill the room with the sound of my pussy as he prepares me for my next high.

He eases three fingers inside me when I'm shaking over his face. I'm spilling over his fingers.

It's too good to care about any of the mess we've made. The mess he's made of me.

Let me tell you, taking that dildo yesterday is nothing like the feel of being stretched and filled by Milo.

"Oh God. Milo, that feels so goddamn good." He shudders under me, even as he's slamming my body onto his thick shaft, touching something deep inside me.

"Say my name again, Racquelle."

I can barely hear him over the slapping of our skin and the slippery sounds of my pussy taking him deeper. I'm too blissed out.

Has he asked me something?

I've fallen into the blue again and I'm not trying to get out. The only thing keeping me upright is his dick inside me and his hands squeezing my ass.

"Say it again," he demands.

My hands cover his as I moan his name, "Milo."

On an exhale as he drives into me harder, "Milo."

And in a scream, when I finally meet the edge and fall over it, "Milo."

Chapter 17
Diamond

I wake to arguing that's rising in volume outside the bedroom. Somehow I'm under the blanket again. Where Blue was once beside me is no longer warm.

Not *baby*.

Not *Blue*.

Milo.

I'm naked, so the sheet will have to do as I get up to see who's here.

If I'm honest, the two voices sound identical. The only reason I can sense a difference between the two is by how much thicker Milo's drawl is.

I get close enough to the door that I can hear the voices a little better. I would put something on and go out there but something tells me not to.

"You're in a shitty mood," Milo says to the other man.

There's a grunt and then, "Can I stay here or what?"

"Don't piss me off. Your room is down the hall," Milo responds.

"I'm not gonna be here long. I'll just stay on the couch and leave in the mornin.'"

Milo sighs long and deep. "T, wassup? You hidin' from somethin.'"

"Not in the way you think."

"How do I think?"

Another grunt and then a scoff. "It's Drea, alright? She's with this fucking dick. He's... It don't matter. I'm gonna sleep on the couch and drive back tomorrow. I have work."

"Whatever, bro," Blue says.

Bro?

His brother is here?

Then I hear his heavy steps coming back toward the room. I skip, hop, and jump back into the bed before he can find out I was snooping.

I do my best to rearrange the covers back on the bed but it's not that great of a job. Somehow, Milo notices in the dark room.

"Did I wake you up?"

I try to fake like I was much more asleep and croak out, "No, I'm always up at two in the morning."

He turns on a lamp before getting back into the bed. "Smart ass. C'mere," he pulls me toward him with ease and now I can't imagine not going with him.

"Why are you up?" I ask into his chest, my lips brushing the warm skin there. He might blow me off, but I think that's a perfectly reasonable question to ask right now.

"My lil' bro, Tony, is in the *friend zone*," he says into my hair.

I should not marvel at how I fit into his body like this. With his arms around me, it feels like this spot was made for me. "Huh?" My brain catches up to the fact that he's said something. I was too busy warring in my mind with *he's a mark* and *if not partner, why partner shaped?*

"He's got it bad for his best friend and she's datin' somebody else. Think he drove here after findin' out."

"I can go, if you—"

"Nah, you good right here. Don't think he's stayin' long. Will probably be in Colorado before end of day tomorrow."

"You care for him. Really I can go so you two can talk or whatever." I don't actually want to go. But this could be an easy way out of the house and back to my people if I play this right.

His dissent is just a brush of his chin over the top of my head. "He doesn't like bein' here anyway. Think I prefer him up there anyway. He should be away from all this."

"Tony doesn't—"

"No and I want to keep it that way. Everythin' I touch gets tainted. If I can keep him from this life then I've at least done somethin' right."

He cares for his brother deeply. He could have let business drag his little brother under too, but he probably doesn't tell Tony anything. He shoulders the full weight of Dupont on his own. And to be surrounded by all these people that don't know what it's like to wear that kind of responsibility...

I could be the one to do that and I can't tell him. Not outright. And certainly not now.

This isn't my opportunity to leave. But it is a different kind of opportunity. "You think I'm tainted?"

"Know it cause you're mine." I push away from him, but he holds me tight. "Don't gotta be scared of the things you don't understand. You don't know what it means just yet. That truth is somethin' you faced the consequences of and now you're here." His words rattle in my mind when he adds, "Fear of the unknown is different from fear of the misunderstood. You're scared as hell of Sativa and Indica and you don't know anythin' about them."

My first instinct is to get defensive. I don't though. The desire to remain in the protection and warmth of his arms, too alluring to ruin just yet. I consider and respond more thoughtfully. "Isn't it like the rule of thumb to avoid big ass reptiles for safety?"

"Yea. Outdoors. In the wild." He looks down at my face and runs a thumb over my jaw. "You saw how chill Sativa is."

"What's your point?"

His thumb takes a lower path to my neck, where I know he's searching for my pulse point. "They aren't even venomous. If you found one in the wild, it's more likely to eat other snakes that *are* venomous than it is to ever attack a person. But you judge them because they're big and black." It's minimal but there. A self-deprecating chuff at his own expense. "Gotta say that it's somethin' I can relate to."

I had no idea where this conversation was going, but now that he's getting closer to the point it's heartbreaking. "Milo, I—"

"It's whatever. Reptiles are the most negatively inspirational animals around. Widely feared for just existin' and doin' what other animals are doin'—survivin'. Unlikeable but at the top of the food chain." He chuckles at whatever is going to come out of his mouth next. It's a sad sound really.

"Dogs and cats hunt their food, too, but most people don't run the other way, havin' panic attacks and shit, when they see them. What's the difference? The fur? I don't know. Shit never sat right with me. I keep the gators, for obvious reasons, but they're way more interestin' than everyone else's pets."

With gentle fingers, I touch his face. Eyes searching for something in mine are warm on my own face. "I'm sure people aren't using their pets for what you are either..." I hedge, trying to lighten the mood. I understood what he was saying. There are so many ways I can relate.

"You have nothin' to be scared of with me, Racquelle."

"I have plenty," I say, knowing he'll miss my true meaning. I could ruin everything by falling for him. And here I go wanting to be his strength when I'm so close to getting what I want.

He is a mark and getting close was the plan.

I just didn't expect the lines to blur so easily.

He accepts my words at face value and that is the best outcome for me. "One day. I'll figure it out. As soon as I take care of Junior. I gotta do somethin'."

"Like what?"

"I don't know yet. Need people to know that you're mine. It's the only way I can keep you safe since people already suspect. Maybe they'll think twice about doing to you what..." He trails off and I don't fill the space with what we both know goes there.

"Yours?" I ask instead. Is it stupid to be hung up on that? Yes. But I couldn't mask the dreamy quality of my voice if I tried.

He holds me tighter. "It's out anyway. Might as well put some respect on the name, bae."

"Uh-huh," I brush him off, getting comfortable to sleep again. "Go to sleep. You're talkin' nonsense."

Milo turns off the lamp, but doesn't let go of the tight hold he has on my body. It never occurred to me that it would be difficult to separate my feelings from the act when I began concocting this plan. I am so far entangled with this man. A blurred line is the least of my problems. It'll hurt more than just him when I have to leave.

I have to leave.

I can't stay. I don't deserve to.

Ugh, fuck!

"Just you wait," he assures me. It does nothing to calm my nerves or doubts. I'm thankful that I don't have to respond because he's fallen back asleep, with a snake in his arms.

Chapter 18

BLUE

"You trippin' for real." I look at my friend across from the diner table. There aren't many food spots for miles around the warehouse besides this one. Since we're going in for a long day, it's best we eat before. I haven't been here in a while because I've been caked up with Racquelle at my spot for several weeks.

Something I'm not at all sorry about.

I know a lot of my people eat here, so it's not uncommon for a couple of us to be here at a time. We might be the reason this place is in business since it's so far on the edge of Clayton Terrace.

Like today, I recognize a lot of them in the booths having their own conversations. Vert, Marcell, and Geno are in the booth behind us eating, but still watching for any signs of trouble.

The cracked green leather of the booth squeaks as Redd fidgets, readjusting how tightly he has his arms crossed. I don't care how tight he crosses them. I'm not getting involved with that.

"You have no issue with your brother going after Steph? What the fuck?" Redd's skin is light enough that his flush of frustration is apparent under the multitude of freckles and to the tips of his ears. I know he hates it, but it is telling about just how much he does have a thing for my best friend.

It's not my fault that he hasn't made a move or something.

The waitress drops off my steak and eggs on one plate and his Southwest omelette with extra hash browns on the other. I start shaking hot sauce onto my eggs, ignoring Redd's attitude. "About to be forty-one years old. I'm too old for that mess. Why would I?"

"Man, so am I." I can see the smoke coming out of his ears. Too many thoughts about *his woman* with another man. But, we both know that's not his girl. "It's not right," he says, taking the bottle of hot sauce from me for his own eggs.

We both eat in silence while the noise from the diner continues around us. It's not that I don't care about my friend's feelings. It's just that I don't actually know anything 'bout that. *I hate speculating.* That shit is annoying. He's been high-key stalking her, but I have zero clue to what end.

I just thought he was a cracked nut.

All of us are a little fucked up to be able to do what we do on a daily basis. His crazy is probably no better than mine.

Only different.

Ain't no way my girl could be with some other dude. He'd be DOA if he tried to get close. That's his fault for not locking shit down sooner.

"Guess I feel some type of way that they didn't tell me, but it ain't my business." I put a hand on his shoulder, leaning over the table. "And really. I don't give a fuck." When Tony was at the house the other night I figured he had reached his wit's end, but I didn't think he was gonna try to get with somebody that quick. Definitely didn't think it'd be Steph of all people.

Kinda surprised she went for that.

"You ain't shit." Redd says. "What if your brother dogs her? He's all tied up in Colton's baby mama."

I wipe a napkin over my mouth and set it on my empty plate. "Yea, not my problem. She's grown, can make her own choices." I shrug, prepared to leave the diner and get back to business. Then I realize, "Aye, I could go down there with her and check on this man to see if he is makin' the moves he's supposed to." I scratch my chin. "Yea, it's a good cover. And I can see what's up with T."

He glares at me, shoving the last bite of eggs into his mouth. My men wouldn't dare give me shit. But Redd is crazy and often plays cavalier with his life.

"That doesn't make you feel better?" He doesn't respond and I drop a couple bills on the table. Standing from the booth I wait for the guards to do the same. To Redd, I shrug again. "Shiiit. It's done now. I'm gonna talk to her on the ride there."

"I'm comin'," he asserts, standing from the booth, too.

"You're not. Need you here to hold everythin' down. We can't both be gone right now."

He crosses his arms again, shouldering out of the building. "Man, what the fuck?"

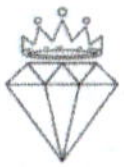

"Soo, you and lil' bro?"

Steph looks like someone has struck her. "Are you really going to do this?"

"I am," I say, watching her every now and again as she checks herself in the visor in the rental. The flight wasn't long, but I spent that time working and she did the same. Now, she's primping and shit to see Tony. "How long you been creepin?"

"It's not like that. Your brother is very respectful," she says, giving me a look that implies *I'm not.*

"Oh. Unlike me?"

Her eye roll is a tangible thing though I have my eyes on the road." Unlike any of you and your people. Redd included."

Weird that she mentioned him. "What do you know about Redd?"

"I *don't* know anything." She dabs at her lipstick and she closes the mirror. It thunks against the roof of the car. Seems like I struck a nerve. "Well, besides the fact that he has the uncanny ability to pop up when I least expect..."

My eyes narrow as we get close to my brother's house on Mason Ranch where he works as the ranch manager. She probably isn't wrong about Redd, but I'm not gonna confirm anything. Him looking out for her, even in this creepy stalker way, benefits me. I like for my best friend to be safe. No one will keep her safer than that crazy motherfucker.

"Didn't answer my question."

She rolls her eyes, "Couple weeks. It's *new*. He hit me up when he was in Clayton Terrace and we just got to talking."

"That lil' shit."

"What?"

"He was in a pissy mood at the crib the other day. Didn't tell me he was comin' either, just showed up all late and shit. Come to find out, he was mackin' on you while he was here."

Her head tilts to the side. "Don't do the big brother thing, okay? I like him and we're just seeing how it goes."

"So, you're gettin' off and gettin' gone?"

"Do you have to be so crude?" She's looking out the window at the mountains passing to our right. I'm in her line of sight so I shrug, waiting for her to answer the question. "No, I'm not. We—we haven't had sex."

My lips curl in disbelief. "At all?"

"No," she says with no inflection in her tone to give anything away. I can't believe this Boy Scout hasn't even tried it. A couple weeks? God damn, he is definitely the better brother.

"On purpose?"

"Yes, on purpose. He was very upfront about that."

Now what Redd said about him being tied up in Drea makes more sense. I don't have the heart to tell Steph though. *Not my business.* Tony's more gone for this woman that I think he even realizes. Maybe Steph will be the one to change that.

"You like it, I love it," I say, as noncommittally as I can. It doesn't matter to me whether those two are getting any. This is what I sacrificed for him to be able to do. *Be a Boy Scout while I remain the monster.*

"I do," she responds and then adds, "What ever happened to your dancer?"

"Nothin'." Though it's far from the truth. She has had far too much happen to her since Steph and I last talked and it's my fault. By keeping her at my place, I can keep her safe, but she's also in more danger. If they only suspected before—it's confirmed now.

Blue has someone he cares about.

A vulnerability to exploit.

"That's not what I meant." She bumps into my shoulder. "Did you ever hook up with her or something? I don't know what you do…"

"What makes you think I do anythin'?" She lifts an eyebrow. I haven't exactly been discreet or dishonest about not wanting to be in a relationship. "I could be a good little boy like Tony."

"I actually *know* both of you. So that lie doesn't even begin to fool me."

"Sure you do, sweetheart." I tell her a version of the truth of the situation. "She's aight. I'm watchin' her, makin' sure she's good."

Her face scrunches up in a way that should be reserved for small fuzzy animals and not the grown ass man that I am. "That sounds really sweet, Blue."

I mock her dumb face and add, "Don't appreciate the surprise. I can be a gentleman."

"Sure, sure. Glad you took my advice then," she says distractedly since we're pulling up to Tony's place. I'm thankful that she's not fully paying attention and grilling me more about Racquelle. She is not someone I'm ready to share anything about.

I want to keep her all for myself, even in friendly conversation with my best friend.

I park in front of his house and grab my bag and hers from the car. Tony's dog, Milli, is already barking and jumping at the door before we get there.

My brother opens the door and his dog shoots out, darting to me and then Steph when she sees I don't have any free hands to scratch her. Steph drops to a knee to show affection to the brown Lab.

Tony has an annoyed look on his face. It usually does look annoyed, but I know it's even more annoyed because we're here uninvited and on the day that Drea's opening her new coffee shop and bakery.

Tony doesn't know I'm here for work. And I'm gonna keep it that way for now. I leave my bag at the door and let those two do whatever they're *not* doing. I'll meet them at Drea's new spot later.

After driving around the tiny main street in Alpenglow Ridge for way longer than I'd like to, I finally walk into the bakery. I spot Steph and Tony easily because they're two of the tallest people in the building.

Mireya, Drea's daughter, grabs me by the hand, dragging me over to where my brother is. She tells me about how busy they've been and I listen to the teenager's account of everything. It's this kind of mundane shit that makes me grateful for my decision to separate my life from theirs. Especially when there's so much goodness here. I could never have this peace and normalcy. It's far out of reach and that's the best outcome as far as anyone is concerned.

By the time we reach my brother she hugs us both, "Ant! You're here! And look, Uncle Blue is here too!" Tony's nickname from Drea and her daughter is Ant. Apparently it's hilarious to them both because he's so big in comparison to them.

I know that my brother is an important part of Drea and Mireya's lives. It makes me wonder why he's even bothering to date my best friend and why she's even here right now. I guess he was planning to come without his new girlfriend until I showed up. I smirk to myself, watching him squirm in the hole I *may* have helped him dig.

"Who are you?" Mireya asks with curiosity in her voice that is as innocent as a young person could convey with her head leaning to one side.

Steph approaches her, unbothered. "I'm Steph," she says, holding out her hand. "And you must be Mireya... Is that right?"

The girl nods, expression unreadable. Doesn't say another word to her.

She glances at her mother for confirmation, and Drea gives a tight smile that's very brittle.

This ain't going how Steph probably imagined.

I step into the awkward huddle, pretending like I don't notice the temperature drop. "Well... this is nice and awkward."

There is so much tension in this group and clearly secrets that are being kept. When no one says anything I decide to intervene.

Could I have left it alone? Sure. But this was a problem for my brother that I'm a small bit responsible for. I plan on being here for a least a few days since Colton wasn't home when I drove by earlier. Letting him have some time to talk to Steph is probably the best thing for him right now.

"Drea," I say, tilting my head toward the bakery counter. "Show me around? I've never actually seen the inside of this place."

She hesitates for a second, but eventually sighs and gestures for me to follow her. "Come on, then."

We leave Steph to navigate the lion's den, Mireya trailing a few steps behind like a tiny bodyguard. Colton's kid or not, I like the girl.

Drea glances at me as we walk past the framed photos and old-school charm of the bakery's new look since she bought it. "Steph, huh?"

I lift a brow. "What about her?"

"She's with Tony?" She stops near a side door, arms crossed. "Seriously?"

"Looks that way," I shrug. "She's good with Tony. He's the one who wants to build a family and shit. That's not for me."

"Yeah, but girlfriend?" Drea shakes her head. "Wild. I didn't even know he was talking to anyone."

Neither did I until Redd made it clear that he had a problem with it. "Not until about a month ago. She grew up with us. We were all friends. You know, played basketball together. Long story." I lean against the wall. "You okay with it?" Can't help but be a little bit nosy since this development has caused a ruckus in my life.

She gives a half shrug in response and then lets out a long exhale. "I mean, it's not like it's my business. But it's weird seeing him with someone and not tell me about it."

Fair point.

There's something like jealousy in her voice, mostly surprise though. Drea's never been petty like some of the others around here. Maybe that's why Tony always kept her close. Beats me on why they aren't together though.

I look for the woman in question and find her standing in line with T by the register. Steph moves through the bakery like she belongs here, even if the glares say otherwise. She's got that unshakeable poise, that high-polish grace that makes women either want to be her or cut her down to size. Gotta admire how she handles her own.

Drea studies me a moment, arms still crossed. "So what really brings you out here, Blue? You haven't been back in forever. And don't say it was because of my opening though I am grateful you came."

I flash her a grin, but it doesn't reach my eyes. "Love supportin' small business."

She narrows her gaze. "That is not an answer."

"Exactly." I give her a wink before walking past her. "Come on. Show me the kitchen or somethin' before T pulls me into a heart-to-heart."

By the time I circle back to the front of the bakery, I find Tony posted up near the bathroom hallway like a watchdog. His eyes cut straight to me.

"Brutal, bruh," I say, smirking. "You said they liked you in this town."

"I know you can't help yourself," he says low, grabbing my arm and yanking me into the alcove like we're teenagers again. "But could you keep your comments in your head?"

"Nah" I lean against the wall and cross my arms. "Am I gonna have to rescue Steph before they get the pitchforks?"

The two of us are evenly matched. Same height, same build. We're only a few years apart. I wouldn't intentionally intimidate my little brother because I have love for him. I did everything our Pa wanted so that he could escape the dark while I found a way to thrive in it. Some people were made for this life, my brother was not. Don't hold it against him, but there is a certain level of respect that I require regardless of anything else. He's treading a thin line.

"Why did you come here?" he asks, teeth clenched.

I play it light, losing the drawl in my voice like he has after being away from Louisiana for so long. "I don't understand what you mean?"

"I left so I didn't have to deal with your bullshit." His voice drops into a hiss. "I wouldn't have to deal with any of this, had you not showed up here with her."

My lips hike on one side, still a little amused by the predicament he's in. "You didn't want to see your girlfriend? How was I supposed to know?"

"By asking!" He lowers his tone. "Could have called me and let me know you were coming. You've never been to visit without announcing. And you damn sure never participated in anything my friends have hosted."

"Wait… You don't think me being here is only about you." *A little honesty never hurt anyone.* "It was kind of a two birds, one stone type of thing."

Confusion overtakes his face as he processes what I've said. "What does it have to do with then?"

"Well if you were in the biz, I'd tell you. But since you decided to be the 'good brother', it's a need-to-know kind of thing. And you don't need to know."

A sound like a growl comes from him in what I imagine is frustration. "Why are you here, Blue?"

I sigh and it seems to frustrate him more. "I'm checking on something," I reach for a blunt, but there isn't one so I pull on my ear instead. *Why didn't I roll one before I came?* "I'm checking on someone. You know who."

I see the moment he realizes who I'm talking about. "What did he do?"

"Like I said, need-to-know basis. You coming into the fold or what?"

"No," he shakes his head firmly. "Definitely not."

"Don't worry about it then. Spend time with my best friend, oh I mean, your girlfriend. I'm going to make myself more familiar with Colton's baby moms."

I walk out of the alcove he's pulled me aside in, but I don't go find Drea again. I've honestly had enough of the drama at this point.

My priority, outside of checking on the brother I allowed to live the straight and narrow path, is Colton. If he isn't on track to supply what he said he could, I won't be leaving the state with clean hands regardless.

Chapter 19

BLUE

The true reason I came to Colorado is not one that I enjoy. The mundane reprieve of the bakery opening sits at a stark contrast to the task I'm headed to now.

After an unpleasant update from Redd, I need to calm myself as best I can.

Benefits of flying private is being able to keep my green on me.

I finally light my blunt and smoke it down slowly as I watch Colton's house. The strong smell of pine crowds the smell of my weed in the air. His truck is parked out front and there are several other cars there too.

Like me, he knows there is safety in numbers. He always had a big crew even before I met him. I don't feel unsafe here by myself because there are many reasons why my life is more important than any of theirs. If I get hurt, they know it will come back to haunt them tenfold.

Recognize the risk and mitigate it. That's security that I can trust.

What I can't trust is the destruction of an entire shipment due to a car accident that just so happened to affect only one vehicle. Police ruling it a hit and run. How does one car drive away unfazed while mine blew up like fireworks? Yesterday, while I was celebrating Drea's opening, someone was plotting.

When the final embers of my blunt draw to an end, I toss the roach and crush it to the ground before I knock on the door with the end of my knife's handle. Was gonna wait but try the knob instead and it opens without any resistance.

As soon as I step into the house, the oxygen syphons out. There was a buzz about until everyone of his men began to notice that it was me standing in the doorway.

Colton glances up from his desk at the back corner of the room and stands a little too fast, his boots catching on the cracked floor tile. I don't know why his house is so shitty when he's making enough to do better. Colorado, especially Harmony Hill, has plenty of new builds that would be better than this dump. "Blue. Didn't expect you until—"

"Until you fixed your shit?" I finish for him. My voice is low and quiet. The kind of quiet that people raise their shoulders to instinctively, like they're waiting for the moment my mood will untether. "And yet here I am."

He swallows. "It's... almost under control."

I turn my head slowly. "Almost? It's November."

"We've been tracking the routes already in place. It's definitely not internal." He clears his throat. "At least not on my side. Some of the runners you hired for the Colorado expansion—"

"Are dead," I interrupt, taking another step forward. "Four of them. Van flipped. Burned. No product and no witnesses. That doesn't feel like almost to me, Sheriff."

His jaw tightens. I can see the twitch he tries to smother under his stubble. He gestures to another room in the house, away from his men. Guess he didn't want them to hear me chew him out.

The pride's still there.

Good.

I'll enjoy cutting it out piece by piece. I decline his invitation to move to the other room.

"Give me until the end of the year," he says, eyes darting to his crew like they're going to rescue him now. "I've got a plan in motion."

"You had a plan last month," I remind him. "And last month, my shipments were supposed to double. Instead, I've got more holes in my inventory and whispers about a rat you still haven't caged."

One of his men, a lanky thing with too much confidence and not enough sense, chuckles behind Colton's shoulder.

I don't even ask what was funny. I didn't make a goddamn joke. I just turn, slow and deliberate. When I look at him, he freezes.

"What's your name?" I ask.

He licks his lips. "Ricky."

"Ricky." I nod. "Mmmh. You like your job, Ricky?"

He blinks. "Y-yeah, I—"

I flip my grip on the knife in my hand and flick my wrist, sending the blade toward him. It lands right below his kneecap.

Colton shouts and another of Colton's goons rushes to the guy.

Ricky screams like a dying pig, clutching his ruined leg, blood pouring onto the floor in a copious stream.

I walk over, crouch down next to him, and pull my knife, "See, Ricky... there's a difference between people who work for me and people who make jokes while I talk about my dead men and my missin' money. Guess which one you are."

He sobs something incoherent.

I put the knife's reddened blade under his chin. "You're welcome to stay. But if you ever open your mouth in my presence again, the next hole won't be in your leg."

I stand after cleaning my knife off on his shirt and return it to its sheath.

Colton's shock is clear as day with the pale cast to his light skin. "Jesus, Blue." He runs a hand over his cropped hair.

"Don't bring him into this," I mutter. "Know who you work for."

The room is quiet except for Ricky's whimpers as someone bandages him up.

I look at the others. "Clean this up. And if any of you have opinions, keep them to your fuckin' selves."

As I walk out, Colton follows. "Blue—"

"Keep it."

He jogs to catch up. "Look, I know I messed up. But this ain't like before. Someone's cutting the line before it even hits us. It ain't my people. I swear on my badge."

"Your badge means less to me than Ricky's leg."

He's quiet for a beat, then says, "I heard about the wreck, but that had nothing to do with us. I think it's time to consider that someone is pissed and targeting you. Sure, there could be a rat. Whether there is or there isn't—this rat is reporting to someone."

I stop walking and turn to face him.

"This is supposed to be your domain. You should have some semblance of an idea about what is goin' on here. That wreck has everythin' to do with you. If someone is targetin' me, they're targetin' you, too!" I bark, tone loud and sharp as I jab my finger into his chest. "It was your word that you had this under control. Don't like that I'm here havin' to find shit out because you aren't doin' your part of the job."

"I'm doing what I can." He steps into my direct line before I can open the door of the rental. "This will all work out. It will be the biggest move we've seen. You see my team working hard in there. End of year. That's all I'm asking."

My jaw ticks. "End of year—or else." I get in the car, slam the door, and sit there for a moment with my fingers flexed tight around the steering wheel. Once Colton has gone into his house again, I settle in for the drive I'll have to make back to my brother's house.

With the mountains swiping past me, my mind returns to the woman waiting for me back home and I start to calm.

Racquelle.

I've never been wrapped up like this before. I'm desperate to get back to her.

Wrapped up. That's a weak word for what this is.

Obsession's more honest.

I went to Colorado because I had to. Because the money don't lie and the green don't move by itself. But every second I'm here, I keep thinking about her. How she sleeps in my arms like she's safe. How she doesn't let anything stop her. How she moves like smoke and intoxicates me like it, too.

I didn't want to be gone this long.

Didn't want her to think I left her there without protection. Though I know my men will make sure she's good. I still worry about her.

And now that the issue still isn't fixed, I'm boiling inside—at Colton, at myself, at the whole fucking empire I built that can't keep itself together when I take my eyes off it for five minutes.

But mostly, I'm pissed because I don't know how to say I missed her without sounding weak.

I need to see her.

Not just fuck her.

Not just touch her.

See her.

I need her to know that whatever this is between us, it's not temporary. It's not because of petty family beef.

It's more and I want to be more.

I start thinking about the chains I wear—the ones people recognize. I've had chicks try to wear my gold, claim me with it like it meant something.

Racquelle's different.

A chain feels too... expected. Too obvious.

She's not just some jawn. So I think about what would really mark her as mine. Not a chain. Not a ring.

Time.

She gave me hers one night and made me crave a lifetime.

So I'll give her time of my own.

Not some designer throwaway. Nah, I want something with weight. Something impossible to miss.

It can't wait until I get back home.

Chapter 20

Diamond

"Hello?" My voice is tentative in the empty hallway.

I look at my phone as I'm right outside of Milo's office.

Doubting myself, I look down either side of the hall. There is no way that he could know where I'm at. Right?

I checked for cameras, but I don't think there are any in the house. I couldn't be sure. The second phase of my plan was taking full effect and he was back in Colorado chasing down what was more like a Trojan horse.

It was a little riskier than what I had originally planned next and I was on edge. There were four of his runners in the van we took out, but a large delivery was making its way out of the state. I would have preferred to take the product, it's true. However, there was no way to take on four of Blue's trained team in such short notice.

I needed to wrap whatever this was up and get the fuck out of here before things really hit the fan.

My heart is racing at the idea of being caught right now. I hope he can't hear that on the phone.

"What you doin'?" Milo's voice is as resonant as it always is. He might as well be in front of me. The energy that I usually feel from him is somehow still here, but I straighten my spine against it.

There is no way that he could know where I'm at.

"I was watching videos on my phone," I lie.

"Of what?"

"I don't know. Random stuff. Makeup, hair... couple dances."

He grunts an affirmative sound. "Check the door. I sent you something."

"What is it?"

"You at the door?"

"No…"

"Well, get up and go answer the door." Just then, the doorbell rings. *Was he also on the phone with whoever is here?* I take my time since I'm significantly closer to the front door from his office. I would usually be walking from his bedroom or the sitting room in the back when I'm scrolling my phone. Every small detail counts when you're making convincing moves.

Looking at the figure on the security screen at the front door, I see a man with a suit and white gloves standing in the doorway. "Um, who is this?" I say on the phone as the guy continues to stand there.

"Let him in," Milo says. I trust that this man has to be someone he knows well if he's allowed to be here when Milo's not.

The guy walks over to the smaller sitting area at the front of the estate and I'm following him. He clearly knows this place better than I do.

Milo's voice is loud on speakerphone as he explains. "This is Carlton. He's gonna fit you for somethin' I got."

Curiosity flutters in my belly with that response. "What did you get?"

"You'll see."

The large case he's carrying has several numbered locks on it. Carlton makes quick work of entering some keys and then it opens to reveal an assortment of tools that he starts taking out.

He holds his hand out, waiting for me. I look at his hand with curiosity and then ultimately give him my wrist. Carlton sets my arm over a cushion that feels like silk and clouds. I have no idea what's happening, but then he opens a smaller box and my mouth gapes. My heart races in my chest and those curious flutters turn more tumultuous than before.

"Blue… what is this?"

"A gift. You ever seen one?"

Oh, I have seen one. It glimmers and shines in a way that is unreal. I've seen videos. I've even shared several to my socials that were truly breathtaking. In person, I know for a fact that nothing I saw online could compare to how insane these are in real life.

Somehow, I make my mouth work. "I—Why?"

"Even though we're not in the same time zone, now we'll always be on the same time. To me, time is money. And it will be for you, too." There must be over a thousand diamonds encrusting the time-piece, not watch because that word could not fully encompass how luxurious it is, it is a work of art. Using it just to tell the time is a little silly. But also, I'm sure that this thing cost more than anything I'd ever buy myself.

"I can't take this. It's too much. I can't even pronounce the name of this." Carlton works on sizing the bracelet links until it fits snugly around my wrist, not at all concerned with my protesting or what I'm saying. I expect it to be heavy with how shiny it is, but it's heavier than that. The diamonds on this thing must have diamonds. The pink gold case is impossibly shiny and the setting even has baguette diamonds to mark each hour. "How much did this cost?"

Carlton begins to tell me, but Blue speaks over him. "It doesn't matter. Think of it as an early Christmas present. I've got one and ours match. I'll show you when I get home."

"You have a pink gold AP?"

He laughs a throaty sound and it does something dangerous to the organ already beating too hard to be safe. "Nah. Mine is yellow gold, but in a similar style."

"Why would you do this?"

"Mine, remember?"

God, no. This is not the moment to suddenly have a conscience. I don't have one. But... fuck. I cannot accept this gift. There's too much meaning behind it. "I can't, Blue."

He ignores me saying instead, "I'll be back soon. I've just been delayed a little longer than I wanted."

I could unclasp the watch from my wrist, but I find myself turning my wrist to one side and the other to marvel at just how much it reflects even the low lighting.

There is a final snap of Carlton's case where he has efficiently repacked his things and stands there.

"Let him out. I want to make sure he's gone before I let you go."

"You're going?" I *need* him to go, so that I can get back to what I was supposed to be doing. But I'm overwhelmed with the gift he's given me. It was a reckless monetary decision on his part. He doesn't know how close to ruination he is, but I can't tell him that.

Since he doesn't know, it makes the gift even more special.

Shit.

Why is my heart squeezing?

I need to get my shit together. He is a mark!

"Gotta get back to this money. I'll hit you up later and you can show me how it looks when you're drippin' down this drip."

Despite myself, I smirk at his dirty mouth—on speakerphone no less, he doesn't care. "Be careful what you wish for," I tease.

He groans a pained sounded on the line. "Can't tell me that, I'll have to leave them right now and head to a hotel."

"Are you not staying in one?"

"Nah. I'm at Tony's. He wouldn't leave Alpenglow Ridge to visit my ass. If I'm here then we can spend at least a little time together."

I never would have thought that underneath the hard exterior was a man who could be thoughtful and caring. Blue is a caretaker. I never want for anything ever since I was brought to his home. He's even gotten me things that I never thought to get for myself.

It's over the top. It's unreasonable—just like him keeping me hostage here. But, it's sweet... in his fucked up way.

"That's good. Enjoy your visit. Don't worry about me."

He told me that he wanted to keep his brother out of the business. I couldn't know what that cost him to do. What sacrifices he made to let Tony do that. It's clear to me now how isolating that must be for him. His only true family removed from his dark reality.

He has all these people around him, but he might as well be alone. How can he trust anyone when they're all employees?

And then there's me.

When he finds out, I know that it will not end well for us. Us being this relationship that he is cultivating like a rare cannabis strain. So much effort and stepping out of his comfort zone for me.

All of this is an illusion.

But I'm the only one that can see the cracks in it.

I'm not falling for him.

My place is at the top, not under him. It'll be too late for him to decide if that place is beside him or above him.

The light bounces off of the watch face a few more times and then I see the inscription: My Diamond with the date we met.

Shit.

"I'm gonna be worried."

I'm going to miss you when I'm gone.

"You'll be back before I know it, right? It's just a few days. I'm as safe as I could be at your house."

"Yea," he says noncommittally. "Be good, Racquelle."

"Bye, Milo."

"I'll never get tired of you sayin' my name," he responds before ending the call.

I'm fucked.

"Everything went as planned. We were able to divert his attention away from the California grab and now he's following the wreck in Colorado. Do you think he'll be home any time soon?"

"I don't know. His lock was more difficult than I thought it'd be for a home office. I'm gonna keep working in here until I get a sign that he's coming back."

Difficult was an understatement. It took me two days trying to get this door open to this office. It wasn't like I had proper tools, so I had to get very crafty with what I could find in the house since I couldn't leave.

Not just because he didn't want me to, but because the guards outside each of the entrances were told not to let me.

Ordering food? Acceptable.

Ordering clothes? Also acceptable.

Going anywhere, including a hardware store? Absolutely not.

I'm still proud of myself for actually getting in. The space was fairly neat and organized. There were minimal files or anything that screamed important information. I started looking through drawers and under any of the decor for a secret passageway or something. But it wasn't too hard to tell that he must have everything electronically stored.

Then I go to the laptop bag. It had a few pockets and I found exactly what I was looking for in the largest section.

There was a little black notebook that had his crude handwriting on it detailing all the planned routes and locations of drops in the near future. I could have gotten this information on my own, but written out so nice and neat makes my life a lot simpler. I take photos and send them to Liezel.

Now, I can start sifting through this laptop. It was unlocked since I'm sure he didn't find a need to. Being essentially the monopoly on weed, allowed him to be lax in this area. Caught a lucky break there because going through these files is going to take a lot of time.

Hours and hours of it.

Scouring each one to find something, anything that could point out just what happened between the Lafayette and the Duponts that made them cut ties so quickly. It was a snowball of poor choices and deplorable behavior after that. It was the reason that I was here in the first place.

Then I see it.

A folder that I could only describe as nondescript. I would have passed it, if I weren't actually looking through every file on this computer.

The name is just a date, but I open it.

There is a news video clip linked in the folder. I open the video and instantly things start to click into place.

There are files from Allen who, I deduced, is working with Milo's money now. I go back and back and back even further until I find the same date.

And, of course, the date of the video and the moment the numbers become jilted line up perfectly.

I found it.

Here is the reason why Dupont and Lafayette fell apart. I know it and I can fix it.

I send that very thought to Liezel in a text message. I begin duplicating the information and sending it to our account when I hear a voice I very well did not expect to hear.

"The fuck you doing?"

Chapter 21

BLUE

There's no worse feeling than coming back empty-handed.

I spent almost a week trying to figure this shit out, breathing thin Colorado air and checking on every damn checkpoint in the grow circuit. The runners were clean. The shipments logged. No one seemed off, and yet—I'm still missing product and it's even more clear that there is someone out to get Dupont. But why?

The time to be concerned is right now.

If no one fears me, and the consequences of fucking with *my shit*, all of this will fall apart.

But if I start hurting people who haven't done anything wrong, then people will jump ship, I'll lose good people because they have sense. I wouldn't support myself if I were them and there is no blame in that.

Is this the point that I accept trying to cut out the Fayes without a proper replacement was bad business?

Fuck.

For shit to look different now is not helping anything. It's not skimming, not like before. This is tighter, subtle and strategic. A hole punched clean through my business like someone knew where the weak spot was. Not big enough to sink me, but big enough to make me sweat.

Don't know who the fuck that could be making me sweat like this though.

I don't have answers. And I fucking hate not having answers as much as I hate gambling.

Still... as my car crunches into the gravel of the drive and the familiar front porch light kicks on like a beacon, a calm I didn't know I'd been missing crawls up my chest.

I'm not used to this feeling—this *home* feeling. It's been years since this place felt like something was beating inside it.

And the reason for it is inside.

Racquelle.

The woman with a body like a weapon. The woman who showed up bleeding and still too damn beautiful to be real. I keep delivering her my favorite foods to eat even when I'm not there and more recently a fucking hundred thousand dollar watch she didn't even ask for.

If she's mine, she's gotta look like it.

Even when I don't want other men looking at her. I need to know that she's being spoiled like a queen.

Fuck.

A queen.

My fucking queen.

I keep thinking about her resilience and her strength.

Then my thoughts stray to her lips and the way she said my name like it didn't belong to a monster.

What she doesn't know is that I would be a monster to keep her safe. I would do anything so that she doesn't experience the pain she already has because of my name.

Yeah.

I'm in deep.

And fuck it. It was about time that I found somebody who could handle me.

Anything I give, she takes.

My knife, my fingers, my dick. She'll take it all and look fucking good with something smart on her lips.

So here I am. Taking the steps two at a time, nodding to my men at the front door, and stepping inside. I've been chasing this moment for miles. I got my ass back to Clayton Terrace as fast as I could just so I could see her. It's almost one in the morning, but what do I care? Being here is the objective.

The TV's off.

No music.

The house is quiet, save for the ticking clock I pass by in the hall.

I head toward the back, expecting to find her curled on the couch on her phone still or maybe sleeping. She's gotten very comfortable with the sitting room in the back. I know Indica and Sativa scare her a little still, but it's easy to forget they're there at night.

As I pass the hallway, I hear something.

A faint rustle.

It's coming from my office.

I freeze.

That door was shut when I left—and locked.

I move slowly, silently.

Hand on the doorknob and it opens with no resistance.

There she is.

My voice comes out low and steady despite the myriad of emotions I'm feeling right now. "The fuck you doing?"

Racquelle, in my chair with my laptop open. One of my black books in her hand, the one that doesn't get shared or stored digitally. Her eyes snap up when I enter, wide with a guilt I haven't seen on her before.

The kind that's not from being caught in a mess—but from *creating* one.

She bolts up so fast, the chair wheels squeal behind her. "Milo—wait—"

Something stirs in me. A feral feeling that rises in intensity along with the quickening breaths in her chest. "No." I hold a hand up. "Don't start lyin'. Not yet. Want to enjoy the truth of this moment for another ten seconds."

Her lips part, ready to spit something out, but she closes them again. Her hand releases the book like it's burned her. The sound echoing in the office that's thick with tension.

I step inside, close the door behind me. It clicks with something final I don't want to name. "Want to tell me why you're going through my shit in the middle of the night, in a room you're not supposed to be in?"

Her voice is soft. Much too calculated to not know what she's doing in here. This was no accident. "I wasn't snooping."

"Could've fooled me. Why else would you be in here?"

"I was—looking for something."

"Ya find it?" I snap, snatching the book from the table. *How would she even know to look for this?* "Want to tell me what the hell you were expectin' to find in here?"

I could pretend that it was happenstance.

That her finding my ledger of all the weight we're moving and through who was an accident.

That maybe, and by the looks of it, her getting the door unlocked and looking through my files on the laptop is also a fluke.

She could just be nosy.

However, all of those excuses I'm making, for my sanity's sake, go out the window when she swallows hard, adjusting her stance to something firm and unmovable.

She raises her chin and it only goads the monster that she tried to coax out of me before.

She's indignant?

She's standing on business?

She forgot who I was.

I'm gonna show her.

In a flash, the energy changes in the room as my anger rises. Racquelle is smart enough to ease her way from behind my desk, but I'm faster and larger.

Her back is against the wall before either of us can process what just happened.

Like a predator to prey, my instincts guided my actions.

My hand is around her throat and her eyes are wide in disbelief or fear.

I can't tell.

I blink. "You think I deserve this?" Her mouth opens, but I squeeze a little tighter. "You think I deserve the knife you put in my back?"

"I think you don't know what you have in your hands," she throws back. "I know what kind of man does the business that you do. I know what kind of man makes men disappear when he lifts his hand."

That silences me.

Not because she's wrong, but because she knows.

Not everything, but enough to make me question what any of what she's saying has to do with her presence in my office.

I move closer, my hips pressing into her and eliminating any semblance of space between us. Her pulse thrums under my hand, but now there's anger blazing in her eyes. "You got a lot of nerve goin' through my books for someone who *needs me* to protect them."

"I didn't ask to need you," she bites back. "It just ended up that way."

"No, you didn't," I say, and I'm close enough now that I can smell her hair products and whatever infuriating scent that is all her. "But you let me take care of you anyway."

Her breath catches when she feels me hard against her stomach.

Even when she's betrayed my trust—I want her. And if that isn't fucked up, I don't know what is.

"Why?" I ask, voice quieter. "Why come here?"

In a tone that matches my own, she simply says. "I didn't."

Waving the book between us, I hold her gaze. "You don't expect me to believe that you found this kind of information by accident. Things that could fuck all my shit up if it got out."

"I didn't come here to look for secrets." That wasn't an answer.

There are too many things that aren't adding up. "Why do you know how to look for them then?" I counter.

That shuts her up. Her eyes dart around, looking for what I don't know, but she won't meet my gaze.

Fuck.

There it is. That flicker of something I didn't want to believe.

She's not just some girl caught in the crossfire between me and the Fayes.

Negative energy pulses around us. I don't know if it's me or her causing it.

I fucking hate gambling. I had no idea that I was gambling when I had a heart for two fucking seconds. My teeth grind over an outburst I can't afford to make if I plan to get any answers at all.

Racquelle feels the shift. She squirms in my grip still firm on her neck. "I don't know what you think you saw," she murmurs, trying to make space between us. "But I swear—I wasn't trying to take anything. I just—needed to know."

"You want to know somethin'?" I say, voice like thunder in the small space. "You should've asked."

She shakes her head as best she can with my hand still around her throat. "Would you have told me?"

I grin, but there's no warmth in it. "Not a fuckin' chance," I sneer, but I'm unsure if that's true. I've told her a lot. More than I've told anybody who wasn't there to see the truth themself. I'll lose myself too quickly if I start recalling all the information I've given her in pillow talk and otherwise. "But I'm gonna show you."

The silence between us grows until it's loud enough to scream. Racquelle stiffens, her eyes pleading for space or for any reprieve.

Even in her fear, she's beautiful.

Maybe more so.

Chapter 22
Diamond

"Don't do this," I try to reason with him. "It's not going to end well for you." I can't help that it sounds like a threat, but that is what I'm telling him. A threat.

He was a mark.

I played my part just like how I was supposed to.

The hurt and betrayal in his eyes crawls under my skin anyway. No amount of rationalization could save me now.

I should have done this differently. I know that now.

Maybe he would have heard me out. We could have allied peacefully.

But, Liezel has what we need to carry out the third part of the plan.

All while he held me in that office, the solution we needed was in motion.

"Ha," a humorless laugh comes from his full lips as he secures the last of my restraints to the bed. "You're threatenin' me when it's you tied up to my bed?"

He had a point.

From his perspective, I was definitely in the worse position between the two of us.

"Please, Milo. Let me explain."

"Enough," he grabs something else and moves from the foot of the bed to sit beside my head. "Don't want any more of your lies. Only truth. And I'm going to get it."

A gag.

Oh shit, it's a gag.

He buckles it behind my head and my teeth instantly sink into it. It's too dark in here. When he's not on the bed anymore, he's basically invisible.

I feel a prick on my thigh and moments later, I lose consciousness.

I wake with a sore jaw though at some point the gag was removed from my mouth. It's dark in the room and I don't know what time it is.

The small amount that I'm able to lift my head is just enough to catch Milo's profile only partially illuminated by the heat lamp in the large enclosure at the back of the room.

My forehead begins to sweat before he can reach me.

I can't see now that he is blending into the darkness of the room. I know for sure he is doing something I won't like.

No, *no, no.*

"Don't panic, it's not the best idea for you."

My breath comes at a rapid pace. "What are you doing?"

"Nothin'." The bed depresses near my feet and then the horrible sensation of something slithering up my left leg makes me freeze. My heart is beating up through my ears as I try not to move at all.

"We'll start small." He says and I hear a knife's signature sound when he removes it from his hip. I can still feel the snakes moving around the bed, but I can only keep my focus on so many things at once.

One slithers over my arm and the other is moving over my stomach. I hate how big this bed is now because there are moments when they aren't touching me at all and then out of nowhere, the sensation returns of their muscular bodies taking advantage of new ground. They may not be venomous, but I'm sure a bite would hurt all the same.

He walks to where my arm is still outstretched by the bindings. I know better than to pull on them. My shoulder is healed and all. However, not strong enough to withstand a similar injury. I grit my teeth when I feel his fingers on my right forearm. "You're right handed?" He asks, already knowing the answer.

I don't respond or give him the satisfaction of seeing how nervous I am. Even though I can't see him, I have some weird feeling that he can see me.

"Wonder how thick your skin is…" he says. It's a taunt. I already know his knife is out.

What had I thought before? I was glad that it wasn't the pointy side that he was sticking in me.

Yea. That ends today.

"What were you doing in my office?" He asks, grip still tight on my hand.

I press my lips together, trying to manage the overwhelming sensations assaulting me at once.

There's three sharp pricks at the heel of my palm. They bite into my skin though I know they aren't deep. It stings and it's even harder not to jerk on my restraints to get away from the acute pain.

Then his mouth is there, licking over the cuts. It stings but feels entirely different as the soft, warm feel of his tongue over the spot is doing something to me. It shouldn't be doing anything like this.

The moon shifts from behind the clouds, casting the room in an eerie glow. I'm thankful for that small bit of visibility. I don't know for how long I will be though.

"You know I came home, hopin' to see you and relax after the shitty trip I just had." He chuffs, the sound cynical and cold to my ears. He gestures to my left arm which still has the AP fastened tight to it. I hadn't thought about the watch, but now I wish I weren't wearing it. There's disgust on his face when I look back at him. "Thought you'd bring me some peace." He brings my hand to his mouth again but this time, he kisses where he's cut me and I shiver.

His lips are gone before another four small nicks are stings against my palm again.

He shakes his head, watching the blood well up from his marks and begin to run down my arm. Milo's voice is too calm as he asks, "What did you find, Racquelle?"

Shit.

I know he broke something in me because I shouldn't enjoy this. Enjoy is too strong an emotion. It's like I can't help but try to squeeze my thighs when his lips meet my hand, soothing the sting before I can truly feel it.

I squirm and squeeze, unable to help how his voice and his mouth are doing things to me that I can't control.

"Different blade today. Don't worry. It will scar."

I can't see what he's doing to my hand. All I know is that the anticipation of what he will do next is killing me.

Four more cuts follow and they hurt, like he's cutting deeper than before. It hurts with the first, but by the time he gets to the fourth, I scream.

"Let's try an easier question." His face is above mine now. A tiny droplet of my blood just at the corner of his mouth. He's untethered—Rage in his eyes though all his words are calm. "Why are you here, Racquelle? You prepared to die for the secrets you're keepin' from me?"

I want to come out of my skin. I wish I could tell him, but I know I can't.

Am I willing to die for this?

I have to be. It's not only my life on the line.

If I die then too much will fall apart without me. Too many people rely on me now. Whatever I do from this point forward, has to be around getting out of this house.

Or at least to my phone—a phone.

Tears track down my face, as I think quickly. He wipes them away with his thumb, pressing the finger to his mouth taking that alongside the blood still slowly dripping from my hand.

It's crude.

So crude and wrong.

Still my mind skews the wrong direction.

Just like the first time he showed me his blade in malice, I throw caution aside and lean into the possession he has over me.

If Milo wanted me dead, I would be.

I know that without a doubt.

He's already executed multiple men just to have me to himself.

Changed his business.

Changed his lifestyle.

My voice is tentative and broken when I say his name softly. "Milo, please."

His eyes meet mine, depths soaking in everything of me at his mercy. It's not only anger simmering in those eyes, but betrayal.

I betrayed his trust.

Something he doesn't give to anyone.

"Listen to me, please," I beg. Pride long gone when I am so vulnerable.

His jaw works, but he sits back. Giving me space.

Rocky, you have to make this work.

You have no other choice.

"After my mother passed I went looking for my father." I swallow deeply, allowing the pain of her passing to bleed into my words because it is the truth. Missing parts of the truth, but still true. "Searching led me here to Clayton Terrace. Off Topz was hiring and I got the job… and you found me."

Skepticism remains on his face, but he asks, "Did you find him?"

I nod, not ready to tell him what I know he won't want to hear.

Swiping the blade along his sleeve to clean it. He returns it to the sheath and begins looking for something under the bed that I can't see.

A small box is in his hands and he opens it to pull out… a bandage.

My hand stings immediately with whatever he's cleaning it with. "Don't want you to bleed out," he explains as he applies a bandage over my hand.

Saying nothing, I wait for him to finish tending to the damage he caused. Milo makes no attempt to free me from where I'm restrained on the bed, but he does remove the snakes at least. He carries one in his hands while the other has worked its way up his arm.

I breathe a sigh of relief that I'm the only snake on this bed again.

He returns to the bed, sitting between my legs still spread wide with only the thin cotton material of my sleep shorts between us. They do nothing to disguise the wet spot that only grows with his proximity. He doesn't comment on it, just runs a finger over the dampness.

I can't close my legs to keep him from making it worse and he knows it.

He rubs a slow circle around my clit. It's too slow to truly make me come, but it's more than enough to tease me.

"Milo, I—"

"That's enough talking for now."

Rocky, you have to give him what he wants.

You have no other choice.

"That feel good?" He asks, the same slow, teasing pace setting my nerves on fire.

Time he spends with his gloved finger exploring the dip and swell of my lips to the hood of my clit. Over and over. Moments that become minutes of his ministrations. My brain gets fuzzy as lust rises in his focus on my body.

I start to speak, but snap my mouth closed. He said no talking. I nod my head.

"Can you take more?"

I nod my head again.

He reaches for his hip and the knife is back out. Lifting the leg of my shorts, he cuts them open from one side to the other so my pussy is completely exposed to him.

Milo makes quick work of cutting the top flap of my shorts so that it isn't in his way. For too long, he just looks at the knife against my thigh. The flat of the blade rests along the crease with the sharp serrated edge closest to my sensitive flesh.

Oh, fuck.

Please, I beg emphatically in his direction.

He doesn't hear me, but he smiles anyway, taking a moment to readjust the glove on his hand.

With some maneuver, he flips the knife so that he holds the wide blade in his hand.

"Been here before," he says, somewhat distantly as he recalls our first night together. "This handle's a little bigger, a little rougher." His eyes flick up to mine, where I'm already breathing harder and faster. "Can you take it?"

I don't know if I can take anything right now. My nerves are on fire while I'm trying to stay sane and resist what I know he's doing.

This is torture.

And it's just the beginning.

He notches it at my entrance without my response. He wasn't lying. It is bigger. It is much rougher too. The callous texture is already uncomfortable against my skin. But I have no choice. I can't go anywhere without hurting myself. I have no plan for this.

Milo doesn't shove the knife inside me.

No.

He leaves it right there, like a taunt.

I don't know if I want it, or if I want to get away from it.

Like I knew it would, I'm curious about anything new this man wants to show me. Even though it is a little twisted and a whole lot sick.

I shouldn't want it.

I *don't*.

The index of his opposite hand resumes the slow path around my sensitive clit, throbbing with need.

Fully exposed I know he can see how I'm desperate for anything—everything he has to give me.

He fucking trained my body.

His smell assaults me.

His energy presses against my will.

His hands tease me.

Goddamn.

I'm at his mercy and there is nothing I can do but take it.

I nod, shallowly. Barely a movement but it gives him the answer he needs.

"Look at how you're dripping already," he says, rubbing the handle through my arousal. There's entirely too much of it for the circumstance. *I can't help it.*

I moan when the rough texture makes contact with my sensitive clit. Bucking to no avail, he doesn't let up, rubbing it back and forth. A devilish smile takes over his face. "Here, I like it right here," Milo says, repeating the motion over and over, playing my body like a fiddle.

I want more and—then, it's gone.

He pulls away from my body, out of reach on the massive bed looking down at me. "No, no." He sucks his teeth. "You won't come that easily."

Our eyes meet and the truth of what's in store for me settles like a boulder in my stomach.

I shake my head, *no*.

But he just nods, his lips curling down in a mocking frown. "Answers. Need them, or you'll never come. Understand?"

I hesitate but ultimately agree. What choice do I have?

"Need your words, Racquelle."

"I understand," I bite out.

"Good girl," he says, lining the knife back up to my pussy.

Cursing my body for not getting the memo that we aren't supposed to be enjoying this, I can hear the sloppy sounds of just the very tip of the handle going past my opening the slightest bit and then coming out.

For whatever reason, it's a very intense sensation. The knife breaching me that small amount and then coming out again.

In and out.

Out and then back in.

Then he adds circles to my clit and the sound of my wetness grows louder in the room.

"Who is your Pa?"

I cannot tell him that.

No way in hell can I tell him that.

I wished he would drop that line of questioning and move to something different, but I should have known that he was smarter than that.

Sure, I may have fooled him so far with my tits and helplessness, appealing to his baser needs. Then falling into something more because he needed someone.

That someone could have been me if we had met in another life.

But we didn't.

We met in this life.

And for better or worse, our paths crossed.

This can't be where my story ends.

I told him before and I still mean it now.

Deeper the handle goes.

Deeper.

Deeper.

"Milo," I gasp. "No," I say, unsure if I mean the knife or to the question he's asked me.

It's too much.

It's not enough.

I clench and clench, each contraction of that muscle going against the logical response of my circumstance.

But, fuck.

It feels so good.

"Tell me," he says, pressing the knife until the full length of the handle is inside me.

My head falls back to the bed. I can't watch what he's doing to me anymore. My head is foggy and conflicted.

I don't know how long he can keep this up.

I'm so close to coming on his knife. Again.

I should be ashamed.

Tears fall from my eyes, rolling down my face to my ears.

I can't tell him.

He stops, removing the knife from me entirely. Using it to cut the rope from one of my legs.

I think that he will move to the other leg but he doesn't.

He takes his pants off. It's quick and suddenly it's his warm skin under my body. Strong and sturdy. Kryptonite for my resistance.

He holds the one leg he's freed just under the knee to keep my legs open for him.

"Why can't you tell me?" He asks, genuine curiosity in the pinch of his brows.

I simply shake my head. *I can't answer that either.*

The broad head of his dick is hot and insistent on my pussy. He swipes it through the slick path from my clit to my ass. I make a silent prayer that he doesn't try my ass right now.

But he doesn't do any of that.

I can see how hard he is. Feel it, too.

But he doesn't enter me.

Frustrating and patient, he continues to tease me in this way.

I mewl out of my mind, I'm over stimulated and not stimulated enough.

Four times he's denied me.

"Milo, please," I beg, voice desperate and unrecognizable to myself.

"Please, what?" He asks, with an oblivious look on his face. As if he doesn't know what he's doing to me.

My head falls back again. I can't get frustrated when I'm in a situation of my own making and I know it could be *a lot* worse.

"I just need one," I murmur.

He hears me with nowhere for me to hide. "Need one what?"

Before I can respond, he shoves into me with one thrust. The breath is knocked out of me as my heart sets off on a gallop in my chest.

His hips are flush with my body. As deep as he can get which is *so goddamn deep*. Stretched tight over the girth he's kept from me all night. The fit is perfect. The sound of relief comes from my chest at finally being filled.

With my leg still in his grip, he has the right amount of leverage to pound into me at a punishing pace.

He fucks me like he hates me and loves me just the same.

Again I clench, getting so close, I'm using all the strength I have to help myself.

He doesn't touch my clit, doesn't slow down for the strokes to truly satisfy my need.

Milo grabs onto my chin, forcing me to look at him as he pumps into me.

With gritted teeth he asks me again and my heart sinks.

Lips pressed together, I shake my head, preparing for what is inevitable.

His smile lacks all joy, but he knows what he's doing to me is fucked up and cruel.

He stops, pulling out of me.

His big hand stroking himself until he releases all over my stomach. He rubs it into the skin there and on my thighs. Carefully avoiding any areas that could be too enjoyable for me.

With a hard bite to my calf, he leaves me there—marked, unsatisfied and alone.

Chapter 23
Diamond

Waking in a stupor, my body aches in too many places. At some point, my restraints were removed after I had finally fallen asleep.

Looks like you played something right, Rocky.

Still alive another day.

I do some stretches, waiting in the room to see if Milo will come in to check on me or something.

He doesn't.

I need a shower, badly, but I also need to reach Liezel. I scour the room to see if my purse is any of the places I normally keep it.

It's gone and my phone is too. *Figures.*

Hurrying over to the closet, I unzip my suitcase. Inside are all the neatened bundles of twenty and hundred dollar bills I made at the clubs. It's not the safest option to have this much money in one place like this, but no place is safe than Blue Dupont's house. Of that, I can be sure.

I move stack after stack and check under the lining. My right hand stings under the bandage, but I'll worry about that later. I switch to my left and dig a little deeper until my fingers brush what I'm looking for.

In a few moments, the burner phone powers on. I say a quick thank you that it's not one of those cheesy ones that has some trilling tone for when it turns on.

I dial the number I know by heart and blessedly, the line clicks over and I hear my friend's voice. "Who is this?"

"Lee, it's time to enter phase three."

"Rocky, where are you? I got everything you sent me two days ago and then silence. Where's your phone?"

Two days? How has it been two days? Was I out for that long?

Shit.

"I'm still at Blue's. He caught me getting all that stuff to you. Look, I don't know how long I have to talk, so just put everything we talked about into effect and wait for my call."

"Why are you always in some shit every time you call me?" Her sigh is heavy on the line then she curses under her breath. "When are you coming home?"

"I don't know…" I'm not dead. A miracle for sure. But I don't know what Milo has planned. All I do know is that I have to get as much confirmed and in place as I can. "I'm going to find a way out, but it's—"

"Complicated," she finishes my thought. "Just tell me if you're okay. I can come get you. You know that, right?"

"It's too—Don't worry about me for now. I'm fine," I say that as my palm stings again and I realize that I don't know that for certain at all.

I have to trust that what I have executed will be enough to carry me through to safety again.

"Rocky," I hear the watery quality of her voice. "It's too much. We can do something else. Anything else. I'll never forgive myself if we lose you. *I can't lose you.*"

"You aren't," I tell her with as much conviction as I can manage. My body is still covered in the evidence that I am not in control here. My future still rests in Milo's hands. "I need to go. Wait for my call. I love you, okay?"

My friend agrees though I can feel her uncertainty and fear through the phone line. "I love you. Please be safe. I'll do what I can from this side."

I sit in the closet for a moment where I acknowledge my role in this mission and then return the phone in the lining with the money and ID card.

When all this began, long before I came to Louisiana, I didn't know where it would take me. Taking Lafayette was the goal. An alliance with the Duponts was supposed to be the safer option. One that would allow me the opportunity to deliver on the promises that I made to my people. If I can't follow through then it means I don't believe in myself or what I have to offer. *I must.* If no one else will, then I have to.

Leaving the closet, I strip out of my tattered shorts and sweaty tank top. The last thing left is to remove the bandage Milo put on my hand. It looks different, like it was changed at some point while I was sleeping.

I'm careful with the adhesive trying not to disturb the cuts underneath. Nothing could have prepared me for what was under the gauze, cream and tape. With a tissue, I remove some of the thick white cream over the damaged skin.

On my palm just above the wrist, it spans the width of the lighter skin there. A name. Not his real name. But the one that is symbolic of fear and respect. In all caps, the four somewhat jagged letters are red and stark.

B-L-U-E.

He carved his name into my hand! What had he said?

Don't worry. It will scar.

Why would he do this? The tender way he pressed his mouth to my hand was at complete odds with the action itself. Of all the things I thought he was doing, it never occurred to me that he would be actually branding me.

Fuck.

I step into the shower and begin cleaning myself, being extra gentle around my pussy that's still sore from his teasing. It was meant to be a punishment.

I know that, but I know what the reward could look like.

I remember the way he ruined me in my apartment and the night he let me in that small bit to see the version of him that was before this current one. He let me see Milo. And I know that means something.

Though my situation is dire, I find myself wanting the reward—the ruination. The way his body was made for mine is undeniable. At either end of his attention, positive and negative, it lights me up just the same.

Gentle cleaning leads to a more thorough massage as I recall what he did to me.

With a frustrated huff, I stop before I get anywhere with my fingers. I know it's senseless to even try and get a quick orgasm myself. I've been in the same position before. *Nothing will help me get there.* Milo has completely taken over my pleasure like a bulldozer and my delicate tinkering will do nothing to ease the ache—only frustrate me further.

Besides, my hand is sizzling with the soap and warm water. I'd likely hurt myself more trying to do anything about it.

If he said they would scar, then I'm sure he knew that for a fact. I would have his name on my hand for the rest of my life.

Why would he do that?

Further reassured that his goal is not to kill me, but to get answers can work in my favor.

Men are so easy.

I have to remember that. As long as he underestimates me, I can use this to my advantage.

Turning off the water, I grab my towel and quickly dry off.

When I turn the corner out of the room, I'm stopped in my musing by Milo standing there tall and imposing with a snake around his head. The thick body like a head band where the arrow-like head bobs out toward me.

"Have a good shower?" He asks as if everything hasn't changed between us since the last time I saw him.

I take a step backward but Milo grabs me by the arm. My grip tightens on the towel I have around me.

"Where you going?"

"I don't want to be in your way. Just gonna go get some clothes and—" My words cut off abruptly as his head lowers to mine and he takes my lips in a kiss that lingers. One moment, I'm nervous of who I'll find and then the next I know it's Milo.

Milo, the protective man who opened up to me and showed me how he fought for respect. Or Blue, the man who demands everything with nothing in return, but what he's willing to give.

It's Milo who pulls my body into his and kisses down my jaw to my neck. He inhales me deeply, lips leaving a burning path to my shoulder. I feel the weight before I recognize that it's not his hand on my other shoulder.

My eyes snap open.

His snake has begun to make a path for itself over my shoulder. I don't know what to do, so I hold my arm out like some kind of paralyzed tree and it takes that opportunity to explore my left arm. I'm grateful it's not my healing hand that it's making its way toward because I haven't ruled out that this massive thing won't eat me. It's heavy and if I were weaker, then it might be a struggle to hold it up.

Blue pays the snake no attention as his hand squeezes my waist. He nips my neck and then back to my lips. I'm breathing hard and my pulse is racing.

Why is it that nothing with this man is simple?

Just a kiss and I'm holding a moving predator that weighs as much as a barbell on one side and giving into a much larger predator taking in my very essence for his pleasure.

"Come here," he says.

I think he's talking to me but he isn't.

The snake extends its head away from my arm back to him and Milo places it back into the wall-width glass enclosure.

"Gets easier, don't it?" He asks me now that he's closed up the tank.

"What does?"

"The snakes. I think Indica might like you more than Sativa does."

I blink several times. *Is he serious?* "Excuse me?"

"Before," he gestures to one side, "you would shrink back. Even when you first saw me with her constrictin' around my head. But then you were holding her, just fine."

"Just...fine?"

He nods and then sits on the bed. There is already that box from earlier there.

The clothes I picked out lie on the bed next to him and I snatch them getting dressed quickly. If he notices my nerves he doesn't comment on it at all.

Holding his hand out, he asks. "How does it feel?" I place my right hand in his and he looks at his knife work.

I look down at my hand that hasn't started bleeding again, but still angrily screams his name. "It's tender," I respond carefully.

With the diligence of a medical professional, he cleans his hands. There's care but unmistakable pleasure in the process of him applying that cream from before and a new bandage.

"Let's go eat and we'll talk." Not a question or a request. I don't validate it with a response, instead I just follow him to the kitchen.

The house feels no different, but when we reach the dining room, there's already four men there. They sit on the bar stools and two others at the dining table.

That is definitely different. Before, I knew there were guards outside of the house but never inside as well.

"This is Marcell and Lonny," he gestures to the men at the bar stools . "This is Benito and Davis," he gestures absently to the table before grabbing some food from the kitchen.

A whole heap of seafood dinner comes out of a thermal bag that he begins handing out. Everyone gets something and then he takes the remaining two containers for us.

"It's seafood night. We'd normally have it delivered to work but since I'm here, we're having it at the crib."

I try for nonchalance when I suggest, "You don't have to have it here. I'm fine on my own."

His lips tip down on one side. "Wish that were true." And he doesn't elaborate.

"I'm actually not the biggest fan of seafood, so I'll just—"

"Damn. I might have known that if you told me the truth. So, how about it?"

I'm taken back at the casual way he's said that. Looking up, I try to see if anyone else has caught on to what he's said. They are unbothered, talking among themselves at the other side of the table.

A piece of his salmon rests on the tip of his fork and he waves it in their direction. "They work for me. They don't care if you're embarrassed. I mean lyin' is pretty embarrassin'."

I drop my own fork. "Lying? What have I lied to you about?"

"Can't put my finger on it just yet, but I will."

I bite my tongue to stop a quip from coming out. There is the thinnest of ice underneath my feet. I can't take any risks.

The harsh way he continues to eat his food like it's pissed him off is the only cue that I have to his true feelings at the moment. "Nothin' to say to that, huh?" I don't say anything. Just begin picking at the food on my plate. It has been a few days since I ate anything so before long I've cleared my plate.

"Rest of y'all, to your new posts." To me he says, "You, come with me."

I gulp as the tall one, Lonny, takes my trash and leaves.

"Don't like repeatin' myself," Milo chastises at the entrance of the long dark hall already.

I follow dutifully again. Never allowing too much space between the two of us.

"Sit," he says and I take a seat in the chair across from his desk in the office that started my downward trajectory with him.

"Milo—"

"Blue," he insists and I suck in a breath. *I don't like that correction.* It draws a clear line in the sand that my access to the man I was beginning to know is gone.

Swallowing, I try again. "I haven't lied to you."

As enigmatic as I've seen him, he turns a folder on his desk so that it faces me. I reach for it and see a myriad of information. My application for Off Topz. Other employment history. My degrees. Several photos that I know were taken without my permission during the time I worked for him. It's all there. He's been keeping tabs on me. And yet...

"What am I looking at?"

"You tell me."

"You have a file on me. You've been... stalking me." My gut tightens. I flip through the papers with some hesitation to not appear frantic. But I need to know what he does know about me.

"Stalkin' is an extreme word. I had a vested interest in keepin' you safe. You needed it—more than once." He taps the desk twice and it brings my attention back to him. "Why is that?"

"We live in a patriarchal society where men feel that sex workers are public property and have zero respect for consent or boundaries," I respond with an eyebrow raised.

"True. I won't deny that. But it's more than that, isn't it?"

I shrug.

His eyes narrow and then he stands from the desk. With deliberate movements, he locks the door and sits on the edge of the desk looking down at me.

"I'm gonna ask you a question. For each one that you answer honestly, I'll let you move on with no consequences."

I gulp. "Okay..."

"For each one that you avoid or lie, I'll take somethin' you're wearin'."

"Huh?"

"Somethin' you're familiar with. You'll strip." He stands. "And you didn't put much on, so I'd recommend you be forthcoming."

My jaw tightens. "I don't wanna play your game."

"Didn't ask." He rolls up his sleeves and sits in his desk chair. "Why are you here?"

"You brought me here."

He tsk, "I'll let you have that since I should have been clear. Why Clayton Terrace when you could have gone anywhere? You show up at my club."

"That was a coincidence." Truth. I only applied at Off Topz because Junior was the man behind it at the time. After he killed Manel for denying him the right to sell his shit in the club, we figured he'd take over. I knew other players went there, sure, but the news about the switch in owners came to me when Chanel told me that the new boss was my first private room request. At the time, it was sheer luck that the man I was looking to ally with came looking for me.

"Do I get to ask any questions?"

His eyes narrow, but he nods, "Sure."

"Why are there men in the house now?" There. Gives nothing away.

"Security is more important than ever. There has been... some things that don't concern you, but concern me very much. Need to make sure I'm prepared."

"For what?" I ask, knowing that he's increasing security because of my measures.

"Ah. You had your question. It's only right that we keep things fair right?" I sit back in my seat and he interlaces his fingers. "You have an MBA."

I sit back in my seat, as well. "That's not a question."

He raises an eyebrow at my tone. "Why are you still working at a strip club?"

"We live in a patriarchal society where men feel that sex workers are public property and have zero respect for consent or boundaries," I repeat, drolly. "The first question any employer will ask is for employment history. They either think I'm punking them and laugh me out of the interview or they solicit me for sex with zero intention of hiring me."

His frown is a tangible thing that affects his energy in the air as it takes on a negative edge. "Who?"

"Ah. I thought we were keeping things fair."

His frown deepens, but he crosses his arms. "Fine."

"Where is my phone?"

"Smashed at the bottom of the bayou."

"What?!"

"Whatever you were doin' in here, can't get out. Can't talk on a phone that don't exist. Now, that was two questions." His lips lift in a devious manner at one side and suddenly, I don't feel as confident as I once did. "First, why won't you tell me who your Pa is if he's the reason you're in Clayton Terrace?"

I swallow the panic and try to respond as honestly as I can. "I don't know what you'll do to him. I haven't really resolved what I need to and I need him alive to do that." God, that was vague. I don't mind taking my clothes off for Milo or Blue. But I know that his patience in torturing me by withholding my release is far too great.

And fuck. I still haven't truly recovered from last night.

Confusion colors his face, but he asks his next question. "Who is your Pa?"

The quiet in the room expands...

And expands...

And expands.

If I have a choice between telling him the answer and anything else, I have to choose anything else.

When it's clear what I've chosen, he commands, "Leggings off and get on the desk."

Not once did I finish that night. My muscles sore from trying to come, but never truly reaching that peak.

It turns him on to be at his mercy, to know that he has this power over me that can't be alleviated without him.

He enjoys that I need him and lords it over me just the same.

I growl and curse, pulling his hair and no relief comes.

He's enjoying this more than he should—If he knew the truth he wouldn't be.

And what's worse? I know it's because he couldn't comprehend that I'm as big a threat to him as I am.

A month passes with more of the same. Except when I'd wake in his arms, it was as if he had forgotten he was Blue no longer and instead Milo took me to the place I was desperate to get to.

Sometimes before I woke and others when he'd wake to catch me looking at him. With my days in this house under his watchful eye, I had nothing to do, but dread the evenings and look forward to the morning.

At night, after he learned of what new ploy had fallen on his business—dealing with the fall out—he would come home and take that frustration out on me. We'd fall into the habit of restraints and games and then questions about who my father was dwindled to nothing when

I gave him nothing. Instead, he would ask about my life, my interests, and my family.

It was a fucked up mind game because what I learned about him came from how he responded to my own answers, like riddles, when my answers were forthcoming. Still I enjoyed it, the mind challenges and him teasing me all night. It was something to look forward to when I couldn't' leave this house because of his growing fear of whoever was attacking Dupont.

In the mornings, he'd be softer with me. Forgetting about the previous day's perils. Clearly at war with what it should be and shouldn't be between us.

In some ways, I felt like I was comforting him after I was the one to hurt him. It was so fucked up. Any semblance of connection I was facilitating between us, I was also destroying with the truth I was keeping from him.

This man was a boat on the treacherous tide as he tried not to take the downfall of his business out on me, not knowing that I was directly responsible.

What could I do?

If this was my penance, I couldn't say that it was the worst he could do.

Chapter 24

BLUE

"Good. You're up," I say, leaning in the doorway of a hospital room in Harmony Hill, Colorado. Unfortunately, I'm still chasing loose ends. With one gone, there's one I have left to check before I can finally get back to Louisiana.

Back to Racquelle.

I'll be the first to admit that I was selfishly keeping her in my home under my guard for my benefit alone. All I wanted was to keep her safe even though I knew all she wanted was to keep her secrets safe. Everyone had secrets and I couldn't fault her for it. But whoever her Pa was held some sort of sacred weight that she was unwilling to relinquish.

Depriving her of the orgasm she knew I could give her was something I enjoyed. I'm a sick fuck, what can I say?

It wasn't always that way though.

In the mornings, I'd let her come on my dick when she was half dead and exhausted from the night before of teasing her. Taking every bit of information she would give me. Finally giving her the relief she craved was the best way to start what would be another hard day.

Never said I was completely cruel. I wanted to keep her and remind her what she could have if she gave me the truth I was seeking. Show her that there were benefits to a life with me if she would allow herself to receive them.

It could be rosy and nice all the time with me.

All I needed was one thing and I was like a dog with a bone. I couldn't let her think I forgot about that elephant in the room.

Just like she'll never forget me.

My name on her hand was sealed with venom. Something extremely mild but highly effective at its job. The tissues are immediately affected if the skin is broken, but not if it is ingested. After making each cut I was quick to remove any of the residue with my mouth, so that it wouldn't do more damage than I intended.

I'll be with her always, from now on.

Back to the woman I'm studying in this hospital bed. She has a bandage around her head. Years ago, she came to me looking for revenge, just like Redd. Kitty, too, had lost someone the same night that he lost his brother.

Under my command, she trained with Redd to become a weapon for me to use against any opp when the time came.

Now she sits in a hospital bed and, apparently, all that she has learned under me is gone. She doesn't remember shooting Colton or why.

Military wannabe, Colton Flagg, was out of his mind on painkillers when I went to see him earlier. The delievery that was under his care to get to Kitty and Thane is missing and no one in this hospital will be able to tell me where it went. For all his months of preparing, there is still nothing to show for it. I'll have to wait until he's coherent to find out what exactly happened.

This car accident that landed Kitty here was all due to the fucking snow, *supposedly*. Thane, my other guard who was driving the car Kitty was in, died in the accident because he wasn't wearing a seatbelt.

Fucking loose ends—*uncertainty*—I fucking hate it.

I'm starting to truly hate that I ever came to Colorado all those years ago.

"Kathryn, do you know him?" I noticed the White man in a chair at the foot of her bed, but paid him no attention. I mean, the dude has a cast on one leg. Definitely not worth remembering though flickers of a name itches just out of reach.

Kathryn, Kitty, doesn't seem to recognize me at all though the way she grips the sheets tells me that she can feel my energy in the room and for that I'm grateful. It can do the heavy lifting, so I don't have to deal with her otherwise smart ass mouth.

I already have a woman besting me in verbal sparring at home.

The man (Michael?) holds her hand until she releases the sheet and patiently waits for him to answer her question, but she shakes her head.

"Oh… Well, that hurts, darlin'," I say slowly, straightening from where I lean on the door. I walk into the room, but the man is surprisingly quick on crutches, challenging me in the middle of the room before I can reach her.

Brave guy.

Stupid guy.

But brave, I'll give him that.

I don't think to reach for my knife because it'd be fucked up to attack a man trying to defend one of my soldiers. Even if it would be easy, this is a very public place and I am not *that* unhinged.

Yet.

Michael tries to put up an argument with me to protect my guard which is hilarious at best. Eventually she puts a stop to it.

"Mack," she says, obviously recognizing how much danger he's in playing with me. *Mack not Michael.* "It's okay. I remember who Blue is by reputation." She asks, "What history do we have together?"

So, there really is nothing there. "Not important." I shrug, deciding I don't have time to rehash everything for her and this is not the place either way. We're in mixed company and I'm not sure if it would help her or be a good use of my time. "If any of those memories come back, you tell me first."

She crosses her arms over her chest, somehow managing to look down her nose at me—even with a bandage on her forehead. "How? My phone was smashed in the accident. I filed an insurance claim for a replacement, but who knows when it will come."

Looking around for a bit I see what I need. Leaning over to the side table, I write my number on a tissue. "Call me if anythin' comes back to you." She snatches the tissue from my hand and I chuff at her. *Only she would dare do that.* "Might not have your memories, but your attitude still fuckin' sucks. Thought some brain trauma would've helped you."

"Well, you thought wrong," she sneers, crossing her arms. "Somethin' else you're lookin' for?"

So many things. "Nah. I'll go." I don't wait for a second longer. There somewhere else I have to be.

I stand outside of my brother's door trying to decide if I should knock or not.

They say bad things come in threes. And the bad things that have come my way are greater than three, within too short a period of time for my liking.

First, the woman that I thought was on my side, is not at all the person I welcomed into my home. She's hiding something. I will find out what it is but still... What the fuck?

Second, since having her in my home, returning home to her at night, I have noticed more people going missing and consequently more of my fucking weed going missing as well.

And as a final straw, my brother, who I never wanted to be anywhere near this shit, has somehow gotten his cookie cutter life intertwined with mine. He was held at gun point by my soldier who remembers nothing of the incident. All because Colton put Mireya in danger and Tony was the one to rescue her.

What kind of parent brings their kid to a drug deal?

Like I said, Colton is a piece of shit dad. Mireya was in that hospital because of him. It seems like somewhat of a miracle that Tony and Drea weren't injured, too.

I don't have a choice, I knock on my brother's door.

The clattering of his dopey dog proceeds him looking through the peephole at me. I can feel how deeply he's sighing from my side of the door before he even opens it. It's cold as fuck and I'm ready to get my ass inside.

"I just got back from the hospital," I tell him without a preamble when I can tell he's still in a shitty mood. Seems like everybody is.

There's no emotion in his voice when he asks, "For what?" He looks like hell, warmed over. Dark circles visible even under his brown skin.

My eyebrows pull down in confusion. *Why the fuck else would I be at the hospital?* "Colton and one of my others were there. I had to try and get the stories straight. Your name came up in both."

He doesn't seem surprised in the least. "So what? Said *one* of your others. What about that Thane guy?"

I shrug a shoulder, "He didn't make it. Dead men can't tell any more stories." And it was true. Something I found to be very useful in my life.

A shudder rolls down his back before he begins to ask, "Did you—"

"Be real, T. You think I'd off somebody in a public hospital? This ain't that. I like my life in the free world just as much as you."

He rolls his eyes. "Look, I don't know what you'd do." *I wish it were staying that way.*

"I know." I take a seat on the couch next to where he's stretched out. "What do you know about that Mack dude?"

He shrugs a shoulder and it's so similar to my own gesture that I smile a little internally. My brother may be a grumpy dick, but he's still my brother. "Good guy, I guess. Works on the Ranch. Lives right next to it, actually. What about him?"

"He was in the room with one of my runners like some kind of bodyguard. Didn't matter anyway because she was useless in terms of information."

"What does that mean?" He sits up a little straighter. "Wait, she?"

"Yea, she. Kitty."

"She was the woman Thane was with when we got to Colton at the cabin. She was holding a gun, kicking Colton's ass just the same."

"I bet. I brought her in myself. Saw potential. But now... I don't know. Too many things aren't linin' up and she can't even remember me."

He turns to face me fully. "Why are you here?"

"I came to check on you." I put a hand on his shoulder, but he shrugs it off. After whatever went down in that cabin, Tony somehow messed shit up with Drea. Don't know exactly what happened there, but she's still at the hospital with her daughter and he's not there.

"You see me and I'm alive, so you can go now," he retorts.

I'm dealing with real shit right now and he's sulking here like an overgrown baby. "What's the big deal? She's just some woman," I taunt.

"She's not some woman. She is the best woman I've ever met. You wouldn't know what love looked like and you definitely wouldn't know what I'm going through. I'm all fucked up waiting for her to let me back in."

He's right. I wouldn't know what love looks like, but I know when a man is down bad and my brother needs that woman and her daughter in his life.

"So why the fuck are you here then? She needs you. You lose her and then what? You just mope around here."

"Look. She doesn't want her life entwined with us."

I'm sorry for it, truly, but I did the best I could to keep that from happening. Ever since Racquelle came into my life it has been impossible to keep control over anything.

Including this.

"Mmh. Sounds like givin' up to me." I say and then think for a second. "I need your advice."

"I don't know if I'm the best person to do that."

"Nah, just be real with me. I think you can give me... perspective."

"Hmm," is all he says and I take that as a cue to keep going.

"You got out. I always thought you were makin' the best choice for you. No bullshit. It really made me respect you. This life, this life is not for everybody. I'm not gonna lie to you and say that I don't love it. I do. But I wonder... when I get ready to settle down like the simp you are for Drea, will I have to give it up?"

My brother may not know the ins and outs, but he knows the consequences of being a Dupont just like I do. "I don't know, man. Look at what happened to Ma. Gone because of whatever shit Pa was into. This girl, whoever she is… She'll always have a target on her back."

"But that's the thing. Pa was movin' shady. He wasn't doin' what we do now. The operation doesn't even look like how he had it. If he were here, he'd be proud." Not that I'm seeking his approval because he'd be reluctant to give it anyway.

But he would have to.

Tony shakes his head. "It's even more dangerous. I've only caught a glimpse and I almost lost my life."

"Ack. Kitty would not have let that happen. Thane was dumb as shit. That got… out of hand. As much as I believe in solvin' the problem myself, karma did it for me."

"My employee did it for you," he corrects and I suppose he's right in a sense. If it weren't for that car accident, I might have more answers right now.

I hold my hands out in front of me. "An accident is an accident. One less drop of blood on my hands."

"Whatever," he says after a shudder rolls over him. He gets up and grabs two beers from the fridge, handing one to me. "What else do you want?" He's trying to get rid of me, but I won't let him do it that easily. I still have more to ask.

"How can I find someone in this crazy world? Is it even fair?" He sits down on the couch, but I choose the armrest instead.

"Nothin' fair about life. You could lose someone just as easily to a car accident as you could to a bullet. If she knows you, then she'll know that." He drinks some of his beer. Picking at the label there, he says, "Bruh, you're a risk no matter how you play it."

"You're right."

"Should I be worried about some woman in your grasp?"

If he only knew. "Yea," I respond simply.

He sits up straight on the couch, setting his beer on the coffee table. "What the fuck? Who?"

I could tell him all about Racquelle, but I don't think it's a good idea when he's so insistent on staying away from Dupont. "Probably best you don't know at this point. Life's a risk, remember?"

Shaking his head, he finishes his beer and leaves to grab another. "I'll take your word for it."

Time for me to get the fuck out of here. I still have so much to do. "I guess as a heads up, I'll let you know. We're takin' Colton back with us when he's discharged today."

"You what?"

"He knows somethin'. Thane's gone and Kitty was only in so deep before she lost her memory. Without what Colton knows, we don't have the information needed to nip this shit in the bud."

His eyebrow hikes up. "I thought you said it wasn't that."

"It's not. I don't need a camera crew or audience. Can't have anybody thinking I've gone soft. I'll get the answers I'm looking for or find out who has them."

"Fuck. Give me your word that you're not going to kill him."

I swig from my beer. "Why?" I ask, truly curious about why he wants to keep Drea's ex alive. Personally, I'd like to end all of Racquelle's exes. This man doesn't deserve mercy of any kind as far as I'm concerned. He put my favorite teenage in danger.

"He's Mireya's Daddy. It would devastate her to lose him after everything that's happened."

My head tilts to the side, "So, what?"

"I can't let you do that."

I laugh with genuine amusement at his suggestion and clarify. "Let me? Lil' bro you don't let me do shit. If I want him, I'll snatch him. Simple."

"C'mon, there's gotta be another way."

I scratch my chin, considering him. Keeping him out of this life was the choice I made. If he wants to be the boy scout he is to protect someone who doesn't deserve it, I won't tell him what to do. "Oh, there is…"

"Shit." He rubs a hand over his face.

If he wants to save that military wannabe, that's his choice to make. "Welcome to the family, T."

Chapter 25

Diamond

I'll be the first to admit that being Rapunzel in this tower was getting old. I missed my friends. I missed my family. I missed my freedom most of all.

After another trip to Colorado, Blue was back with big changes to recover from the most recent near-loss. I say near-loss because Thane, a plant of ours, passed away in a car accident due to winter weather. Like I said, men are so easy. Nina made sure that she could entice him to work with us. From what I heard, it wasn't that difficult to get him on our side since his loyalty was to his friend, Kitty, who was rising up Dupont's ranks. Not to Blue, or Dupont, in general.

That was going to be our package to keep, but there was no one to intercept with no directive from me or my knowledge until after the fact.

One of the changes Blue made was to replace Kitty, who was injured in the same accident that killed Thane. It's amazing what you'll find out just from listening to the guards talking when they think you won't know or understand what they're saying. Lonny got moved up to take Kitty's place running, and now there are only three men on protection duty in the house.

Today, Blue says that there will be a new guard to replace him.

I'm nervous.

Over the past few weeks, I had gotten somewhat used to the guys patrolling in the house. That seems more intense than it was. It was usually just them in all the corners of the house, occasionally walking around. Probably to keep me out of the office, but mostly to make sure if anything were to get past the men outside, there would be no way for them to get to me on the inside.

I had to admit that a part of me enjoyed how precious Blue made me out to be to his men.

But I hated how closely I was watched because of it. I could spend time in the yard, practicing routines, working out, and taking my fill of all Blue's favorite food places that delivered to the property. But, that wasn't living how I wanted. I miss *people* and socializing. And working.

I'm stuck playing the long con and my patience is fraying.

From everything I could tell, in the tiny bit of communication I've been able to have, Blue doesn't know who or what is hurting his business right now. All he knows is that it's in danger.

Before, when I was only here because of what Junior did to me, I was in obvious danger. A danger that I know could still be very real, but not being able to leave this house is extreme even given the circumstances.

There is no doubt that Blue is both possessive and crazy.

Logically, I know it's because he doesn't trust me—which I don't blame him for.

Can't blame him for.

However, I haven't had an opportunity to get to my burner phone and talk to Lee in the past week. He's gotten me a phone to replace the one he smashed, but we both know that it'll be monitored. With how frequently he's been taking trips, I know that she must be doing what we talked about and set up. If there is anyone who could hold things up in my absence, it's her.

I miss her. God, I miss her so much it hurts. But I know that I need to bide my time.

Sometimes, things work in your favor and I'm hoping this new guard will. It's not difficult work, but they will still need to get the hang of it. In that time, I hope that I'll be able to have a conversation without someone listening in.

I sit on the couch in the sitting room at the back of the house. When Blue comes into the house, a wave of his energy expands and expands until it finally fills the sitting room. One by one, his guards follow him into the space, making it even smaller.

Trying not to appear anxious, I flip through streaming channels on the TV.

This is it. New guard incoming.

"Aight. Everybody, this is Lidia. She'll be takin' Lonny's place in the rotation for the time bein'. She came highly recommended so treat her with respect." Blue cuts a look towards me, but I'm too stunned to make any sort of smart comments right away.

It's Lidia.

I blink several times and yes, it's Lidia! The other men introduce themselves to her and exchange their introductions or whatever.

Poker face, Rocky.

Finally, I get my shit together and snark, "Great, another guard. Should I jump for joy?"

"You know what I need from you and it ain't jumpin'," he says.

I roll my eyes and continue flicking through my options on the screen. "I'll have my ass planted right here until I'm ready to work out tonight. Like usual." My head tilts to the side with my sarcastic smile.

The obnoxious ringtone for Redd blares into the room, cutting him off from responding in a meaningful way. Instead, he kisses my forehead before walking off to take his call.

I don't know how he fucked this up, but I'm never been more happy to see anyone in my life. The other men are still talking amongst each other when Lidia sends me a sly smile.

Oh yea.

This is gonna be good.

Several hours have passed of me watching a couples dating show before I finally get off of the couch and go look for Blue. I wanted to talk to Lidia but I've come too far to blow whatever purpose she's here to serve. I have time to investigate that in the future.

Walking down the darkened hallway, it doesn't take me long to find him. The smoke room was empty and there is no light coming from the front of the house.

He sits on the bed without a shirt on. Only a loose pair of grey joggers. He's leaned forward with two of his locs in hand. It doesn't get easier for me to see his scars on display. Knowing what I know. I feel like shit in more ways than one.

"What are you doing?" I ask from the doorway.

"Retwist," he says, wrapping a rubber band around the ends of the two locs he had in his hands.

"Oh." Taking the few steps to the bed I sit next to him. "You'll probably think it's silly. But I thought you went to a salon or something."

"Why would I think that's silly?" He looks at me a beat and I pick at my cuticle, instantly regretting what I've said. "Ah," is all he says. His smug grin making my own turn down.

"What is that?" I say, pointing to his face.

"Should really get your jealousy under control."

"Me?" I scoff. "It's a... safety thing."

He gives me a look and I'm taken back to the night he saw my first glimmers of jealousy flare. In an attempt to divert from being found out, I had let it slip. I wasn't normally a jealous person, but Blue was mine.

Mine?

My mark.

Of course.

"Uh-huh," he retorts. After securing his final twist with a rubber band, he grimaces. Holding his hand, he starts to massage them.

Sitting on the bed, I instinctively reach for his big hand. "Do they–"

"It's fine. Just been overworking them." He doesn't pull his hand from mine.

Following the line of his scar above the most prominent of them, I apply pressure with my thumbs to the tension there. Slowly I make my way up his forearm to his thumb.

His head falls back and he rolls his neck, locs splaying behind his head. "Fuuuck that feels good. How do you know how to do that?"

"Pole dancing is a sport like you wouldn't believe. Our grip strength is important in many ways. This is a recovery massage we learned pretty early on." I press into his palm where the thumb connects, moving my thumbs away from each other. Over and over again until I reach the top of his thumb. Repeating the massage for each of his fingers. He's relaxed back onto the bed before I finish, boneless and relieved.

"This next one, is really gonna get you," I preface before I interlace my fingers with his. It takes both of my hands intertwined with one of his to be able to stretch his palm and fingers. The groan that rolls out of him makes me press my thighs together.

When I release his hand, he scoops me up into his arms, hands on my ass. "You know I'm never lettin' you leave me now, right?"

I manage to tap my chin as I ask him. "When were you letting me leave again?"

His eyes gleam before he kisses my forehead. "Wanna take you somewhere."

With my hands on his chest I hold his downward gaze. "Like a date?"

"Somethin' like that."

It had been weeks since I left this property. Tonight, I'm going all out to finally stretch my legs.

We arrive at a restaurant that I could only describe as luxe. All four guards come with us to the restaurant, but we leave in two cars. Both Marcell and Lidia sit in the front of Blue's night black Maybach in their standard guard clothing, so I didn't have many clues to where we could have been going. This though, was far more luxurious than I was expecting, I'm happy that I had dressed for a true date.

Another thing I was able to do with few limitations was shop online. At first I bought silly things that I thought might irritate him, but he never said anything when the obnoxious flamingo inflatable pool float chair arrived. Even though it's the middle of winter—and he has no pool.

Then I really started buying things I liked. A few new outfits to replace the ones that he had shredded with his knife.

Then I found designer ateliers that would take your measurements online for custom orders. This one I bought on a whim because the model looked fantastic in it. The fabric shimmered like my club clothes but not nearly as cheap looking. Thankful that I was able to have it tailored now because I'll actually be able to show it off.

The slinky black dress hugged my every curve until it reached my ankles. Brand new red-bottom spike heels let the long line of the dress shine without me tripping on every step. I absolutely looked the part of a woman who would be eating at a place like this. I had also purchased a smaller clutch for the evening that was just large enough for me to slip my burner phone into it along with my other things.

I hadn't worn makeup for a long time with nowhere to go, but tonight I was primed, blended, lined and highlighted to perfection.

Using the highest setting on my flat iron, I straightened my hair and added an elegant curl to the ends. I needed so much humidity-proof serum to make sure it didn't expand as soon as we walked out of the house. A little bit of edge control gel finished my look off, swooping my baby hairs back into the straight style.

She cut zero corners, is what I'm saying!

She is me.

If looks could kill...

Marcell opens his door but Blue is the one to open mine. I step out of the car and take in the sight before me.

When Blue had come out of the bathroom, hairline edged up and crisp down to his beard that had been trimmed... I knew I was done for. His hair was twisted up neatly and he smelled like my legs were going to spread or maybe I needed to bend over right then and there.

It took me a little longer to realize he was in a pressed black shirt and slacks. I had never seen him in anything other than lounge wear or the tactical clothing he wore when he was working. This look... was... lethal. He looked much too good for my ovaries to take.

Standing in the mirror with him behind me, I knew I need to get a picture of the two of us. I pulled my dummy phone out of my bag and snapped a few. We looked good together.

Better than good.

We looked right–like we *belonged together*. It's the same thought I had in room five all those weeks ago. It felt inappropriate then and now it feels even more so.

In my heels, our height difference was a little less pronounced so he didn't have to bend as long as he normally did. Blue's lips pressed to my neck as his hands rested on my hips. I snapped the photo at the moment my shoulders relaxed.

Looking back at the picture, I couldn't help but confirm—we look like we belong together.

A King and his Queen.

Chapter 26
Diamond

"This is where you take me for a first date? Should I expect the Met Gala next time?"

Blue chuckles, swirling his wine that the sommelier brought us with the third course. "Just a step above Off Topz, huh?"

I nod my head, placing a tender slice of the pork into my mouth.

Dinner's been going well. I haven't had any French-Creole food since I have been in Louisiana, which is a tragedy in itself. La Récolte was only open on the evenings for the weekends with a reservation list that spanned months–in Clayton Terrace–color me completely impressed.

The lighting here was low, warm and intimate. The wall to ceiling window overlooked the wrap around deck that sat just above the water. There were others in this restaurant, but I couldn't hear them and I could barely see them. For all I knew, it was just the two of us.

"Another good investment, then," he comments.

My jaw drops for a moment before I gather my composure. Dabbing my napkin to my lips, I ask, "This is yours?"

His head tilts, "Why the surprise?"

"This is not the kind of *investment*, I'd picture you making."

"Fair," he says, sitting up a little straighter. "My real estate agent was the one to suggest it. I was skeptical. Restaurants aren't as lastin' in this economy. Too high a turn-over. Fine dining, different story."

I wish that I could actually talk business with him.

A formal education only offers you so much. Learning in real life and becoming successful is something else entirely. I could learn so much from this man–could show him a thing or two as well.

In another life, I could ask him the questions I truly wanted and not the ones that I must to keep my cover.

I bite my lip to refrain from doing that and he continues to tell me about a few other restaurants that he has in his portfolio.

Somewhere between the fourth and fifth course, I excuse myself to the bathroom with Lidia as my guard, thank goodness. I had almost forgotten that the guards were here. I don't think I could do what I was planning if it had been Marcell or Benito.

I nod my head toward the exit that leads to the opposite deck and Lidia follows. She stands guard at the door so that I can get my burner phone out of my bag.

Questions on top of more questions all assault me as I finally get to dial the number I know by heart. When it clicks over, I rush out, "How did you manage to pull this off?"

"Oh, hi. How are you? I'm good, thanks for asking."

"Lee," I hiss. "Don't sass me! I only have like five minutes to even talk."

Liezel clears her throat. "By *this*, I'm guessing you mean Lidia."

"Yea. Thank you for my new personal bodyguard."

Lidia snorts a laugh, but is quick to return her focus to the door. She may not be a true part of Dupont, but I'm still in danger. Blue's claim on me was not without its own repercussions. I'm grateful that Lidia is actually qualified to protect me if anything were to go down.

"To answer your question, we've just been following the plan. Infiltration is easy when they're scrambling. They needed people, we were there to step in. Lidia is very well qualified, and highly recommended."

"By us?" I question.

"By us," she confirms. "Now, we have one of our own to protect you should anything go down."

"Incoming," Lidia says, moving to the door to open it for Blue.

"I gotta go. This is brilliant work. Talk soon!" I quickly end the call, stuff my burner away and pick up my dummy phone that Blue gave me instead. I snap a picture of the waterfront now that the sun is beginning to set.

His energy whips around the space as I look out onto the water.

"Thinking of jumping?" He asks in his deep tone at my ear.

"No," I respond, tucking the phone back into my purse.

"Good. Wouldn't advise it." His body presses mine to the railing, hard and imposing behind me. Blue points off into the distance and I follow where he's showing me. A small light flickers in the horizon among cypress, tall grasses and more dense plants.

"What am I looking at?"

"Tell me what you know about the bayou."

My brows pinch, unsure about this line of questioning. "I don't know..." My voice waivers. "There's a lot of them here."

"Know what lives in them?"

Despite his warmth still pressing close to me, a chill slips down my back.

He flicks his wrists and there's an ominous *plonk* in the water before us.

"What was that?" I say, turning to face him but he doesn't give me space.

"Look," he says and my eyes try to see what he's showing me.

Then I see it.

Obscure shapes begin to move in the distance.

"Milo..."

He runs a hand down my arm over the goosebumps. "That was a chicken breast that I just threw. It's been some time since I've needed to come out here. Chicken is good, but I know they prefer somethin' a lil' different. Lil' bigger."

"Milo..." The shapes are moving just as slowly as before but there are far too many of them.

A warm palm dips under my skirt to run over my calf and up to my thigh. Kneeling behind me, his face is eye level with my ass. "You see it yet?"

I squint at the shapes. I don't know for sure, but I figure there are only so many things it could be.

"Milooo," I whine when his tongue dips into my puckered hole. He's tentative, a soft brush of his warm tongue exploring me there.

"Blue," he corrects.

Oh, fuck.

No.

I tense and he smacks my ass, now fully exposed with my dress over my hips. He stands, covering me from anyone who could be walking past in the restaurant and thankfully from Lidia. I've been lucky that no one is on the deck–that could change at any moment.

"Hands on the railin'." With two of his fingers at my lips, he commands, "Suck. Get 'em nice and wet."

"I don't want to play this game. We were having such a nice dinner. The last course is gonna be ready soon."

He hums, the sound vibrating against my back with how close he is to me again. Wet fingers slide over my hole. I jerk from shock, but he holds me in place with his body pressed to mine. "I'd like a lil' dessert with my answers. That a course you can serve me?" He says into my ear, lips brushing over the shell and nipping the small gold hoops I chose for the evening.

If he asks what I think he will, then I'm taking this next step with him. I can't tell him what he wants to hear.

I'm positive that those are gators that continue to move toward us. "Better hurry 'fore they get here."

"Why?" My back is ramrod straight against him as I try to look for all the signs I missed. There are signs leading to this in my memory and I can't parse through them quick enough.

I had no idea.

My guard was down. He's charmed me. I felt like I was in the clear with Lidia protecting me. But there is not much that Lidia can do to protect me right now without jeopardizing my position.

Even with my position being compromised.

"Relax, Racquelle. You have nothin' to worry about if you just tell me the truth."

My voice is as quiet as a whisper with my eyes on the shapes still making their way toward us. "I've told you everything."

"Who were you talkin' to on the phone just now?"

The persistent thump-thump-thump of my heart in my ears begins to overshadow my hearing. "I-I wasn't–"

"You were." A single one of his fingers slides into my ass and I gasp out a breath. Tightening and then relaxing myself. I know it will only hurt me to resist.

But relaxing brings an entirely different feeling.

The fear of what he would do to know the truth doesn't dampen the excitement from what he's threatening either.

Consequences of what I've done are the least of my worries. I have to face them if I expect to make it out of Blue's grasp to show the Lafayettes what I'm capable of.

Blue is testing me. He's too smart to miss the signs of my suspicious behavior. I shouldn't have chanced that phone call.

I just have to last long enough to find a way out.

I just–

"Maybe I should stop takin' it easy on you, huh? You think one is enough?" He practically snarls into my ear as I press into him. With my hands on the railing, I try to back away from the edge.

"Blue, please," I beg. My mind is a jumbled mess of should and should nots.

Should not be begging him for what he thinks will be enough.

Should be finding a way to not find out what he thinks is enough.

"Ohhh," I moan when a second finger enters me.

I've been here before. He's used two before and I know how good it is.

He bites my earlobe, shocking me out of the hazy feeling of being breached this way. So *publicly*. So out in the open. So close to the edge where his monsters are still heading this way. "Remember how many I'd need to fit?"

Trying to control my breathing, I nod, eyes never leaving the water. "Need your words, Racquelle. Tell me how many."

"Four. You need at least four."

"Good girl. Now, it's been a minute so you might have forgotten the question that burns in my brain. The one that makes me hold on to my doubts about you and want to keep you close all in the same breath. Know you won't answer it. So, who were you on the phone with just now?"

Fuck.

It had been a while since he questioned me. My core tightens in preparation for what my body can sense is coming. Sweat rolls down my back at his proximity and also with trepidation.

I was so close to just telling him.

To let him know that Senior is my dad and why I'm here.

Tell him all about my plan and his role in it.

Especially if it means we can go back to how we were before I came out here.

But I can't do that at all when I know the lengths he's willing to go.

Taken off guard, I thought we had moved past this.

He was waiting.

He was patient in setting this trap for me.

The evening was going so well. I could have even been fooled into thinking that this date was real.

Blue never said this was a date.

He never agreed when I suggested either. Only redirected.

And I missed all of that.

"Can you take more?" His question comes when my silence persists as I try to unfuck the chess board I was not paying attention to in my mind. He was always thinking of how to get what he wanted. I had missed everything.

All the signs.

I'm back in the game now.

I was no virgin. I had done anal before. But I had never done it with any one or anything nearly as big as Blue.

Rocky, you're in for it now.

My agreement is swiftly punctuated with another finger, wedging next to the previous two.

Those fingers I had massaged only hours before. I had helped soothe his aches and he was utilizing the efforts of my labor to send me into a frenzy. The pleasure of his soft coaxing in my back channel is bliss and torment in the same breath. It's overwhelming and breathtaking.

Anyone could see us.

Anyone could hear me though I try to contain my volume. My whimpers were barely subdued. I'm still hoping that I won't cause a scene or attention of someone out here.

That wasn't what Blue wanted though. He always wants to hear me—every sound.

"Nah. I want all those cute little noises you make when you're at my mercy. You're already drippin' down these thick thighs. I wanna clean it up with my tongue but only if you're good and make it to this next finger. You know I hate lettin' any of that sweet honey goin' to waste. What do you say? Are you gonna let me inside this ass so I can get to the honey slidin' down your legs?"

"Fuuuck," is all I manage as I writhe over his fingers. The pinky is not much more of a stretch, but it is more than enough to show me how absolutely helpless I am right now. "Blue..."

I can't think.

I'm all nerves and feeling.

The breeze blowing softly around us is a sentient thing crawling over my over heated skin. Lighting me up and stealing my concentration on anything else.

Maybe it's just his elevated energy pulsing around me like my throbbing clit and clenching center.

None of it could bring me to my body like the feeling of his stiff length rubbing through my folds. With his fingers still inside me, he uses his other hand to coat his dick in my wetness that's flowing just for him.

Blue's voice is infuriatingly calm. He's got all his control in place while mine is crazed right next to my pride at his feet. "Deep breaths. Gonna slide my fingers out. Last chance to tell me something real. Tell me this one thing. You know I've got you. You know I'm keepin' you safe. You're cared for. Have I given you any reason not to trust that?"

Damn him.

Damn him for making me want to give in. For making me want to compromise my mission.

He. Is. A. Mark.

I'm just the distraction.

I'm keeping him distracted.

I believe in my plan.

If I say it enough times, maybe I'll stop being weak for him.

Maybe I'll stop falling. "But th-the gators–"

It's at this moment that he notches the fat head at my puckered hole. It's startling, but not unwelcome from how he's already started prepping me.

It's gonna hurt.

It's going to be too much.

I'm going to take it anyway.

Goddamnit. I want to take it.

"Deep breaths, Racquelle." *How is he so patient?* Why do his words feel less like the foreboding they should be and more like the concern of a passionate partner?

I have to relax. I have to lean into the feelings that I'm fighting for him or this is going to be so much worse.

On my second inhale, he eases himself inside.

If I was whimpering before, then the sounds coming from me now are far more feral. They rip from me as his flared head gets past the ring of muscles that suck him in.

His grunt in my ear only heightens the intense surge of sensation from being filled this way.

"Racquelle," he groans. "You're gonna make me bust right here. Right now. Are you gonna take this nut on the deck? You're loud enough to draw a crowd. Everyone can see how deep you take this dick in your ass from the windows. Everyone can see how you belong to me and only me. You think I want everyone to see how well you take this dick?"

"N-no," I manage, unable to lower my tone or the urgent keening starting from his slow strokes inside me.

"You tell me what I want and I won't have to leave you leakin' my cum at the table while we eat this last course." Blue smacks my ass. It stings and the pain intensifies the bliss of his next stroke. *Did he ask me something?*

"But that's what you want, isn't it?" His teeth sink into my neck and he continues pumping into me at a pace that makes me meet him thrust for thrust.

It was too much.

Then it wasn't.

Then it was heaven.

My heart clenches along with my ass as he takes me higher and higher.

Blue begins thrusting into me in earnest and I'm absolutely lost to it.

It feels so fucking good that I'm completely lost in his words. The ones that keep pouring from him like praise.

"I can't let you go. I won't ever let you leave me. *That's what you mean to me, he growls with feeling in my ear.* "If you think you can get away, just know that I'll cut down anyone who tries to take what's mine."

I want to respond or defend my actions but the heightened sensations are too much to speak, let alone form coherent thoughts. His fingers roll along my folds gathering more of my juices to use in easing his length inside me. Then two of them rest inside me, doing nothing but driving me insane.

"You love being stuffed by my big dick, don't you? Look at you grippin' my dick in your ass and my fingers in your pussy. You wanted it just like this, didn't you?"

"I'm so close. So..." My breath catches at the closeness of the gators now. They have to be at least thirty feet away. "Blue, th-the–"

"Yes, bae. You're takin' me like a fuckin' pro. Keep doin' that." His hips meet my ass. My stomach presses into the railing but I love how deep he's able to get inside me.

There's splashing as the gators finally reach their prize and I freeze in place. I can't count how many. The adrenaline spikes something in my blood. Blue's thrusts never slow as he's reaching his climax too.

I hold onto the railing with all the strength I can muster as he throbs his release deep.

Panting into my ear, he covers me so that my dress can fall back into place. After adjusting his pants to put his dick away, he says. "They'll never reach you. Never get to this deck." He licks the fingers that were just inside my pussy clean. "But you will be finishin' tonight's meal drippin' wet at the thought of them getting to you. Was it worth it?"

I smooth a hand over my hair, trying to gain my composure again. My little clutch didn't get lost in whatever just happened on this deck because of the wrist strap. I'm careful to only remove the dummy phone up my call log.

There are no calls from the evening and I wait for him to recognize what I'm showing him.

His eyes narrow and he asks, "What's this?"

"I was just taking a picture of this view," I explain, a little breathless from what we've done. It's not the complete truth but something in me couldn't let go of the opportunity. Swiping over to my photo app, I show him the pictures. "I've never seen the bayou like this. I wanted pictures to remember this special night together." I swipe further back to the previous photos of us earlier and leave them there. "I thought we looked good together here," I say, looking over my shoulder to him. "Do you think so?

Blue curses before walking over to the railing himself. With his forearms on the edge, he watches his gators continue to splash around the green hued water. "Everyone has their secrets. Some are worse than others. I know you aren't trying to hurt me. Trustin' you is hard after findin' you how I did in my office, Racquelle."

"I'm sorry," I say, fidgeting with my purse strap. *I am sorry*, just not in the way I should be. I wish things were different.

His eyes meet mine and it takes my breath away. Here is the vulnerability that I never see from him outside of his home. Away from the bedroom in the mornings.

This is the eyes of the man who let me in.

The one who I'll burn with my deceit.

That one that will feel all the ways I hurt him as I continue to wedge lies between the two of us.

"Workin' on it. I have to get better. You know that I want to give you more than this. I can. I will. Can you be patient with me while I do that?"

Guilt tumbles around my stomach but I hug him from behind, letting my face rest on his back when I say, "Of, course."

He pull a blunt from behind his ear and lights it for the two of us to share. Probably why he was headed out here to begin with.

One day, I'll have to give him up to step into what I'm building. For now, I can enjoy this temporary bliss.

Chapter 27
Diamond

After our first fateful date at La Récolte, I noticed a change in Blue. He was my Milo again. The one who made me fall and fall hard. I didn't miss our fucked up mind games. He made good on his word to learn to trust me more, in everything but letting me leave his heavily guarded home. Instead, I enjoyed our growing ease in whatever this was as I played Rapunzel in his captivity.

It was nice, but I had to set my feelings aside to finish what I started.

I would have to ask for his forgiveness later.

I would find a way to make him forgive me when the success of my purpose here caught up to him.

The first week that Blue was gone, Lidia informed me on everything I have missed in Atlanta. Her intimidating height and frame were a sight for sore eyes. To have someone familiar in the house made me feel less like the hostage I was and more like the boss I am. I don't know how she recovered from seeing or hearing what happened on that deck but we both are moving past it.

There were much bigger things at hand.

When cocaine became the product of choice because of Junior's stupid decisions, my family—my old club—were stuck with nowhere to go. It was hard to see it happen and having lost people I loved because of it. Either to the drugs he was peddling or fleeing the pressure of his miserable presence there.

Worst of all, my mother.

Because of Junior, she was introduced to the addiction that would ultimately take her life. Losing her empowered me to take what I had learned in my schooling to take from him, in turn.

I had to take everything.

I was sick of how we were treated by men like Junior but learning of our familial ties infuriated me further. I was sick to my stomach and knew I had to do something.

Men are so easy.

Every good dancer knows that.

And there were many good dancers at The Chrome Flame.

I showed them my ideas and invited them to back me in this endeavor to ruin Junior.

Using our feminine wiles, there were several monied men–and men who just loved these ladies–willing to make some extra money boosting green and moving it elsewhere.

The dancers who didn't have loyal clientele, were bait for marks within the Faye ranks or coincidentally, the Dupont ranks. Women like Nina who weren't working the floor yet but had a penchant for getting what they wanted. Men tell all their secrets to the ones that make them see stars after all.

I'll always be grateful for how Lee had followed the plan to the tee. I outlined several areas that could be weakened by a little commotion for the new women in these men's lives–Dupont and Lafayette.

And even better if we could plant any ideas of loyalty to someone else that could improve their financial standing.

"Lee moved to the second location. We're at capacity for the first," Lidia tells me. "If we fill the second, we'll have to start moving it or risk legal suspicion."

"It won't be a problem. I will figure out how to get out of here by then."

"What can I do?" She has already done so much. I had barely formulated a plan for infiltration like this. The highest infiltration I had gotten was Thane and he wasn't very high up or respected in the Dupont family. His partner Kitty was, though she was not one of ours. It was likely better that way.

There were a few of my people in the lower ranks to keep tabs on how Blue was moving, but my original goal was never to trick him. Only to show the Fayes that I could do what they did and better. That I could show them how to be better *with me.*

Over the course of January, Lidia and I were able to come up with a system to communicate back home more effectively, so I could be more hands on with the decisions necessary for my plot.

I finally had a chance to talk with my family for more than ten minute phone calls. No one batted an eye because Milo was able to feel comforted that I wasn't giving his new guard shit while he relaxed with the brief reprieve of our attacks.

We had one close call where Davis was a little suspicious with how much I was laughing after a particularly funny recollection of Lee's newest exploits as Madame Lee. All efforts were going smoothly and it felt good to let off a little steam with my friend.

It's February, and the guard rotation has gotten more smooth, so I'm able to increase what we were boosting from a quarter, to thirty percent of what was promised. Having the exact location of the drops helped. Blue had made no changes to any of the information I'd relayed to Liezel that night. But it was harder for my team with Duponts aware of potential threats. Unfortunately, there were several more casualties.

When we were lifting small bits, it was easier for my people to get it and go. It's more difficult, even with more certainty, to move that kind of weight undetected. I had been thankful on those nights that Blue wasn't here to see my tears for the ones who had fallen. I was gutted by those losses on both sides. My girls were safe, but the men they had been whispering to weren't. They were on the line and that was just how it went. I couldn't spare anyone cooped up like I am.

When Blue was home, he was exhausted. I could tell that this was affecting him and instead of taking it out on me, he leaned into his obsession with keeping me protected. Even when I knew he was starting to lose more than what could be negligible. I let him lose himself even more in my body. And frankly, I was doing the same, knowing that I was destroying us both.

I knew that this was bloody work, but I was still remiss at the cost. It was senseless. If Senior had trusted me to do what I knew I could, none of these losses would have to come to pass. Yet, I knew that there was nothing I could do. Business like this wasn't for the weak and I had to follow protocol. Each name would be remembered and my team sent what was agreed upon to their families if they had them. It was the very least that I could do.

Still, securing this kind of leverage was unfathomable. Years of my hard work and research finally coming into fruition. I wish I were celebrating the highs and lows with my family back home. I had to settle for what little conversation I could have on Lidia's rounds in my part of the house.

March rolls around and this was the hardest. Knowing that we were upping the margins once more, I made sure everyone was armed and protected as best I could. Everyone knew that this was a risk.

At this point, I reflected again on what it would be like to actually work with Blue instead of against him. He was convinced that I was a casualty in this war. I couldn't be the one to inform that it wasn't me *but him*. That hurt even more.

I couldn't go back and I couldn't redeem my actions. If I were to be taken seriously by either family, I had to earn the respect twice over.

For playing both sides and just because I'm a woman.

It was his side who spilled the most blood and my numbers were relatively unscathed. Blue was working with skeletons, literally and figuratively, as we held over three months of his product.

Any business missing that much would surely not last long.

April comes sooner than I expect. And now, everything has gotten far more tense. After so long of him flying under the radar, Lee has pinpointed Junior's location. *And that is bad for him.* If Lee found him—then other people certainly could too.

But that—that's my way out of this house. My way to leave and step into the power that I had been amassing from the safety of my enemy's home.

All without his notice.

It's the first week of May and I send a fateful text message to Blue's second-in-command.

Like the person I've heard he is, he calls Lidia's phone immediately after receiving it. "Lidia, the fuck is this?"

"It's not Lidia," I say onto the line with all the confidence of someone who knows they're landing an expert move.

There's a pause where I'm sure Redd is trying to put the pieces together, but I don't make him work for it. "I have what you want. As long as you help me, I can get it to you before week's end."

No one hates the Lafayettes more than Redd Blundell. I'm gonna serve Junior up on a silver platter.

"Help you how?" he questions with skepticism thick in his voice.

I look to Lidia who gives me an encouraging nod. She's just as ready to go home as I am. "I need out of this house." He laughs, no, guffaws on the other line. I grit my teeth and let him have his fun. "I can tell you where Terrell Junior is, unprotected and unarmed."

That shuts him right up. There's a click and then Redd asks, "How do you expect me to get Blue's most prized possession out of a house that's armed to the teeth? Even against me?"

Running the pad of my finger over his name on my palm, I take a deep breath and tell Redd, "Leave that to me. Do what I say and you can have the revenge you've always wanted."

Chapter 28

BLUE

You know what's a really good natural stress reliever?

You don't have to guess, I'll tell you.

It's killing the men that have been on your must-kill list, but out of your reach for months.

Before me, Keith Brussaud, Ervin Mallard and Lawrence Lafayette are strung up by a single arm to a random pipe in my warehouse. It's cold, they're wet and let's just say that plenty of my men are happy to take their stress and frustration out on them as well.

After some digging and not that much effort, Redd had figured out who took Racquelle from the grocery store that day. Like Junior, they were hiding and staying out of reach for very good reason.

Well, they showed up in Clayton Terrace again.

Big mistake.

My knife itches in my palm to finally get the retribution they deserve for hurting my woman.

Not the knife that laid claim to her body, forever letting her, and anyone, know that she was mine.

This is my K-bar. And it's been too long since she's tasted blood.

It was extremely unlucky for them that my memory of Racquelle's injuries were as vivid as they were, seeing her in front of me that night. The pain that she endured—every moment of her misery in recovering. Crystal clear in my mind.

None of these men would survive.

Though I couldn't be sure that it was because of them that my weed was going missing. I couldn't be sure that it was because of them that my men were dying trying to protect what was mine. I could be sure that my patience had little to say to uncertainty. Elimination was a sure thing for these three. They were high enough in Junior's ranks that he would absolutely feel their absence.

I wanted him to feel it.

It was personal, but I wasn't willing to fuck up my hands to end their miserable existences. My people had felt that enough to pitch in to this retribution beat-down. It would make it last a little longer than necessary.

Working smarter, not harder. That's just good business.

Slipping the blade into my external sleeve, it glimmers in the hard lighting of the open room. Venom drips only slightly at the hilt where I've coated the blade.

Lawrence is first. The throat would be too generous. I look for a spot that has the fewest bruises already, and I'm happy to find that there are many of them. But right between his ribs, looks good to me.

A clean entry is good for me, bad for him.

With his body weight contorting from the pipe, I can hear the ligaments pop as he jerks from the effects of the venom.

I hope that he will remain conscious for the duration of it.

Keith is next. I don't need to deliberate for this piece of shit. He kept her from screaming in the lot with a hand to her mouth. After wiping my blade on Lawrence's pants, I make sure it's ready for a new entry. With the arm that isn't tied to the pipe, I slip the blade directly between the bones above his wrist, slow at first and then twist when I remove the blade.

There is no screaming that I'll miss from his pain today. *He's earned it all.*

And finally, Ervin. He was the genius with the syringe and later the one who knocked her unconscious with his boot at my doorstep. My grip doesn't falter when I bring my boot up to his head with a kick and then plunge the knife into his chest right over his heart.

The three of them flail in agony as the culmination of their beatings and my venom takes them on the most miserable journey to their end.

I'm certain there are more who deserve a similar fate, but I want that motherfucker, Junior, on the end of my blade more.

I was up until late in the night working over the three men responsible for most of Racquelle's injuries. I chose to stay at the warehouse and clean up, only taking a shower and quick nap before the next work day came.

And per usual, it was more shit I didn't want to deal with on my desk.

More money lost, more product gone.

Chasing down whatever new attack was causing my empire to bend, near breaking, didn't excuse me from the day to day responsibilities that fell to me here. Even more so now that we were losing people and consistently having to shuffle duties between who was left. No matter how mundane.

"Boss, Kitty's here to see you," crackles through the line. I really had not expected to see her here after she had been staying with Michael. *No—Mack.*

As far as we could tell, she didn't remember anything damning and couldn't have been telling any secrets. When I got a call from her a couple of weeks back, I thought something was up. Knew she wasn't responsible for whatever leak or mole or rat I was dealing with. Was willing to pick her up and everything but chose to send someone in my stead because I had enough to deal with.

Once she got here, I had to explain to her, as best I could, why she started working with me. I'm thankful that last night alleviated most of the rage I had over my circumstance because dealing with Kitty is trying, even in the best of times. I don't comment on her disrespect because she doesn't have the three years of seeing why I deserve it at the ready. Her memory is shoddy.

I do my best to summarize what I can. "You showed up at my house. Not here but at my family home. You had fire in your eyes. I figured you were high or somethin'. Nobody talks to me like that and lives." I narrow my eyes on her in a way that suggests she should get a clue about that fact. I might not be ready to flip, but that could be triggered by anything at this point. "But it turns out that you and I had mutual goals."

Her eyes go big as saucers, but she asks, "What were our mutual goals?"

"Revenge."

"Revenge?"

I nod, surprisingly comfortable telling her this truth. "Both wanted revenge. The night you lost your Nana was the night I lost a good friend and a valuable soldier. The Lafayettes set up Lewis, Redd's brother."

It was the night that everything became clear.

Lewis went to a house party to sell some green. Not unusual for a low tier guy. Redd didn't have a problem with his little bro in the life since he was always more proud of this shit than I was. Plus, Lewis was an eager little punk.

That night, there was a mix-up or maybe it was intentional. His bag had more coke than green and it was only one person's fault. Junior was at the party, but Lewis refused to sell the snow. Accused Junior of setting him up and shots were fired.

That's all I had found out anyway.

Redd was livid, wanted to go after him right away. But I knew it would start a war that we weren't prepared for. Had to hit back in another way.

Kitty's voice breaks my reverie, "And that's how I ended up workin' for you?"

"In a way. We're still beefin' with the Fayes. You said you wanted in and Thane came too. Trained hard. Rose quick. Ran green for me until one day the green didn't come back. Thought you were stealin' from me. You beat Colton down pretty bad up there and then I find out you were in a hospital and remember nothin'. Luckily, I found my shit and you weren't blabbin' to the cops. I didn't wanna deal with that… complication."

And now Colton's missing. Not dead, though I tried my best when Tony brought him to town. I hoped it would scare him shitless. But I haven't heard from him since.

"And what about Ethan?" Thane or Ethan was her childhood friend and the runner who died in the accident that took her memories. I knew they were close and that loss must have hit her hard.

"Yea. Knew he was takin' some off the top. He was the type. Problem resolved itself, didn't it?" She flinches, but I don't give a fuck. At this point, anybody who steals from me can disappear. It's made my life a hell of a lot easier.

There's hesitation, which is unlike the woman at all. I already know what she's gonna say before she opens her mouth. "I've been gone for months now. What if—What if I don't come back at all?"

"Why would you do that?" My brows furrow. That is not what I expected. I fully thought she was gonna ask to come back. *More news I don't want to hear.* If there's something I need, it's more competent people to do this job. "Convenient that you forget all about the reason you were in this to begin with."

"Yea... those are the only memories I do have... So much loss and I just want out."

I don't need anybody here that doesn't want to be here. It's a liability. I tilt my head to the side. "Comes at a price," I say. I've never had anyone willingly walk away from Dupont. Not alive. But I can't look weak either.

I tell her that it'll cost twenty large to make her way out. She made that in a couple months, easily. I don't need the money, but I might with how things are going. It will at least keep her out of my hair for a while and away from my desk.

My phone vibrates on the table and I pick it up on speakerphone when I see it's Redd.

There's heavy breathing, but Redd's voice is clear, "I got 'em. They're comin' for you."

I stand, looking down at the phone like it's grown legs. "The fuck?"

"That bitch finally showed his face and I took the shot. Blood for blood," Redd replies.

My mind is in complete disarray as I try to think of anyone, absolutely anyone he could be talking about, knowing that there is only one man that it could be. "Told you to stand down. Let us handle it." Like businessmen, I don't add because I butchered Junior's men just hours earlier.

"I've been waitin' over a year for this, Blue. Lew had more life to live. I couldn't let it stand no more. He made a mistake gettin' comfortable in Clayton again."

"Fuck," I start the protocol for an attack. First shooting a text off to the team at my house. With the warehouse video feed connecting from room to room that guards are in, sounding the alarm from the app. "You fuckin' idiot! They were waitin' for your dumb ass."

Twenty people rush into the room and stand guard around the table.

Looking back at my phone, there are nine cars all pulling up to the front of the warehouse.

This is the last thing I need. *Lafayette men ready to take my team on for this.*

"Blue," Redd pants. "They're takin' me."

I pull at my locs, thinking over what my next steps should be. "Who? What the fuck? Who is takin' you?"

"The cops found me," Redd says and the blaring sirens start up in the background.

"That's not a problem. Did anyone see you?" I ask.

Silence.

"Redd, did anyone see you?" I ask again. Fuck, I hate repeating myself.

His voice is too calm for his circumstance when he says. "A few folks maybe."

"Maybe? What the fuck?! Tell me you aren't this dumb." I huff a long suffering sigh. "You're on your own for now. I have to deal with whatever Faye Senior wants here. Go with them and say nothing until I come to get you out."

"Heard." The line clicks and I grab my knife again, prepared for whatever might come our way. "With me," I tell Kitty when she's just sitting there in shock.

With panic in her eyes she asks, "What are you doin'?"

"Goin' to have a chat with Lafayette Senior to see if we can't come to a deal."

Chapter 29
Diamond

He doesn't speak right away.

My presentation of what the family dealings will look like moving forward is more organized and formal than anything he's used to. I'm confident in my work as it's this very same brain who earned her spot right here.

The office space that we're currently in is not too far from the town center of Clayton Terrace and its luxurious finishing make this feel more like an actual business instead of the back alley transactional crap Junior had reduced us to.

The sophisticated conference room had been decorated before I chose the space. When I walked in, I knew this was the place for me. I didn't flinch at the color palette of deep navy and gold accents. Even the mahogany wood table reminded me of him in a way that was comforting. I was finally out of his grasp and free to chose and do whatever I wanted. Subconsciously, I had chosen—

Nevermind that.

With Liezel here now and Lidia keeping an eye on us—mostly her—I am comfortable in my position and the far end of the table by the large screen behind me. I slide my Birkin to the side of me on the table and go through all of my plans. My agenda was clear and well thought out. No stuttering and no shrinking to fit whatever meek idea he wanted of me.

I've bled too much to be silenced by a man who never once held me when I cried.

Especially not when that blood once came from his son.

I killed him. Not with my own hands, but it was me who signed that death warrant. I gave the command that put a bullet through his skull. I only wished that I had been there to watch the light fade from his eyes.

Like I had to watch when my mother's light left the world, never to return again. Because of Junior.

Because Senior denied me what was mine to begin with. If he had acknowledged me all those years ago, the coke would have never made it's way to The Chrome Flame. I would have been sure of it.

No matter, I did it for this. For the room I now sit in. For the table I was never allowed to touch.

Until now.

My father leans back in his leather chair at the opposite end of the table. He just watches me. Fingers tented beneath his chin, eyes sharp for his age and disinterest with this business anymore. I know he doesn't see a daughter when he looks at me. He sees a threat.

A successor.

An executioner.

And maybe, for the first time, a true replacement.

"You really thought you'd waltz in here and the family would be waitin'?" My father finally says, his voice like old gravel—worn down and jaded by time and a hardened life. "You trying to prove somethin'."

"I'm not trying," I say flatly. "I already did."

He tilts his head, and the room shifts around that tension. I didn't expect him to come quietly. That's why everything became bloodier than I wanted, initially. I'll give him the cheatsheet version because despite how he has treated me, I still want him to be onboard with the direction the Lafayettes will be taking moving forward.

"I took out the damage your son couldn't see coming," I continue, keeping my voice low and clear. "With the choices he was making for this family it would be up in smoke and ashes and crawling with negative legal attention before the year ended. I've cleaned up more of his mess in three months than he managed in three years."

He doesn't interrupt. That's how I know I'm finally getting through to him.

"I brought back money, real money. Consistent and not at the cost of destroying the lives of our clientele. And I did it without asking for permission, and without using your name to shield me."

His jaw sets, but he still doesn't say anything. I look over to Lee, who gives me an encouraging look and lifts her eyebrow silently saying, "Do it, girl. Finish him."

My gaze flicks to Senior. "You can pretend that this is still about me trying to earn my place with you. But we both know the truth."

He narrows his eyes. "And what's that?"

"That it was always mine."

Silence.

Then laughter—low and rasped. He pushes up from his chair and walks to the window, slow, deliberate steps like he's dragging the weight of decades behind him. He glances over his shoulder, the edge of his mouth twitching upward like he both resents and respects the answer.

"Junior had my name," he says. "He was blood. He was—"

"He was weak," I cut in. "And weakness rots everything it touches."

That hits him. The stillness that follows feels like the moment before a fuse meets flame.

He turns to face me fully. "You killed my son."

"I saved your family. It was a mercy kill and probably a better end than he was heading for anyway with how many different drugs he was playing with on a consistent basis."

His silence is approval.

It's not love.

It's not pride.

It's a tactical acknowledgement—one leader recognizing another. But when he walks toward me and places a hand on the back of my chair, there's something else in his eyes too.

Fear.

"You're one bad woman. I couldn't predict that this was what was comin' for this family when you stepped foot in the house before," he says, and his voice holds something close to reverence. "That's what makes you better than him."

I let out a breath and smooth the front of my suit.

That's it. The box I didn't want to admit I'd been waiting to check. Not affection. Not belonging.

Just *recognition.*

The daughter made in the dark image of her father. And now she's sharper.

He lifts his hand from the chair and offers it.

I take it and just like that, *I'm her.*

The head of the Lafayette family.

Not everyone will be clapping for this arrangement. There is still a small faction of Lafayette that remain loyal to Junior's memory and what he stood for. Old dogs clinging to dead loyalty. They won't bow. Not easily.

That's fine.

They'll break.

Or they'll be broken.

When I informed him of the hit, and all that I had orchestrated, I allowed him to notify our people of the next move. Head straight for the Dupont Warehouse. Nine cars, each with four of our men. Ours, mine, it's all the same now.

He makes the call and places the phone on speakerphone. Before it connects he says, "Don't want to lose any more of my men." What he's not saying is clear, *no more bloodshed to prove a point.*

The next in command at the ready is Jalen Lambert. Competent and not a part of Junior's drugged out lackeys. "Umm, sir. Do you want us to go in?"

He wasn't addressing me but I'm sir now. "Send them in and wait for our next move," I say.

"You heard her. Rush 'em and wait."

After the phone call, my father leaves for the small office to have a conversation that will change everything. It's just Liezel and Lidia here in the conference room for a moment.

They both come to my side and hug me. I feel the new weight of Lafayette and it's an accomplished feeling as much as it is a burden. One massive hurdle cleared and one more that still stands in the distance.

They release me and Liezel begins collecting everything from the room while Lidia goes to guard the door again. Can never be too careful now with more targets soon coming for my back.

I press a hand to the inside of my wrist, where my pulse flutters like crazy. A finger brushes over his name. The slightly raised letters taking me back to that time.

It stirs something in me. Something too close to regret... or maybe grief.

I have to leave it behind though. I must push it aside.

I didn't just climb the ladder. I stepped into my power and left everything else behind.

Nothing is more important than the money.

Repeating it in my head does nothing to make it feel more true.

I think of Blue. His scent. His hands. His laugh like smoke in his lungs. He still doesn't know who I am—what I've done.

But he will.

And when he does, he'll either destroy everything trying to get to me... Or stand beside me and rule what's left of it.

I'm hoping for the latter while trying to accept that it might be the former.

And if he does get to me, it won't be to cuddle.

Either way, the blood's already on my hands. I made these decisions knowing exactly where they would get me. No hesitation because my feelings for him couldn't cloud the plan that was already in place.

And I'm not done yet.

It's time to take the call that I have been dreading.

Chapter 30

BLUE

I don't want to call Senior.

But what choice do I have?

Redd put a bullet in his son, against my direct orders, but a life has been taken. Not just any life either.

The head of the Lafayette family.

I hate that son of a bitch more than anyone else. Maybe even more than Redd.

Might be more upset because he was the one to end that fuckers life and not me.

I rub a hand over my face and make a different call first.

The phone rings and rings. She's not picking up. There hasn't been a single time since I've known her that she hasn't picked up the phone.

Where is Racquelle?

Have to trust that my team is keeping her safe.

The next call is more important right now. Damage control or mitigation takes precedence. I'll check on Racquelle as soon as I'm done with this shit.

It's been a while but thankfully, Senior's number hasn't changed. The old man picks up on the third ring.

"You've got some nerve callin' me," he says without preamble.

"This wasn't my shit, Terrell. Redd acted against my orders."

"I know," is all he says. A heavy sigh rings weary in my ears. "In this life, you can't get attached to much. Never did I ever want to bury my son. Your kids ain't supposed to go before you are."

I expected fury, not resignation. "You sound awfully resigned about it."

"Well, my daughter came to tell me that it would happen. But there was nothing I could do about it."

Something sick and cloying crawls up the back of my throat. Carefully, as if I'm edging up to a bomb, I ask, "Your daughter? Didn't know you had one."

"I didn't either. Until recently. She's gonna be takin' over the family in Junior's... absence."

My mind works a million times a minute.

Redd is about to be down for a sentence he shouldn't be serving because he decided to take matters into his own hands.

The last of my profits are gone without a trace after months of chasing and coming up empty.

Bad things come in threes.

And now Racquelle is— "Who's your daughter?"

"Well, you might know her as Diamond. Worked at Off Topz a while back."

Through gritted teeth, I try to keep my voice as contained as I can. "Where is she?"

There is silence that crackles on the line.

Too much fucking silence.

"Hello, Blue." Her sensual voice slips through the receiver and into my ears.

My heart drops to my stomach as my rage rises to the surface.

It's the most disorienting feeling of finding out something you didn't know was being kept from you.

Weeks of inquiring about who her Pa was to find out like this?

For all this time I thought she wanted to protect him from my world. To keep him safe from the consequences that she had already endured with her connection to me.

But that couldn't have been farther from the truth.

"You're a Faye." It comes out as stupid and lame as my observation of her being new at Off Topz so many months ago.

Months of her living in my house. I kept her safe *in my house* all while she knew that she was the daughter to the very people who were destroying my operation piece by piece.

"I'm actually *the Lafayette* now. I'm running this thing."

Disbelief is a pungent thing in my brain. "You—What? How? Why?"

"Well, I'm happy to explain everything. Would you like to meet for coffee or dinner? I'm free—"

Her voice is casual as she speaks. I still don't understand. "Nah. Tell me what the fuck is goin' on right now."

"Ah," She chastises me over the phone. "You don't make the calls here. I'm in control. I don't owe you an explanation." In a softer tone she says, "But, I'm willing to give you one if you let me."

"Racquelle," The sound of her name guts me and I try to process how much I've fucked up. How she made me look like a fool. Everything I lost while she sat comfortably in my house. That night in my office she must have taken more than I could have realized. That is an obvious fact now. God, I'm so stupid and blind. "What did you do?"

"Long story, long—I'm your supply chain management team and inventory control. Seeing as how I am in possession of more than sixty-five percent of your stock, you can defer to me moving forward."

I blink at the wall. Then my temper rises to a fever pitch. "Why are you doin' this?"

"Because I am a woman in a world dominated by men. The only thing you all know how to respect is force. So. Here is your pressure. Do you feel it?"

Do I *feel* it?

Fuck. Yes.

Months. Weeks over weeks I went to her for comfort and it was her who had been causing everything that was going wrong in my empire. She was right. I was down on product and losing money every day just to maintain what was left.

I want to know how.

I need to know why.

How could she align with the very men who hurt her?

"These men—Racquelle, they left you broken and bloody on my doorstep as a message to me."

She tuts, "A small faction of my men. They followed Junior without question. It is a problem we're resolving on this end. Everyone who matters supports this next chapter for the family."

"What is this?" The ground has opened up and swallowed me whole. Everything I thought I knew about this woman... Raw emotion suffuses my next question. "Who are you?"

"None of that is important. While I have you on the phone, I'd like to discuss a time to go over our next steps." She says with no inflection to give me any indication that she is feeling or understands how deeply she's cutting me.

"Next steps?" I scoff. "You think I'm gonna work with someone who smiled in my face and laid in my bed ALL WHILE THEY WERE GUTTIN' ME?" My voice rises to a level I've never used with her.

I've never yelled or screamed at her.

It's not within my character to do it either.

I'm spiraling as my mind tries to make sense of all the signs I missed. How I couldn't see that she was somehow responsible for all the bad things that have happened in the past six months.

Despite my yelling, Racquelle's voice is reasonable, like she's giving me an option as innocent as left or right. "What choice do you have?"

My hand rests on my knife as I fight to keep my voice at a reasonable level. "Between workin' with an enemy or bettin' on me? The choice is simple."

"Don't do this," she seems to stumble over the "M" consonant in my name before correcting to, "Blue. I don't have to be an enemy if you can be reasonable."

"Reasonable?" The laugh that rises from my chest tastes just like venom as it poisons the air around me.

Making this call in the privacy of my office was a smart idea. I don't know how my men would react to seeing me like this. Appearance is everything. This woman has made me look like a fool in more ways than I can even begin to process right now. "Oh, is it *reasonable* to do business with someone who tricked you and lied to you?"

Her slow exhale sits heavy on my shoulders. "For one second, I need you to think. *Think rationally.* Consider that I am the other player in this game. Not the woman who you brought to your home and kept there. Before you, the plan was always the same. Then you took me. I did the best with what I had and when you stop to think about it, I've done better than most.

"I can help you succeed and do even better numbers than you were doing before. It doesn't have to be hard, but it will be different. That is a promise."

She might as well stop wasting her breath. This is a betrayal that cuts deeper than any I've had to deal with in the past. No one has ever hurt me like she just has. I *cared* for this woman. I went against all my better judgments to do right by her. To keep her safe and protected while I settled things. "What you're saying means nothin' to me. Just like none of your words meant anythin' in the past six months."

"You're thinking emotionally—"

"Damn right I am! I claimed you. I protected you. I stood by you even when I knew you were lying to me." I drop into my office seat, the weight of all that has come to light, hitting me like a freight train. I put my face in my hands, defeated. *Fuck. She played me.* "How could I have known you kept all this from me? What more could you want from me?"

"Blue—" The sound of my name on her lips is a siren's call. Noise meant to lure me to my demise. This woman used me and brought about the destruction of everything I built. I lost good men and women. She stole from me.

"Fuck. That." I seethe.

She attempts to gentle me with her tone. That sultry pull present at my eardrums. "I never wanted it to be this way."

"Bullshit. If I see you again, it's on sight. I've got a knife with your name on it. Come find out what it means to cross me."

I end the call with half a mind to go end every Faye life in the building right now. The thought scratches my mind and leaves just as quickly.

This is not the kind of boss I am.

This is not how I do business.

But those Fayes don't know that.

I get Geno on the phone immediately. "Round up the Fayes and bring them to the main room."

"What are we going to do about Kitty's boyfriend?"

"What?" I ask, unsure of what the hell he's talking about.

"Mack? He came here looking for her? We're holding him with the other Fayes in the storage room."

This fucking dude is a goddamn thorn in my side. Why is he so annoying? "Bring him, too."

"Heard," he says before I end the call.

I grab a gun from my weapons cabinet at the back of my office and make my way to the main interrogation room I spent the better part of last night in.

When I walk in, they're all on their knees with their hands tied behind their backs. It's lucky for them that the blood from last night has already been hosed down or else they'd be kneeling in it. The use of cold water on Junior's main guys has only made the concrete even colder under their knees though. *Good.*

It's cold and damn near dark with all the lights turned down. We never use heating down here because it's not supposed to be comfortable.

"What is this? Why are you doing this?" Someone says in the room. Not someone, *fucking Mack.*

I ignore the question and instead ask one of my own. "Have anymore men comin' to lay down their lives for your stupid decisions?"

Mack opens his mouth again. "Actually—" I'm at my wit's end so I fire off a shot into the space. It hits the ceiling above and pieces of the concrete rain down on us.

"No one is talkin' to you." I bite out. "All you Fayes are going to die if someone doesn't tell me what you're doin' here."

Finally one of the Lafayette men speaks up, "We only brought the men who came with us. Got the go ahead when your second popped his son." He looks around, seeming to count the men in the room and is obviously confused by Mack's presence. *Join the fucking club.* "The fuck is that?"

Someone from my team shines a flashlight directly on Mack and now I've got to address this nuisance before it gets any bigger. I stomp over to him, pulling him up by the arm. "Mack? What are you doin' here?"

"Mack?" Kitty recognizes him immediately, coming over to his side. I roll my eyes at the two of them.

"Hi, butterfly," he says to her and I can't stop my lip from curling. *Butterfly.* Who is this marshmallow?

She barks to one of my men, "Loose him. Now." He looks at me and I just nod. With Mack released from the zip tie she asks, "What are you doing here?" *I'm sick of this sappy shit.*

Clearing my throat loudly, I question. "You mind takin' your lover's spat somewhere else? I'm tryin' to get biz done in here?"

She flips me the bird and ushers him out into a corridor just outside of the room. The door closes behind them and I turn back to the Lafayettes remaining.

They may go back to Racquelle alive, but they aren't going in the state they came.

"String 'em up and work 'em over. Find out everythin' they know about the new head of Lafayette," I command, storming out of the main room to figure out what I'm going to do about the snake I helped rise to the top of their family.

Chapter 31

BLUE

There's deep buzzing that mimics the one in my skull when I step through the guarded door to the more heavily guarded room.

There are men in every corner to keep an eye on the inmates plus extras in-between.

I'm impatient as I wait for the line of men to enter the room.

This is the very last place that any of us wants to be.

The weight of how I've failed Dupont is very apparent with my presence here. How could my second-in-command fall to this fate?

How did I let it get this bad?

There's families here to visit loved ones that are incarcerated. There's elderly visiting young men. And here I sit, waiting for Redd.

He is the last person that any of us could have guessed would be locked up. The least violent, usually choosing to hack your shit into oblivion or whatever the fuck it is that he does on his computer.

He may have been the one to teach me to fight and still continues to teach now, but it's very rare to see him doing anything outside of the gym.

Well, he won't be doing anything for the next eighteen months. He screwed us all over when he took those shots in broad daylight with too many witnesses. They've got to make an example even if it is a far shorter sentence than he deserved for premeditated murder.

I can understand his motives, but I don't have to agree with them.

Creating an understanding with local law enforcement when I first started making enough money to warrant serious consequences was important. Those alliances allowed me the kind of leeway to broker a deal that could ensure that my best friend wouldn't be spending the rest of his life in this hell hole.

Finally, Redd sits with his neon outfit and generic slip-on shoes. "Orange truly doesn't suit your colorin', know that?"

"Shut up," he says, flipping me the bird and making his cuffs jingle.

My next quip dies on my tongue as I realize that there will still be many months where I won't have my friend around. Even with the best I could do, he'll be serving time. This is the life, but it's been so long since any of my men had to take a fall for anything.

"Man, wipe that look off your face. I knew what I was doin'. Was prepared to sit here for way longer. Lew can rest easy knowin' his brother got that fuck back."

I nod, jaw clenched. "It fuckin' sucks bruh."

"I'll make it until it's time to get out this bitch." Then he thinks for a moment. "You know what would make it better?" I sit up a little straighter, prepared to do anything else I can for my best friend.

"Tell Steph to write to me. They allow that shit here. Know they read 'em and shit, but it'll probably smell like her." I just look at him dumbfounded. Of all the things he could have asked for. "You know it smells like ass and jockstraps back there." He nods his head toward the hall that he came from. "A letter from her desk with that posh ass letterhead and everythin'... You never did tell me what perfume she wears."

Throwing my hands up, I ask, "How the fuck would I know that?"

He shrugs, jingling again. "So, you'll tell her?"

"Yea," I say. "I'll do what I can." Redd takes my response with the kind of acceptance that is more weighted than I would expect for a letter. It's just a letter. One that I don't think Steph will write but I'll do whatever he asks of me at this point.

"What you gonna do about Diamond?" He asks.

"Not doing shit. Took an L and now I'm moving forward." A massive L that I don't know when I'll be able to recover from but a loss is a loss.

Confusion is an unwelcome emotion on his face. "Why are you so bent on not working with her?"

"You know why," I snap.

"And that is? She's runnin' the Fayes now. You know she has her shit together. Fuck, she single handedly served us our asses all under your roof. She's capable as fuck."

"Keep your voice down," I growl. "She didn't hand us shit."

"Why are you so butt hurt then? Imagine what she could do working with us."

"You want to line up with somebody so spineless?"

Redd's brows pinch, still confused as ever. "How is she spineless?"

"She was at my house—"

His head tilts to the side. "You took her there."

"She lied to me for months—"

"Technically, she answered everything you asked her. You didn't ask any of the right questions and that falls on you." *It did fall on me.* I failed Dupont. The L I'm taking, I earned. As bitter of a pill as it is for me to swallow, I couldn't deny that she bested me.

Crossing my arms, I say, "Lying by omission is still a lie. I can't trust her."

"Have you considered that she needed to protect herself too? You fuckin'—" He looks around. "You fucking kidnapped her after she showed up that night and were actin' crazy caveman protective about her. Like a fuckin' Neanderthal! She did what she had to. If she still managed to hand you your ass, then you need to ally with her instead of fightin' her." He stabs a finger into the tabletop, making his point. "She could clearly sweep us off the map if she wanted to. But she doesn't. Why do you think that is?"

I grind my teeth, hating every bit of sense he's making. "I don't know, but I can't trust it. I should have killed her."

He scoffs. "Yea right. We both know you couldn't."

"Fuck."

His smirk is too jovial for his circumstances. "Gotta admit she is a far better partner than Senior or Junior. And it sounds like Senior is leavin' it up to her anyway."

I narrow my eyes on him. "When the fuck did you talk to her?"

Casually, he responds, "A couple of days before I popped Junior. Call a spade, a spade. You're pissed that you fell for the jawn and she still has your heart. Probably more so now. What's so bad about that?"

Gritting my teeth, I ask, "Did you miss that bit earlier about trust?"

"She offered you a fair deal."

I squint at his observation. "How much did y'all talk?"

"A fair bit. She's bad, man. That's no lie. I wouldn't have taken that shot just to spite you." He sucks his teeth. "It's a good deal."

I put my face in my hands, rubbing my eyes with the heels of my palms. "I'm not convinced. It's a gamble and I fuckin' hate gamblin'."

"You get the girl and you get the business back? Seems like a two birds, one stone kind of thing." He waits for me to look up at him again. "That's good business."

It's a stark contrast in the cutesy building I'm pulling up to the place that's keeping my best friend. It's been a while since I talked to her and I have to admit that I want to see a familiar face that has nothing to do with Dupont.

"Damn, you look like hell," Steph comments when she sees me walking through the front door of her office building. The tiny receptionist that is supposed to greet me has been too scared to actually do such whenever I show up.

Steph gives Allison a smile on my behalf and we head back to her office.

"You know, I do have a home. You could come by and see me there."

"Too risky," I respond. The last thing I wanted was to get her involved in a capacity like that. Who knows which of my movements were benign tracked. She is my agent, after all. This could still be considered a business meeting.

She rolls her eyes. "Fucking Duponts. You both are a piece of work."

"Trouble in paradise?" I ask, looking around her office. She's got pictures of all her clients cutting ribbons in front of their new businesses and properties. There's several awards on the walls, too. It's clean and organized. And I catch a hint of whatever the smell is that Redd seems to be obsessed with. It's coming from a small teardrop looking vase. The steam flowing into the air on a constant stream.

Her head tilts to the side and she slowly says. "We've been broken up for months, Blue. What are you talking about?"

"Oh," is all I can manage. "Guess I'm out of the loop."

"I'll say. You've been out of everything for months. Ever heard of a phone?"

"Had a lot of shit on my plate. My mind's been preoccupied keeping the business afloat."

"Trouble in paradise?" She parrots back to me.

"Yea," is all I say. "That would be one way to put it."

She checks her watch then clicks on her computer a few times. "Well, I've got time."

After a long sigh, I tell her everything. Nothing incriminating, but everything about Racquelle. How we first met, protecting her and then her staying at the house. I recognize that those months where I had her in my house weren't conventional, but in this retelling to Steph, I leave out the part about her not leaving. Then finally, I tell her about the ultimatum that Racquelle gave me.

She listens patiently, waiting for me to give her all the details. I realize that I haven't actually talked to anyone about her. Not like this.

Hardly think Redd counts.

Steph interlaces her fingers, nodding her head when I finally finish relaying all the details I can. "So... You took her to La Récolte, but I had to meet you at the hole-in-the-wall barbecue place? Is this why I find these choice pieces of property for you? So I can get the scraps?"

I tilt my head at her attitude. "I was cravin' barbecue."

She rolls her head, cracking her neck. "Wow, you really took my not letting her get away to heart then."

"What do you mean?"

"When I said that, it was in a… I don't know, I thought you were about getting off and getting gone. What happened to that?"

I glare at her. "She's not like that."

"She's a dancer at Off Topz, I highly doubt she's *not like that*."

"Aye, watch yo' mouth." She raises an eyebrow. "I'm not gonna lie and say I don't care about her still. Fuck. I hate it but I do. She's clearly more than a dancer at my club. She's not even a dancer at my club. She's a fuckin' boss."

"And now you can't respect her anymore?"

"What are you talkin' about?"

"When she was a dancer, your employee, under your control—you liked how she was strong and fierce and about her money." Steph sums up everything I thought about Racquelle to accurately for my liking. I did like all those things about her. It made her stand out in my eyes.

"Yea, so?"

Her eyes narrow as she continues to explain. "Now, she's all those things but she's a competitor. Not just any competition—the winning side of the competition."

"Steph—"

"Nah. Nope." She puts a hand up. "You said your piece and now I'm gonna say mine. If you lost, then admit that. If she were a man, you'd give her props and move on. But because you slept with her, 'claimed' her, you're pissed that she bested you?"

"I'm pissed that she lied to my face for months! Why is no one understandin' that?"

"Because it's dumb and so are you!"

"The fuck, Steph?"

"Don't what the fuck me. I know what you're like. You fucking like this girl. And I'd say more than like with how you're acting like you don't have any GD sense." She looks up at the ceiling, as if in prayer. "Am I doomed to make all Dupont men accept the loves of their lives? Please tell me that is not my curse." She completes her prayer with her fingers dragging across her chest in a cross pattern.

Looking back to me, she says, "She's the only one I've ever seen you talk about this long and I'm sure you did not make it easy for her to go. If she's smart, and she clearly is, she did what she had to.

"If she lied, then it was for a reason. Forgive her or don't. But to let your business fail because you're too proud is dumb as hell. And if you could see that then you're missing the whole point of business. The money. So are you really 'bout it or not?"

"Nothin' is more important than the money," I murmur. "I don't enjoy how my *friends* are gangin' up on me."

"Oh yea?" She laughs at me. "How is he?"

My look is bland when I say, "Incarcerated."

Steph crosses her legs, sitting back in her pantsuit. "Okay, smart ass. You know what I mean. It's a big deal."

"Well he was gettin' on my ass earlier so I'd say he's doin' as well as could be expected."

She looks out of her window in thought for a moment. The pensive nature of her look out the window makes me think that I've missed more than I thought while I was caught up chasing Racquelle's tricks. Steph continues to look out the window when she says, "That's good, I guess."

"He did have one thing to request." Now to the point of why I truly came here. Which was not to get my ass handed to me by yet another high-power woman. "He wants you to write to him."

She finally breaks her stare from out the window, turning wide eyes on me. "Me?" She leans forward, putting her elbows on the table with her head on a fist. "What am I supposed to write to him?"

"Hell, if I know. But shit. He's locked up Steph. You can't throw him a bone?"

"No," she says drolly and I give her a look. "Fine. One letter is all I'm committing to."

Standing from the chair, I pat my back pocket to make sure I'm not leaving anything in her office. "Better than nothin' and it means my job here is done."

I am already to the office door when she asks, "So, what are you going to do about Diamond, Blue?"

"Nothing to do. She gets what she wants apparently."

Chapter 32

BLUE

The sparkles off the face of her watch only brings memories from the first time that I saw her.

Shiny and captivating.

Too good for me.

She had always been too good for me but I just didn't know why.

In my mind I wanted to protect her from my world. Little did I know that she was the force that would change it forever.

Thinking over what Steph and Redd, said, I have to acknowledge that I may be acting stubborn. With everything I know, there was no way that I could miss how amazing Racquelle is. She pulled off something no one else could just because she's her.

No one could have infiltrated my operation so thoroughly. No one could have taken Lafayette so brutally.

It's because *it's her* that she came out on top.

What drew me to her that night was not the bling of her outfit, though it certainly was the first thing I noticed. It was that energy of hers.

How bold she was.

How unafraid and unapologetic she was.

When she saw what she wanted she went for it.

Did she not show me that the first night she met me challenge for challenge?

She could have walked away when I teased her with my knife. I was completely ready for her to say, hell nah, and kick my ass out. But she was game.

Never scared.

Fuck and that I loved.

Loved it.

Love.

She never backed down. Even in my house, she took everything I had to give and still came out stronger on the other side. Why the fuck would I want to let her go? How could I not fall hard for her and hoard her to myself?

I asked the questions.

I did.

But was my goal to know her secrets or just to know her?

Fuck.

I toss her watch on the bed and get my snakes out. Letting them out onto the floor, I remove the tattered pieces of that first outfit I cut up from the back rock they always hangout on.

Before she came, I had been getting them accustomed to her. I didn't know I was introducing my snakes to another one.

It was me telling her that snakes get a bad rep and here I am calling her one like it's an insult.

Was this me being a sore loser?

I couldn't tell. My pride was hurt and I knew from all appearances that I looked like a fool. People would talk and likely come to that conclusion.

They didn't know her.

She was unmatched.

I had to be impressed by what she had accomplished even if it came at my expense.

I could make this right.

I could get my empire back, if I got my head out of my ass.

How she managed to beat me at my own game is a complete mystery. I never knew and on top of it all she still was a comfort to me. I don't think her feelings, her concern, her passion was fake.

When I said I wanted to have something real with her, I meant that. And that was with her held against her will. Fuck, I had held her against her will and she still showed me compassion. I put her through so much and she was still thinking about me.

The only choices I had right now were to bow to her or lose my empire to the woman who took it.

If she had gotten Senior on her side and put the Fayes in a place to best me, then who's to say what she could do if I were to re-ally with them again…

Redd was right. Racquelle could save Dupont just as she was able to destroy it.

Did I really want to lose her and my empire?

There was only one right answer.

I hear a noise at the front of the house that should not be happening. There are no guards here anymore with her gone. And I always lived alone.

My front door opens and I freeze.

Who the fuck could that be?

Putting my snakes back in their enclosure, I grab her watch off my bed and put it into my pocket.

Pulling my knife, I make silent steps to the doorway and out the hall.

"Who the fuck is here?" I bellow down the hall with the sound of footsteps in my foyer.

Then, a bag goes over my head and I can't see shit. Blindly, I swipe my blade, but with a chop to my wrist, it falls from my hands.

"Got 'em," someone says to my left but there are already three men on me. One holds my legs while two more have my arms. "Headed your way," they say while I'm restrained.

I thrash and flail, but I don't earn any give for myself. "Man, put me down." I complain, helpless in my home. "What the fuck? Who are you?"

The one who was speaking before says, "We don't want to have to tape your mouth, so come quietly and you'll get the answers you're lookin' for."

DIAMOND

Back to the place where it all started.

Off Topz looks totally different to me now that I'm no longer an employee here.

Except it's nothing like it was when I first stepped foot in here.

You could say that I've been using my newly acclaimed power to do... just about whatever I want.

It feels good to be Queen.

The changes that I knew needed to be made were being checked off a very organized list. Cleaning up all the trash that Junior had created in his shitty reign was more work than I first suspected from the outside. But now that I'm here, I can do what's necessary to mitigate the impending demise for Lafayette with precision. I was having a great time doing it, as well.

There were even new ideas I had and wanted to put into action as soon as I was done with the meeting that would begin in just a short while.

Off Topz is empty aside from the kitchen and Chanel who was more than happy to work tonight. Several of my new personal guards are here making sure that nothing happens tonight.

I sent Lee and Lidia back to Atlanta to keep watch over The Chrome Flame until I needed to make the changes I had planned for it.

There's a mess of writhing black fabric being carried to the table I'm sitting at. I remain quiet while they place him in the chair and readjust his restraints before finally removing the bag from his head.

It takes a few moments for his eyes to adjust, then he focuses on me. Muffled words form behind his tape.

Guess he didn't come quietly.

I expected as much.

His energy is a ravenous thing through the space with how upset he must be right now.

It's a welcome presence that I missed, actually.

Standing, I walk over to him in my silver tailored sheath dress and red bottom heels. Makeup fierce, like I might be on the pole tonight. My hair thick and wavy around me. I look like sin and his savior all in one. With careful movements, I remove the tape from his skin.

He doesn't say anything after I remove it, just watches me walk over to the bar top where Chanel has left the main speakers' control tablet.

I ask, "Shall I put something on for us, baby?"

I make it back to the table where he sits, fingers hovering over several different options. I decide on something low and sensual, really setting the mood.

"Not your baby," he states calmly. "Blue."

My head tilts, taking him in. I've never seen him restrained before and I've got to admit that I like how the tables have turned. "I think I prefer Milo," I purr.

"What the fuck is this, Racquelle?"

"So you agree, Milo and Racquelle are having a nice dinner?" I ask, undeterred by his attitude.

"Whatever," he says, checking his surroundings. Then, they land on me, assessing. *Smart.*

I'm still the most dangerous thing in this room.

I reach into my handbag and pull out a familiar item of his and his eyes sharpen to points on me. "Why do you have that?"

I'm careful to remove the blade from its sheath, serrated teeth shining in the club lighting. It's the knife he used for his claim on me.

Though we both know it was there with and without the scarring.

Placing the knife on the table between us, I say, "It wouldn't be a date without one of these." I pause for a moment, looking deep into his eyes. "Between us anyway, right?"

"How am I supposed to eat with my hands tied?" He asks, chair rocking with the movement.

I smile and clasp my hands under my chin while I look at him. He looks good in a long sleeve navy tee and black tactical vest. At least he's been keeping up with his exercise routine in the month we've been apart. Strong shoulders and biceps still cutting obvious lines through the sleeves. "We'll just talk for now. Once we get that out of the way, I'll decide whether you can eat." I wink at him and sit back in my seat to cross my legs.

"Racquelle," he says carefully, trying to find patience, as he is the one tied up at my mercy now. "Why am I tied to a chair in my own club? What is this?"

"Remember how I said that I was free to sit and talk business over dinner? I just found out that you're also free right now. I love how that's worked out for us."

He raises an eyebrow, only grunting at my methods to secure this date. I feel a strange sense of glee being able to have this conversation.

Everything has led us to this moment.

"Does this mean we can start?" When he doesn't respond, I take that as my cue to begin. "Perfect. First, we should go over the most recent events. As made apparent, I've been named and crowned the head of Lafayette. Everything that this family stands for is clear and present for any who dares look into us. We are the largest holder and facilitator of arms and cannabis in the South, from this point forward." Milo opens his mouth, but I put a polite finger to my mouth indicating that he should be quiet. "That might be a little difficult to understand at present, but please save any questions for the end of this presentation," I say with a smile.

He rolls his eyes but allows me to continue. "While," I cough, "staying at your home, I was able to secure, as previously stated, over sixty-five percent of the cannabis being moved by Dupont from Colorado." An apparent fact to him, but the next is not. "And California." His mouth opens to speak but placing a finger to my lips again, I say, "The green that was believed to be obtained by Dupont was actually a reggie decoy and not the actual grower's supply from SoCal."

He blinks several times and his brows furrow in concentration. "How—"

"I'm getting there," I assure him. "Currently, we are holding the product in two undisclosed locations with the proper storage, maintenance, and security to ensure that all product is ready to be distributed. And what do you know? I'm actually sitting in front of someone who needs product to sell–and probably fast–in order to regain control over his dropping profit margins. What are you at right now? Five percent?"

He grinds his teeth. "So, all this just to work for me?"

"No, no, no, no." I stand grabbing the knife and walking over to where he's bound. "See, I don't want to work *for you*. I'm proposing a partnership. Selling, you are better than anyone has ever seen. But everything else, that's my wheelhouse. Together? We'd be untouchable."

His wary eyes track the knife in my hand. I pull his long locs away from his face. My lips brush his ear when I say, "Seventy-thirty split."

"Pretty generous," he points out.

"I know," I respond, running a finger under his chain at his neck. "I could give you twenty right now and sacrifice nothing. To account for damages from December to May. You know, when you held me in your home and away from my work?" He frowns, but I sit in his lap and kiss the corner of his mouth. "I can be very amenable when I want to be."

He leans away from me to catch my eyes. "Stop playin' with me, Racquelle. Not taking thirty. Sixty-forty."

My dress rises up over my hips as I straddle his lap to look him in the eyes. My elbows rest on the table behind me as I consider his offer. His, however, drop down to where he can now see I came to this meeting with no panties on. Never said I would play fair.

In fact, I have zero intentions of playing fairly.

"Fuck, you're already so wet," he comments as he listens to the sound of my finger running through my bare lips.

"You won't be taking sixty... right?" I ask when I raise that finger between us.

"Another," he commands, even with his hands bound I can feel that weighted energy surrounding me and the space.

I slide my middle and index fingers inside of me, only gasping slightly when I push in and out once. "Like this?" I ask.

Removing them, there's a few moments of us both seeing my glistening fingers between us.

I bring my fingers to my lips, but he leans forward to catch them in his mouth before I can.

With the space cleared on the table, I scoot back on the surface to lift my pussy up where he's eye level with me. Milo is just a breath away from me, but I move back out of his reach.

"Ah, before you can have that, there's one last detail that you need to consider."

"What detail is that?" He says, licking his lips clean.

Never go to waste.

Moving my heels to the ends of the armrests on his chair, I give him a full view of what my power looks like. "Do you remember…" I begin, "when you started to experience a consistent decline in the quality of the cannabis you were getting from Lafayette before you cut ties?"

The bomb settles between us and I allow him to think through what I'm saying. Precious moments pass where I can hear the gears grinding in his head, tracing back my maneuverings to long before we even met.

"The reggie… That was you?" I nod, my eyes crinkling with the wonder in his for me. "Fifty-fifty," he barks.

"Thought you might say that," I giggle, letting this last accomplishment fill my glow to the top.

"I love you, know that?" He says, eyes flicking between mine. The energy shifts in the room again.

Warm from him and bright from me.

Wrapping my arms around his neck, I admit. "I love you, too."

The chair rattles as he struggles in the ties again. "Goddamn, loose me so I can finally eat, woman."

"One thing left to do," I say, standing again but kneeling in front of him.

"What's that?" he asks.

I cut his shirt open before answering, "Don't worry. This will scar."

Using the same knife he used on me, I make five small cuts above his heart in the shape of a diamond before licking the wound clean, like he did for me.

I grab the bandage and cut cream, carefully applying both to the mark I've just given my mark.

Coming up from my knees, I remove his ties with the same knife and what remains of his shirt.

He cups my face, licking into my mouth.

He deepens the kiss before saying, "My biggest mistake was not tellin' you I had fallen in love with you that first night I saw you glitterin' across my path. Partners is better than I could ever deserve. This empire is ours."

"Ours," I say into his lips between kisses. He slips the AP back on my wrist and, "Guess what?"

"What?" he asks, still kissing my neck.

I smirk, waiting for him to stop kissing me and look at me. "Think I'm able to cover how much your dick is worth now."

He laughs deep and resonate, holding my waist. "Show me," he says.

Taking my time to remove his pants and boxers, I look up into his eyes. I know what awaits me and though I've had him in my mouth plenty of times, I'll never get used to his size.

The weight of his girthy dick is unmatched.

I spit onto him to make it nice and easy for me to stroke him how I want.

Being on my knees is not a symbol of giving up my power, but a statement of taking what I want.

I worked hard to have the control and the upper hand.

There is no need to prove myself because the work speaks for itself.

I'm taking exactly what I want.

The money.

The power.

Milo.

"Don't need much, bae. I'm 'bout to nut just knowin' I have you again," he says, holding my hair out of my way.

My tongue circles his crown, proud and taught. I work him in, needing to take him as deep as I can down my throat.

His groan vibrates through me all the way down to my core as he climaxes in my mouth.

The taste of him is on my tongue, musky and so him. "Swallow it," he commands. "All of it." His hand is reverent on my face. "Show me that it's gone."

I stick my tongue out to show him it's nice and clean.

"Good girl," he says, running a hand over my chin to catch the drool there. "Now, show me that ass. I'm hungry."

THE END

Thank you for reading Into the Blue! I hope you enjoyed it! The series continues with Redd's stalker romance up next!

WRITTEN IN RED: Coming SUMMER 2026

Read the first chapter by subscribing to my newsletter **HERE**.

Catch up with the other couples in this book with these stories:

Whisk til Peaked — It follows Blue's brother, Tony, and you'll see Blue quite a bit. Two best friends, Tony and Drea, get snowed into a luxury resort and must face the secret feelings they've had for years.

Roped on the Ridge — It follows Kathryn Jeann after she gets into a car accident with a sunshine cowboy, Mack. They agree to be roommates and help each other heal after she loses her memory and he breaks a leg.

Please don't forget to leave a review as it helps other readers find my stories and enjoy them as well!

Alpenglow Ridge

Saddled with Finesse
Verse to Acclimate
Whisk til Peaked
Hope by the Horizon
Roped on the Ridge

Shades of Vengeance

Into the Blue
Written in Red

Zea is a passionate storyteller who brings romance to life with heartfelt emotion and unforgettable characters. A lifelong lover of love stories, she weaves her background in anthropology into crafting tales where swoon-worthy heroes fall hard for their strong, relatable heroines.

Living in the picturesque mountains of Colorado with her husband, daughter, and a spoiled, posh cat, Zea draws inspiration from her surroundings to create warm, vibrant settings readers want to escape to. When she's not writing, she's indulging in her other loves: cooking, hiking, designing clothes, or curling up with a romance novel and a plate of sweets.

Zea is dedicated to connecting with her readers and invites you to join her on this journey of love, laughter, and happily ever afters.

Want to be the first to hear about new releases, exclusive content, and special offers?

Sign up for my newsletter at

www.zeakayleighgalan.com/news

www.instagram.com/zeakayleigh

www.facebook.com/zeakayleigh

Signed Book Shop